Junction

Still Ticking

L. A. Evans

'Junction: Still Ticking' by L. A. Evans
Published by Elizabeth Guttridge in 2021
LAEvansBooks@gmail.com

Printed and bound by Amazon

First Edition

This novel is entirely a work of fiction. The names, characters and incidents portrayed in it are the work of the author's imagination. Any resemblance to actual persons, living or dead, events or localities is entirely coincidental.

ISBN: 9798717780063

For Bethan and John

Prologue

July 22nd

My index finger on my right-hand twitches**.** It sends a wave of angst through my rigid body. I can't move anything else. Open your eyes, I tell myself, but I can't. I hear faint voices around me, but I can't quite make out what they're on about. They seem to be talking medical nonsense. I hear the clattering of metal against metal, the beeping of machines and the occasional sound of snipping.

Then, I hear a drill start to whir and I feel pressure. Pressure being placed on the top of my head. There's no pain, but a feeling of someone or something pressing down on my skull in short bursts, rattling my brain. What the hell is going on? Why can't I move? I try to talk but my lips won't bloody open.

It's hard to hear the voices around me, but occasionally some clear words seep through the distortion such as: burr hole, brain fluid, tissue. What the actual?

I can smell disinfectant, blood and some sort of sweet, sickly stench. I can sense rummaging around me and the sporadic brush of material against my skin.

A female voice chatters away, using medical terminology I don't understand but she seems to be talking her way through a procedure. A medical procedure. An operation.

Oh … my … God. I'm being operated on. And I'm awake. Do they know I'm awake and that I can hear almost everything that's going on? No, of course they don't otherwise they would stop. Are they bloody idiots or something? My gut churns and my pulse races. I hear someone talk about 'BP rising'.

Come on, woman, get a grip, sort yourself out. You can get through this; you can get through anything. You're strong, you know that.

But I'm panicking and I can't stop. What the hell has happened to me? Why am I suddenly here, with my life firmly being held in a stranger's hands? Clearly an incompetent one at that. I don't know who this surgeon is or what her background is. What if she makes a mistake, what if she's … pissed? You hear these horrific stories about surgeons operating whilst intoxicated and families losing loved ones as a result. I have absolutely no sodding control over this situation, none. I need control. I have no idea if I chose this surgeon or if I paid for the best. Was this a planned surgery or did something happen to me? Think, for God's sake, think!

I remember driving my car. Yes, that's it! Where was I going? Shit … No idea. Who was I with? I don't think I was with anyone. No, I was on my own. I was definitely on my own. Was I on my way here for a planned surgery, perhaps I have a tumour? Oh God, I'm dying. No, don't be bloody stupid. I would remember if I was having planned brain surgery. Wouldn't I? I don't think this surgery was planned. Something happened whilst I was driving.

Suddenly, images flash in front of my closed eyes. A car is looming toward me. It came out of nowhere. My foot is pressing hard on the brake but I'm not slowing down quickly enough. The sound of squealing brakes pierces my ear drums. I can feel myself being thrown forward and an unbearable pain across my chest. The burning smell of rubber singes my nostrils.

I crashed. Oh shit … I crashed.

And here I am now, on an operating table *awake*, with my fate being held in the hands of a stranger.

'She's crashing!' I can hear someone exclaim.

'Start compressions,' I hear a female say.

My body lightens. I suddenly feel as though I'm lighter than air itself. I can move my fingers more now. This is freaking me out, what the hell's happening now? Are they going to notice me waking up and stop? I hope so. They have to notice.

Then the panic I felt vanishes. Gone. Where I don't know, but a strange feeling of inner peace fills my body, replacing it. I embrace it. It's a wonderful feeling. I'm no longer scared or panicked; I can feel the terror slipping away and being replaced with calmness. I open my eyes with ease.

A radiant light burns down on me from above. The light gets bigger and brighter. Is it growing or am I moving closer to it? There's no longer a gravitational pull rooting me to the ground. I'm weightless and know that I am floating. I turn my head to look back to the ground and I see the distancing operating table below with surgeons rhythmically pressing down on my chest and I can faintly hear a lifeless tone playing on the heart monitor.

'We're losing her,' the same female voice says.

The bright light is all around me now. There's an overwhelming feeling of tranquillity and joy which consumes me from head to toe. I'm being pulled further into the light. Where is this taking me? Wherever it is, it's somewhere I *want* to go. I want to forget everything that happened to me during the last couple of months. I want to forget what *he* did. Focus on the light, it's soothing, it's somewhere I need to be, somewhere I want to be.

Through the light, a translucent hand reaches out toward me. Its palm is open, urging me to take it. I want to. I really want to. My body is warm, with … what is this? Love? I reach out.

'Charge to three-sixty … Clear!' The woman bellows.

A gravitational pull tears me away from the hand's grasp. No, no I want to stay within the light. I strain my arm and grapple with the air, struggling to reach the outstretched palm once more. Please, take my hand whatever, whoever you are. I need you. I need this feeling to last forever.

'It's not your time, Zoe,' a voice in my head says, as clear as day. 'Not yet.'

Not my time? No, no, you're wrong, I'm ready. I ... I want to feel this peace and serenity. I want to forget. Please.

'You still have a life to live, Zoe. You need to find your *own* peace first.'

This time, a male surgeon's voice roars, 'Clear!'

The light above me is fading as I'm being pulled back toward the operating table. I turn my head to face my destination. The serene tranquillity I felt by the light is now extinguished and utter horror replaces it.

'What … the … fuck? No, no, no! Stop! Please … that's … that's not me!' I cry, but it's no use. No-one seems to be able to hear me.

The sleeping body of a brown haired, freckly, overweight woman lies beneath me, surrounded by doctors. A male surgeon holds the paddles firmly to the woman's chest.

'Clear!' One final surge of electricity fires through the woman's chest and the pull is immense. Dragging me toward the table.

I shout out again, ‘stop, stop, stop! Please, someone help me!’ Yet again, no-one hears. I try to fight it, legs kicking, arms flailing but I’m helpless. The power of this electrical surge is too strong, and I am sucked into the body of this fat, brunette stranger.

Part 1

1

17th June (5 weeks before the 1st car accident)

Staring at the picture hanging on the wall opposite to me, I ponder over Paula's last question, 'How did that make you feel?'

I thought pictures in a counselling room should be calming. Maybe a painting of a beach or a sunset or something else equally relaxing. Not this one. This was a picture of a rhino grazing on a twig of dead tree, surrounded by a barren, African landscape. He looks sad, lonely and vulnerable.

How did that make me feel? She's responding to me talking about being sent to boarding school as a child. Well, it was shit. My parents packed me off to boarding school in Taunton as soon as I hit secondary school age. The school was at least seventy miles away from home in Swindon. This way they could focus on their careers and let someone else raise me for as much of my youth as the school terms allowed.

One summer holiday when I was fourteen, I returned home, a shell of my former self. You see, I was bullied. I wasn't the muscular, toned woman I am today. I was weak and pathetic. I was spotty, overweight and a bit of a loner growing up and the kids used this to abuse me.

The worst episode of bullying happened in the school canteen just before the end of term and my return home for the summer holidays. I sat alone, as normal, and ate my lunch in total silence. Once finished, I stood up and pushed my chair back under the table and noticed a puddle of blood on the seat of the chair. Knowing that I had to walk from my table, to the scrap-bins to deposit my used tray and then out of the canteen, whilst wearing a thin blue summer school dress soaked in period blood, was soul destroying. There was nothing I could do. I had to get out of the canteen as quickly as possible and hope that no-one saw the red seepage all over the back of my dress.

But they did. Of course, they did. Everyone saw, including my sister Mel. The table of bullies laughed, pointed, cheered and made sure that everyone else's attention was on me. Before I knew it, the whole room erupted in laughter.

I legged it out of the canteen and spent the rest of the day up in Sick Bay, where they washed my dress and gave me fresh sanitary towels. I refused to go back to lessons that day and just sobbed in my Sick Bay room.

The bullies didn't forget. In fact, they made sure everyone remembered. For the remainder of term, I was nicknamed Carrie. Unfortunately, I didn't have the ability to enact vengeance on the bullies with telekinesis so I became an even bigger recluse than I was before and I decided to starve myself.

Mel didn't stand up for me back then. She was twelve and she was scared of being bullied herself. She had loads of mates in school and was always one of the popular girls. She obviously wanted it to stay that way, so she distanced herself from me. I was so jealous of her.

Although Mel didn't actually join in with the bullying in school, she didn't protect me or have my back. That was a very lonely feeling and something I never forgave her for.

When I first told my parents about the bullying, my father's response was, 'Well, just lose weight, no wonder they pick on you when you're *that* size.'

He was right. I didn't want to be overweight anymore and I knew that if I starved myself, I would not only lose weight but with any luck, my periods may also stop. This would prevent anything like that from ever happening again.

My father was very regimented. He was an army Major and lived his life by rules and discipline. He wouldn't tolerate anyone moaning or complaining about things that were within their control. His motto in life was to just sort it out, make it right and suck it up. He was the epitome of the 'stiff upper lip'. His name was Richard Davenport, and from what I heard, his regiment had nicknamed him Major Dick, although no-one ever dared call him this to his face for fear of being court-martialled.

'I hated boarding school,' I tell Paula. 'I was bullied because I was fat and weak. I took control of my life which lead to the eating disorder we discussed in our last session. Yet I came through all that and that's why I'm the way I am now.'

'What do you mean, the way you are now?' Paula asks. 'Do you like who you are now?'

'Of course, I do! I look fantastic. I'm healthy and fit, not like I was back then. I'm now at my perfect weight and I don't want anything to stand in the way of that.'

‘What about what’s inside? Do you like who you are and how you treat others?’ She asks.

That’s a difficult one and not one I really want to answer. I don’t think I’m rotten to the core, but I’m not liked by people. I’m black and white. What people see is what they get, I don’t pussy-foot around people’s feelings. There’s only one person on Earth I need to look out for, and that’s me. No-one ever looked out for me growing up so why should I look out for anyone else? People think I’m selfish, I don’t think I am. I’m strong and independent. Anyone who thinks differently is just jealous of what I can offer that they can’t.

‘I’m true to me. I’m independent and strong. I’m always in control and this makes me strong. People look up to me. If they don’t like me, it’s just jealousy,’ I say.

‘What makes you strong Zoe?’ She asks.

What a stupid question, doesn’t she know me at all yet? ‘What I’ve been through in my life, of course. How I was disciplined enough to lose weight and make myself beautiful, how I was bullicd but grew stronger as a result, to name a couple of reasons.’

Paula continues her questioning. 'You mention control and self-discipline a lot Zoe. What do you think would happen if you didn't have control of a situation?'

'I always have control. I *have* to have control otherwise things will go wrong, and I will only have myself to blame.'

'Do you think it's possible to *always* have control Zoe?' Paula says. 'Some things in life are out of your control. And if you try to control every aspect of your life, you may miss opportunities that can be incredibly positive and influential on your life.'

I disagree. If you're in control of your life, you won't miss out on opportunities because you'll create them. You'll live your life how you want to and not be influenced by others or have your life dictated to you.

'I don't think that's the case,' I say. 'I make my own opportunities. If I don't think something will make a positive impact on my life, I won't pursue it. Simple.'

Paula says, 'Ah, yes, but there are sometimes situations that you think will have a negative impact on your life which may not always be the case. Why not be open to things outside of your comfort zone? You mentioned in your last session that

Tom wants children, but you don't. What's stopping you from exploring this as an option?'

I agreed to pay privately for some counselling sessions after Tom found out about my affair with Steve, my brother-in-law. Tom only took me back on the condition that I sought help for my 'issues'. One of those issues being that I didn't want children. I didn't want to get a divorce from Tom, that's far too costly and he would have ended up getting half of my money. So, I complied with his demands and accepted counselling.

He thinks the reason why I don't want children is because I have a fear of putting on weight. He's right to a degree, I don't want to put on weight through pregnancy, not when I've worked so hard to get this body. However, the main crux of the issue is that I just don't want children. I don't have a maternal bone in my body. Perhaps that's because my parents weren't maternal, I don't know. But, ultimately, I don't know what parental love should be, so it's a lot easier to just avoid that situation.

'What's stopping me?' I ask. 'I just don't want children. Full stop. There's nothing anyone can do to sway me on that one.'

'And that's your choice Zoe,' Paula says. 'No-one should pressurise you into doing anything you really don't want to do. Just make sure you are certain of this and make this clear to Tom. He has a right to make his own decisions too.'

I say nothing to this. There's nothing else to say. What's she suggesting? That I tell Tom directly that there's no hope of ever having children together because I don't want to and then *let* him decide to leave me? No chance. I can't afford to lose my money to Tom.

When I agreed to have counselling sessions, I didn't think I would actually have to speak as much as I have done so far. I've always been very cynical about therapy. How can talking about issues or concerns help? You just have to sort it out, make it right and suck it up. It's only you who can do that. No amount of therapy can help with that. This session is proving that point. She's just irritating the shit out of me. I don't need to be here, there's nothing wrong with me. Not anymore. And that's all credit to me. However, if it means Tom and I stay married then I'll have to grin and bear the remainder of these meetings.

Thankfully, the session for today is nearly over. Paula gives me some exercises to do before we meet again. She sends me a couple of videos about letting go of the past and embracing change, for me to watch and annotate with my thoughts and asks me to bring them along with me next time. As if I can be arsed to do that.

She also suggests I try to give Tom control to make at least one big decision before our next session, whether it be a holiday booking as an example or some home decorating. Something bigger than just what to have for tea or where to go for an outing. She can suggest this all she likes, but I'm not letting Tom make these big decisions alone. I'll consider compromising a bit but that's as far as I'll be pushed.

Today's meeting ends on one last bit of advice from her. She suggests that if I ever feel anxious about control slipping away from me or feel an argument brewing as a result of me losing control, I need to apply a little pressure on the centre of my forehead by using my index finger. I need to mentally allow my finger to absorb the tension and anxiety of not being in control and then release it by casting it into the atmosphere. What a load of mumbo-jumbo, I'll never lose control.

2

June 24th (4 weeks before the 1st accident)

This afternoon is going to be a long afternoon. I have my least favourite client coming into the gym at three-thirty for a one-on-one training session. Pete the Perve. It's days like this when I wonder why I'm still working. I don't need to work but it's better than staying at home and generally I'm doing what I love the most. Not this afternoon though.

Pete is a six-foot, overweight, balding man. He's around my age but looks fifty-odd. The stale stench of cigarettes lingers in the air when he's around. He repulses me. Not because of the way he looks necessarily, although that doesn't help, but more the way he acts.

He was referred to my gym by the NHS a few months back, due to him having a heart attack. Premature heart disease they called it. I call it being obese and stupid. He comes once a week for an hour-and-a-half session with me. He only wants me. He doesn't seem to be losing any weight so I'm almost certain he binges on burgers and beer throughout the week and only comes to the gym in order to see me.

Generally, I view him as a harmless, pathetic excuse for a man who's a little inappropriate and sleazy. I can handle him. So, instead of asking someone else to be his personal trainer and potentially lose his business, I agree to continue seeing him.

Five minutes after his training session was supposed to start, I hear his SEAT Ibiza roar into the carpark through the gym window. It's such a typical boy-racer car. One you'd probably find being driven by a total prick, looping around Weston Super Mare promenade, windows down with some God-awful hip-hop music blaring. It's blue with white racer stripes plastered across it, from the bonnet to the boot. It completely sums him up.

'Alright beautiful,' he says as he waddles into the gym.

'Good afternoon Pete,' I politely reply. 'Thanks for being late, yet again. Right, let's get you warmed up first.'

'Ahhhhh you can warm me up anytime petal … hah … hah,' he says whilst rubbing his hands and circling his sloppy tongue around his lips.

I smile that awkward 'you repulse me, but I have to remain professional' smile. The only thing that's going to get me through this afternoon is knowing that I'll be seeing Steve at six o'clock, after work.

Tom thinks I'm going to be going out with Karen after work for a bite to eat. Karen is the only person I really talk to at the gym. She's alright in small doses but I wouldn't really fancy socialising with her too much. I'm not really into the same things as her. She loves reality TV when I don't really see the point in people going on TV in the vain attempt to get fame. She's also into drum and bass. Whenever I hear drum and bass, I just hear noise. I'd much rather listen to some sophisticated classical music. However, she's very useful as an alibi when lying to my husband.

A couple of months ago, Tom and Mel found out about my affair with Steve. Mel hated me for it, she finished her relationship with Steve and moved to New Zealand, disowning me as a sister. I guess I deserved it.

Tom and I agreed to work through our marriage. In all honesty, I only stayed with him so that he didn't take half of my inheritance through the divorce proceedings, hence why I have to attend counselling. But Steve was suddenly single, and I just couldn't stay away from him.

Steve served in the army for ten years and worked his way up to Sergeant. He's no longer in the army, instead he now works in a fitness boot camp after a shrapnel wound affected the mobility in his leg a little. Enough for him to change his perspective on life. I have a lot of admiration for him and finding him very physically attractive means I'm somewhat addicted to him. I know it's wrong. I know I shouldn't cheat on Tom; he deserves better than that. Yet, I just can't stop myself.

'So, you gonna join me so we can get hot and sweaty together then Princess?' Pete says, bringing me back to the mundane present.

'No Pete,' I reply sternly. 'You need to work a bit harder I think, you're not quite as hot and sweaty as you should be.'

I ramp up the treadmill. Let's see the fat bastard sweat. Pete starts panting and puffing. Thankfully, that shuts him up for a bit.

Whilst Pete huffs and puffs away, I start playing with the gym keys dangling from my neck twiddling them around my fingers. I cast my mind back to Steve and the first time we met, almost fifteen years ago. Mel had been dating him for about three months and she finally invited him over to meet me and our parents during the school summer holidays. He was a year younger than me and one year older than Mel. He was good looking even back then, but I worried that he was just another, typical fourteen-year-old-boy, after one thing only, something to brag about to his friends.

He knew about the bullying I suffered when I was in my young teens. Once he started dating my sister, surprisingly he proved his sincerity about his relationship with her by backing me when the bullies started laughing at me or calling me names. He protected me when no-one else did, not even Mel.

Mel and Steve were, what they call, childhood sweethearts, I guess. Together for fifteen years but it took twelve years for Steve to finally propose to Mel. The older they got, the smaller the age gap seemed. I was always very jealous of Mel growing up. She was in a long-term relationship which I never had. Steve was a great catch and I wished he fell in love with me and not her. But why would he? I was overweight, spotty and a loner.

Whereas Mel was beautiful and one of the most popular girls in the school.

Mel and I were close when we were young. We were a united front. But, as soon as she joined me in boarding school and distanced herself from me, it all changed, and I resented her. I couldn't stand seeing her happy all the time, when I never was. I hated the fact that she found such a loving boyfriend and later husband when I had no-one.

Then I met Tom. He was no Steve, but he was kind, caring and didn't try to control me. I ploughed all my attention toward him and our relationship. I didn't have time for anyone else, certainly no time for Mel.

However, Tom and I had been going through a rough patch about a year ago because I got bored. Bored of Tom, bored of the mundane, bored of my life. Tom thought it would be a good idea for us to start socialising a little bit more and doing 'couple' things. We didn't really go out together anymore or do anything together and the affection he showed me at the start of the relationship had dried up. So, we started meeting up with Mel and Steve more often, Tom thought that would bring us closer together. It didn't. It brought Steve and me closer together.

Steve was exactly what I wanted in a man. Well-off, regimented and extremely handsome. He was bored of his fifteen-year relationship and I was bored of Tom. We just clicked.

About four months ago, Steve decided to get a tattoo on his chest of a woman pushing weights. He said that way I was always close to his heart.

I'm snapped out of my daydream when one of the keys falls away from my lanyard due to my excessive twiddling.

As I bend down to pick up the key, I feel a sweaty hand grab my bum and squeeze firmly and meaningfully. I jump back up, swing in his direction, arm raised ready to swipe at him, with a face of fury. I keep control and refrain from slapping him but inside, I'm seething. My face doesn't lie though.

Pete is stood there, all sweaty and grinning through his panting. His treadmill was turned off and he was stood on the floor behind me. He must have turned the machine off whilst I was in my daydream and been stood there gawping at me. For how long, I have no idea.

'What the hell do you think you're doing?' I yell at him.

'Come on beautiful, you've been teasing me for months now. Flirting with me, firing all these innuendos at me. You know you want me!' he says.

'No, I haven't!' I shout at him. The gym quietens, all ears in our direction.

I lower my voice and verging on a whisper, I say, 'I suggest you leave quietly now and find yourself another gym to go to. You are no longer welcome here and will no longer receive training from me.'

'Oh, come on, sweetie,' he continues. 'I meant no harm; I was just playing. No need to be like that.'

He reaches out to put his arm around me. My stomach churns through total repulsion and rage bubbles through my veins causing me to erupt.

'Get the hell out of here Pete, you perve!' I shout again. Everyone in the gym stops to look and stare at the situation unfolding.

His face reddens and his drooling grin fades, it's replaced with sheer anger and embarrassment.

'That's fine, you frigid tart! This gym is shit anyway. I'll take my custom elsewhere.' And with that, he storms out of the gym, leaving me shaking with rage.

*

Five o'clock couldn't come quickly enough. After Pete left, I couldn't concentrate and was just clock watching for the remainder of the afternoon, focusing on meeting Steve later and being able to tell him all about it.

I received a few sympathetic glances from gym-goers once Pete left the gym, but my colleagues didn't approach me. They know me well enough to just leave me be when I'm angry. I'm not a crier so if anyone tried to comfort me, I'd likely lash out at them too.

At half-past-five, after a shower and freshen-up, I send Steve a text: 'On my way, Stephanie.'

We are so careful in our texts just in case Tom were to read my phone. His name is stored under the pseudonym 'Stephanie' and it's become a little bit of a joke name now. It winds him up when I call him Stephanie which just makes me want to call him it even more.

I head off to The White Tavern. Tom hates this pub, he says it's uninviting, dated and the food is terrible. Therefore, it's a safe bet that he wouldn't see me there. It's a good job that I'm such a private person, if anyone else saw me there with Steve, they wouldn't bat an eyelid as they know nothing about me or my life. They'd probably just think Steve was my husband.

The pub is a thirty-minute walk away from the gym unless you know the shortcut. Along the Taunton to Bridgwater Canal. I can make it within fifteen-minutes. I leave my car parked at the gym and make my way to meet Steve. As I leave the carpark, I notice that Pete's car is still parked up but he's no-where to be seen. What a prick he is, he's probably using the gym car park for free parking whilst he goes and grabs a post-gym burger or something.

Ten minutes into my walk along the canal, I approach a bend in the bridle path. I continue my quickened pace around the bend and am stopped short in my tracks. A shadowy figure appears in front of me, blocking my route. It's an overly familiar tall, male silhouette hidden by the evening sun. No, no it can't be. What the hell is *he* doing here?

Instantly, my anger from the day disappears and I start to panic. I know that behind me and in front of me is nothing but water and dirt tracks. I have never seen anyone else on this route, not even a dog walker and I've walked it a number of times before on my way to meet Steve after work. He must have been watching me for months walk this way, ditched his car today after I humiliated him and stood here waiting for me.

I think of my dad and 'suck it up'. 'Pete, is that you?' I ask, knowing full well it is.

The light that was once blocking my view of him, now slowly reveals him, in all his grotesqueness. He says nothing, but just stands there staring at me, a sinister, dark look across his face.

'Pete, what are you doing? If this is about before …'

Silently, Pete starts walking toward me. All I can think of to do is run back along the stony walkway, the way I came. I can out-run Pete. I turn and run as fast as I possibly can in heels but I'm struggling to control my breathing. I try to swallow the panic. Breathe God dammit, breathe! Adrenaline pumping, I inhale and exhale rapidly with every beat my feet make on the gravel.

I can hear him huffing and puffing behind me but he's not gaining on me. I glance behind me and I seem to be gaining some distance. But, with eyes on him, I fail to see a giant rock in my path and trip, buckling my ankle in the process.

Grappling at the ground I manage to pull myself up, but the pain from my ankle soars through me. I let out a pained scream, but I have to get away from him. Suck it up, move your arse, you can still outrun him! I frantically limp along in utter fear glancing behind me constantly.

He's caught up with me and is right behind me. I push through the pain. Limping along and using my arms to try to power me. But it's no use. I feel a tug at my T-shirt, lose my balance and fall to the ground.

Pete wrestles me into the undergrowth. He is on top of me, restraining me, using his full weight to pin me down. I know I embarrassed him at the gym, but I would never expect to be attacked by him. What the hell is he thinking? Shit … what's he going to do? Punch me, kick me, leave me for dead? What will I tell Steve if I'm covered in bruises, or Tom? Oh God, how do I explain this to Tom? This can't be happening. I need to fight back.

'Pete, no, you don't have to do this!' I cry.

I try to release myself from his clenched knuckles, but his hands are firmly gripping my wrists. His hot breath is blowing intermittent exhales of stale coffee and cigarettes in my face. I try to push him off me with my torso, try to move my knee in order to inflict some sort of pain on him. Any pain would do. But he is just too heavy.

My left arm is moved forcefully into the grip of his left hand along with my other arm. I see him wrestle with his belt buckle using his free hand.

No, this can't be happening. No, not to me, no. My muscles fail me, the horror of what is happening takes hold. I lose self-control and shamefully freeze.

'You think you can humiliate me and get away with it?' he spits at me ripping at my clothes. 'You're nothing but a dirty whore, who needs to be treated like a whore. I've been watching you. I know what you've been up to, cheating on your husband. You're a slut and now it's my turn to have a go at you.'

With a savage thrust, pain surges through my groin. I can't scream, I can't fight. The only thing I can do is let small tears roll down my cheeks and wait for this to be over.

3

15th July (1 week before the accident)

I never imagined becoming a mother. My parents were never loving or affectionate. They were heavily career focussed and their way of showing love was to shower us with gifts and send us to boarding school to get the best education possible. Or so they said. I knew the truth. That it was just to get rid of us for the majority of the year.

When Mel and I were in primary school in Swindon, I started to realise then that my parents weren't the same as other parents. We weren't greeted with hugs and kisses by our mother at the school gates once the bell rang at the end of the day. No, we were greeted by 'the nanny'.

Nanny Jane would fetch us from school, take us home, cook our tea and sometimes even bath us and put us to bed. It was only on weekends that our mother would step into the role of 'mum'. Even then, she was useless at it.

Mel and I had a good enough relationship with Nanny Jane. She looked after us, made sure we were safe and even disciplined us. But there was no love. She drew the line at getting too involved with us, for whatever reason. She was there to do a job, and once the job was complete, she'd go back to her own life away from us.

Mother was a high-flying solicitor. She worked long hours and dependent on the case, would often work late into the evening. She didn't have time to be both a career woman and a mother at the same time, so she chose her career. The only time she ever took an interest in our schooling was at parents' evening when she would portray herself as an amazing mother, showering us with affection which was all for show in front of the teachers.

Father spent a lot of time away due to his responsibilities to the Royal Marines. He was based in the barracks at Norton Manor Camp on the outskirts of Taunton. However, he would often travel for six months or more for training exercises, missions and even served in the Gulf War. He then left the army shortly after being diagnosed with prostate cancer eight years ago.

He never had time for us. He never did 'dad' things like playing games with us, taking us out for ice-cream or encouraging us with homework. He was always in a rush and everything had to be done now, without delay. He was a clock watcher. I knew this was because of his army training and discipline but as a child I wished we could just enjoy time with him without him cutting occasions short by saying things like, 'time's up' or 'time's ticking'.

Even during the school holidays, we didn't see much of my mother or father. My father would often still be away during the holidays and my mother still needed to work. She would arrange her twenty-five holiday days around our school holidays as much as possible, but quite often she continued to work throughout her holiday whilst Nanny Jane remained our sole carer.

As I stare down at the stick in my hands that reads, 'PREGNANT' I feel sick. My stomach aches, my head is dizzy and if I weren't sat down at the time of reading the results, I think my legs would have buckled and I'd have keeled over in sheer dread.

I had had a terrible feeling that the results would be positive. My period was a week late and although I'd not had any symptoms, I just couldn't shake the feeling that I was pregnant.

What an idiot I am. I was on the pill. How could this have happened? My hands are trembling, causing me to lose my grip on the stick so it falls to the bathroom floor.

No-one knew about what happened to me three weeks ago. I didn't tell anyone about Pete and what he did to me. How could I? It's shameful. The one time in my adulthood I lost control of a situation, that's what happened. If I told Tom, I'd have had to explain what I was doing walking to the pub after work, on my own and not with Karen. That would have opened a whole can of worms and started a new, fresh, web of lies.

As for Steve, I couldn't possibly tell Steve what had happened. He would have blamed himself. I was walking to meet him after all. Plus, he would possibly look at me differently, perhaps he'd see me as a weak victim. It would have changed the whole dynamic of our relationship.

I couldn't go to the police. There's nothing more that I want than to see Pete rotting away behind bars. But as soon as I tell the police, investigations will start, followed by court proceedings, testimonials, witness statements. My secret affair would be revealed to everyone and my moment of weakness would haunt me forever. No, no-one can know.

I haven't been back to work since for fear of bumping into Pete. I arranged a sabbatical, explaining that I just needed some time off but without going into details. They understood and assumed it was because of what happened with Pete in front of the regulars and my colleagues. I let them believe that. It made me look weak which I absolutely hated but I just couldn't go back to work there, not yet anyway.

I let Tom think the same. I had to explain to him somehow why I wasn't going to work. He works at the same gym as me but on a different shift pattern. He wasn't there when it kicked off with Pete, but he would have heard the gossip. It just seemed the easy option for Tom to think the same.

There was never a time in my life when I wanted a baby. I wasn't maternal at all. It might be because of my upbringing or like Tom said, perhaps I don't want children due to my fear of piling the pounds back on. After all, the last time I was overweight, I starved myself almost to death. Personally, I think it's just how I am. Having a child means you no longer have control of your own life or your own body so for me, it just wasn't an option.

But now here I am, pregnant and I have no idea who the father is. It could be Tom's. We were trying to work things out and one of the things we tried to do was get our libidos back within the relationship. Spice things up as the counsellor suggested.

Steve is also a very possible contender. After all, I had been meeting up with him in secret and we certainly lead a highly active sex life.

But there's one other option which doesn't even bear thinking about. Could this baby growing inside me, be the product of rape?

I look down to my abdomen and all I feel is hate. Hate for what is growing inside me, rotting me from the inside out. I run my nails across my skin, I want to claw it out. It's a parasite growing, infecting me and threatening to ruin my entire life. If there is any slight possibility of this child having a rapist for a father, then I need to get rid of it.

I snatch the pregnancy test up from the floor and toss it into the bathroom bin. Out of sight, out of mind.

*

Returning home after an afternoon run to try to clear my mind, avoiding any secluded areas, I grab a glass of water from the kitchen and make my way into the lounge to have a sit down before a shower.

As I walk into the lounge, Tom is sat on the sofa, head down, back straight and hands on his knees.

'You OK love?' I ask, still panting slightly after my run.

'When were you going to tell me?' he asks. He seems distant and somewhat annoyed.

Oh God. What does he know? Does he know I'm still seeing Steve? He's found out, he must have. My mind starts ticking overtime thinking what excuse or lie I can conjure up to hide the truth. If I weren't sweating already, I know beads of sweat would be forming on my face now.

I clear my throat. 'What do you mean love?'

Tom reaches inside his pocket and pulls out the pregnancy test I had thrown carelessly into the bin. Shit. What an idiot I am, I didn't want Tom to know, I wanted to avoid questions or him potentially trying to make me keep it.

'You're pregnant?' he asks, a small smile forming on his face. 'We're having a baby?'

Great. Here goes …

'I found out this morning Tom. But … you know I don't want children. I can't be a parent Tom, I just can't.'

I can see him start to get agitated, desperation is written across his face. 'Zoe, this could be a new start for us. We can do this; I can support you. I know you're worried about weight and your body changing, but it would all be for a good reason and I'll love you no matter what. You know that don't you?'

I sigh. 'Tom, I know that, but it's my body. I cannot have this baby. I can't!'

'I know it's your body Zoe, but it's *our* baby. I have a say in this decision too. Please!'

This is exactly what I wanted to avoid. Why did I have to go and leave it in the bathroom bin? I could have hidden it in the wheelie bin outside, taken it out with me on my run and disposed of it somewhere, burnt it. Anything. But no, I have to go and put it somewhere for Tom to bloody find.

I sit down next to Tom and take his hand.

'Tom,' I say softly. 'You know I don't want children; I never have. You knew this about me when we met. Please don't guilt trip me. I know it's hard for you to understand but I cannot have this child.'

If he knew what really happened to me and that the child could be the offspring of the devil, he may have another outlook. Not forgetting the fact that he has a one-in-three chance of being the father. If he knew that, he'd be straight out the door anyway. He forgave me once for having an affair with Steve, but he'd never forgive me a second time.

'I know,' he says. 'I just always imagined that if you did ever become pregnant, your opinion might change. At least I hoped. Please, just promise me one thing, you'll think about it. Don't make any rash decisions and let me know. I'll support you my love. I may not agree, but I won't let you go through it alone.'

I reluctantly nod. I don't need to think about it though, I've made my decision. There is no way I am having this child.

After my shower, with no delay, I google 'Abortion Clinic' on my phone and make the call. My appointment is booked for the twenty-second of July at ten-to-three in the afternoon.

4

22nd July (Car accident day)

Today's the day. I was offered counselling before the appointment, but I declined, saying that I have my own counsellor anyway who I'll be discussing this with. Not that I will. What's the point in talking it over with a stranger? She can't change what's happened to me, she can't make it better.

Some people would think it's my fault that I'm in this situation. That I brought this on myself for cheating, being disloyal. But I don't think anyone can or should blame themselves for being raped. OK, so I'm cheating on Tom. It's appalling behaviour, I know that. Although, I'm not sorry. I love Steve. At least I think I do. I get the butterflies and the excitement people talk about when they say they're in love. I admire him more than I've ever admired Tom. Therefore, I believe it's love. I think deep down, I always have loved him. And I'm pretty certain he loves me too. But, is that really a reason for me to suffer such a vile attack? Did I really deserve *that*? No, I didn't. No-one deserves to be abused in such a way, no matter what you've done in your life.

I haven't cried since I froze on that stony, canal pathway. What's the point? I'm stronger than that. If I cry, I lose control again. I must 'suck it up' as my father would say. Get on with it. What's happened has happened and I can't change anything. All I can do is keep pressing forward.

Don't get me wrong, I'm scared. In fact, I'm terrified. I'm terrified of bumping into *him*, of seeing *him* again. He took something from me that he wasn't entitled to and he could do it again. He's still out there, roaming around, living his life, possibly doing the same thing to other women. I probably have a duty to protect other women from him and I know that I should report it but I have to look after number one.

I have absolutely no control over him or the situation and I hate it. However, there is nothing I can do unless I confess to Tom about my affair and then face divorce, losing my money in the process, all whilst inflicting guilt onto Steve. The only thing I have control over right now is getting rid of this baby.

Thinking back to what the counsellor suggested I do, giving Tom control over at least one big decision, I ironically laugh to myself. Well this is one big decision I will *not* let Tom make or even compromise over.

Tom doesn't know that I have my appointment this afternoon. He thinks I'm still 'thinking it over', although there wasn't any thinking required. I know Tom said he would support me and come with me to the appointment if that's what I decided. However, I can't bring him along. It would give him more time to try and talk me out of it which would be a complete waste of his time and energy. It would hurt him too much to actually see me go through with it.

When he finds out that I have gone through with the termination behind his back, he will resent me for it. But I also know that, in time, he will forgive me. That's the kind of sucker he is. If he found out about my continued affair with Steve though, he would never forgive me again. Questions will be asked in my appointment about the reasons why I have decided to proceed with the abortion and I cannot risk Tom being there and starting to doubt my loyalty when he hears some of the answers I give.

There is no way that I will be disclosing the real reason for my abortion to the consultant. What I went through with Pete will remain my secret. I can't face telling anyone about it, owning up to being a victim. I will, however, explain about there being two potential fathers. I feel I have to justify my reason for terminating this baby. I don't think 'not wanting a baby' would be sufficient. I know it's my choice to terminate but I do feel I need to give a decent reason for my decision.

I'm clock watching and I know it. This can't happen quickly enough; I just want it to all be over. I've been for a run this morning and had a play on the piano to try and while away the hours but even that's not helping to distract me.

Growing up, it was expected that I take up a hobby and learn a musical instrument. I chose piano because I had always loved classical music and the emotion one can stir in others by caressing those magical keys.

It was something I enjoyed, even though I was made to learn by my parents. I found it to be a positive release from my struggles growing up. Whilst playing, I could get lost in the music and forget about the bullies, my eating disorder and the loneliness I felt growing up.

As I got older, I started singing. I was actually rather good. I still occasionally do a few gigs in local pubs now. At least I did up until a few weeks ago. I can't see myself singing in public for a while now for fear of who may be watching me.

It's almost lunch time so I decide to make myself an avocado salad. I'm not really hungry but it gives me something to do to kill time.

My phone buzzes on the kitchen worktop. I put down the knife I was using to chop the avocado and glance at the number. It's a New Zealand line which can mean only one thing. Mel.

What the hell is she doing calling me, especially as it must be almost mid-night at her end? I've not spoken to Mel since she found out about the affair and left the UK. I contemplate leaving it ring out to voicemail, but curiosity gets the better of me, so I answer.

'Mel?' I ask.

There's a pause. 'Yeah it's me,' she replies.

I have no idea what to say, this is extremely awkward. 'It's been a while,' I say.

'Look, I'm not going to beat around the bush,' she says. 'Tom's phoned me and told me about the baby. It's late and I'm tired, he kept me on the phone for over an hour. But I needed to call you. I know you must be confused right now and I thought you might need someone to talk to. I'll never forgive you for what you did to me, but you are still my sister and I want to help.'

Great, just what I need. My sister calling me up to stick her oar in. She knows I don't want children, so she's sticking her nose in where it's not wanted. She doesn't want to help; she wants to try to convince me to keep it.

'It's none of your business, Mel,' I snap at her. 'I don't need to talk to anyone about it. I've made my decision. I don't even know why you're calling me. You said it yourself, you'll never forgive me for what I did so why do you care?'

'Woah,' she says defensively. 'I was *just* trying to give you an olive branch and offer you support. I didn't have to you know Zo. I could quite easily be tucked up in bed right now, but no. Tom was so worried about it that I just had to call you. I couldn't wait until the morning. I thought you'd at least be a little confused about your decision. Please tell me you're going to at least think about keeping it?'

And there it is. That's the reason why she's calling me. I knew it. She wants me to keep it.

'Not that it's any of your business Mel, but I can't have this child. I don't want this child! You know I've never wanted kids.' I want to nip this in the bud. 'There's nothing you or Tom can say to change my mind.'

'Wow …' she replies.

'What do you mean by that? Wow?' I can feel my blood starting to boil. It's my body, my decision. Just like Tom, she cannot know the truth.

She starts to raise her voice down the line. 'It's selfish Zo. You can't do this to Tom! Not after everything else.'

She continues, 'Tom loves you, you idiot. Can't you see that? You've got a good man there who will support you no matter what. You can't just go ahead and abort his baby. Please, at least think about this!'

'I don't need to! My decision is made, I'm going to the clinic this afternoon and no-one will be able to stop me.'

'He doesn't know does he?' Mel groans down the phone at me.

'He knows I don't want it,' I say. 'But no, he doesn't know I'm going today and it's going to stay that way Mel.'

Mel's agitation increases, 'You can't do this Zo, you just can't! Tom has every right to know what you're doing. He'd support you; he loves you. No, you just want to do what you want when you want, screw everyone else hey? Typical Zoe, always …'

I move the phone away from my ear and let her rattle on down the receiver. I can't listen to this. I do feel bad, but I can't justify my decision any more than I already have done.

'Zoe?' I hear seeping through the telephone. 'Zoe!'

I put the phone back to my ear. 'I'm getting rid of it Mel. You won't convince me otherwise. You can tell Tom if you want. But I'm telling you now, if you do, I will *never* pick up the phone to you ever again.'

With that I hang up, the phone shaking in my hand. How dare she tell me what I can and can't do. She hasn't got a clue.

She has no idea about why I must go through with this termination. She just thinks, typical selfish Zoe.

I don't care what she thinks. She disowned me as a sister the moment she found out about Steve and my relationship. She's never really been there for me anyway. Not growing up, not in school not even in adulthood. She deserves to be lonely, just like I was.

*

The drive to the clinic is across town. The traffic isn't too busy at this time of day though so I should be there in good time. I haven't heard from Tom yet so I'm hoping I can get there, be seen and be out before he realises, or before Mel opens her big mouth.

Driving along, I turn on the radio to try to distract myself. Turning up the volume I listen to a song I've not heard before. It's a haunting melody with orchestral backing. It intrigues me, so I start listening to the lyrics:

... I've much on my mind and no way to turn,

Should I go back or keep moving on?

The hurt that I feel deep inside of my ...

Suddenly, I hear a horn blast behind me distracting me from the song playing. Looking in the rear-view mirror, I see the headlights flashing from an all too familiar car. It's Tom, Mel told him. He's following me.

My mobile starts ringing on the front passenger seat. I peer at it, and the name Tom flashes up on the screen. I try to reach for it with my left hand but can't quite get it. I fumble around trying to silence it, gripping the steering wheel in my right hand. But I just catch the side of the blasted phone, accidentally nudging it, causing it to fall into the foot-well of the car.

I glance back at the road ahead and see another car looming toward me. I try to brake, slamming my foot down on the pedal but it's no use. I'm going to crash and there's nothing I can do to stop it. I brace for impact. I'm tossed around and around as if I'm in a tumble dryer, the seat belt crushing my chest. Then I slam my head into the steering wheel and … nothing but darkness surrounds me.

5

The index finger on my right-hand twitches. It brings me back to the present and to the intense pain surging through my body. My chest hurts with every breath, rippling waves of agony up to my bruised skull. I try desperately to open my eyes, but they are sealed shut.

There's a repetitive beeping noise seeming to come from the left side of where I am lying. And to my right I can hear people talking, whispering. I strain to try and make out what they are saying but I can't understand a word.

I let out a quiet groan which, only for a split second, helped ease the pain.

'She's waking up!' I hear a male voice shout. 'Nurse, she's waking up!'

I feel someone lean over me, I can smell their sweet scent, it's a gentle floral smell, perhaps lavender. I feel warm breaths across my skin and my left hand is raised for a brief moment then lowered gently back to the mattress.

'Aisha?' A woman's voice says above me, close to my face. 'Can you hear me?'

I groan again.

'She's definitely coming round Mr. Brown,' I hear her direct this in a different direction. 'Give her a little time as she's been sleeping for quite a while and the anaesthetic is still wearing off. We'll monitor her closely, but it would be good for you to talk to her, reassure her.'

'OK,' I hear the male voice say. 'Aisha? Can you hear me? I'm here, you're OK. You're OK.'

I feel him stroking my hand as he says these words.

Why are they calling me Aisha? And who is Mr. Brown? What on earth has happened to me? I try to cast my mind back, what is the last thing I remember?

I remember being in my car, on my way to the abortion clinic, Tom was calling me. I reached for the phone and then …

I crashed. Yes, I remember crashing, a car looming towards me, the smell of burnt rubber, the squealing of brakes, the overwhelming feeling that I was going to die.

I let out a pained cry. I thought I was going to die. I was so scared and had no control. No control at all. Of the car, of myself, of the other vehicle. My breathing accelerates, short intermittent breaths in quick succession.

'Shhh, shhh,' I hear the man whisper in my ear and feel him now stroking my head. 'It's going to be OK Aish, you've been in a car accident but you're OK now. You're coming round after an operation so you're going to feel a bit groggy but I'm here. I'm not going anywhere, I'm here.'

An operation? Yes, an operation. I draw in a big gasp of air as realisation hits me. The voice of the surgeon, the bright light, the awesome feeling of calm and tranquillity.

I remember the voice in my head saying something like, 'It's not your time yet Zoe. You still have work to do.'

What was that? Was that the light people talk about when they glimpse death? Was that voice inside my head my conscience or was it a greater power? No, I don't believe in God.

But perhaps … maybe it was? No, don't be stupid Zoe, it was my mind telling me not to die yet.

The paddles. I remember the surgeon using paddles on me, sending electrical surges to bring me back. I catch my breath. I remember being sucked back into the wrong body. A woman was lying there, below me, all freckly with brown hair and I couldn't stop it. I couldn't stop being sucked into her body. Did that actually happen?

I desperately try to open my eyes again. This time, I'm able to slowly peel back my eye lids, blinking frantically. I take a deep breath in as the light above my head burns into my exhausted pupils.

'There you are, Aisha,' the man says. 'That's it, you can do it.'

I can make out dark hair and a kind smile, but everything is still a blur. His eyes come into focus and they're bright blue and bearing down on me.

'Hello you,' he says through his smiling lips.

The corners of my mouth curl up slightly. I have no idea who this man is, but I know he's here for the other woman, the other woman whose body I now seem to be inhabiting. Smiling is the last thing I feel like doing, but his smile is so infectious that I just can't help myself. I uncontrollably smile back at him.

This is unexplainable. How has this happened to me? Am I going to be cocooned in this body forever now? No, that can't happen. I won't let it. All those years fighting for the body I needed, the body I deserved and now I'm stuck inside this alien monstrosity. I know I'm now fat. That's one thing I did notice as I was being sucked into this body. I can't go back there, I can't be overweight again, not after everything I went through growing up. I wish I could reverse time and not try to pick up the phone whilst driving. What an idiot!

Oh shit, the baby. What happened to the baby?

In the distance, maybe a few rooms away, I hear muffled shouting. It's a female voice shouting, 'Who the hell are you?'

My eyes widen and I see the man by my bedside I now know as Mr. Brown, turn his head in the direction of the shouting.

'Stop calling me Zoe!' the shouting continues. 'I don't know who you are but I'm not Zoe!'

What? We swapped? She's in my body and I'm in hers! This is insane. How could the hospital let this happen? I've a right mind to ask to speak to someone and sue the hospital for negligence. My breathing quickens again, eyes wide.

Mr. Brown sees me start to get agitated. 'It's alright Aish. Obviously, someone's in much need of some psychotherapy! Try not to listen, there's no need to feel frightened. I'm here.'

I'm not frightened, I'm raging. But he's right. She does sound insane. I will also sound mad if I speak up. I need to keep this to myself until I've found a way to get my body back and I will. I will get my body back.

Then the woman, who I now know to be Aisha, screams, 'Get out!'.

There's another pause, then she continues, 'I just need to be alone. Please, get out!'

With that, silence resumes and we hear no more from the distant Aisha.

*

On my own in my hospital bed, I hear clocks ticking, machines whirring and distant hustle and bustle. Well this is boring. I wonder how long I will be incapacitated for, stuck in this bed without being able to do anything. I hate this. I can't do anything until my body heals and I'm able to stand and walk. Right now, there is nothing more I want to do than to find this Aisha's bed and get my body back. I don't know how to get it back, but I have to do something, try anything. But I can't. Not yet. I need to use this time to figure out a plan of action.

Mr. Brown has gone to get a bite to eat. He didn't want to but I insisted, saying he needed to keep his strength up for the both of us. I've yet to find out Mr. Brown's first name, which is a little awkward when he's calling me Aish and I can't say his name back.

Down the ward's corridor, I hear voices getting louder. I can make out a couple of females and a couple of males. One of whom is Mr. Brown.

'Is she OK Luke?' I hear one woman say, a young tone to her words. 'I can't wait to see her. Does she remember everything?'

'I'm sure she's fine,' another, more mature woman says. 'She'll soon perk up when she sees us. Luke's said she's doing well considering, so we just need to be there for her.'

Mr. Brown, or Luke I assume, replies, 'Yes, she's doing OK. A little disorientated but she seems to be fine. I guess the doctors need to monitor her, but I'm sure she'll be pleased to see you all.'

'Let's just try and keep calm, we don't want to overwhelm her. She's been through quite a time,' an older man says.

The dark green curtain separating my bed from the rest of the hospital is slowly swept to one side. Luke softly says, 'Hey you. I've brought some people with me I think you'll want to see.'

He stands to one side while a man and woman, possibly sixty-odd walk in, followed by a younger woman around the same age as me although it's hard to see them clearly.

I can't make out their faces. They're all a blur. I normally have twenty-twenty vision. I try blinking, and blinking again, but nothing works.

'I … can't see clearly,' I proclaim.

'I know Aish,' Luke says, 'But I couldn't find your glasses. It's been an age since you last wore them and not contacts, so I couldn't find them anywhere.'

Great. She wears glasses too, as well as being overweight. Happy days.

The older woman rushes up to my bed side, sits herself down on the chair next to me and grabs my hand. 'Oh darling, we're so pleased to see you!'

'We need more chairs, I'll go get some,' the older man says, leaving the room.

The younger woman plonks herself down on my bed next to my right leg. I let out a groan.

'Ooo, careful Gemma,' Luke says. 'She's very fragile.

'Sorry Aish,' Gemma says jumping back up from the bed, a massive grin on her face. 'I'm just so excited to see my bestie.'

The older man returns with three additional chairs stacked one on top of the other. He separates them in a semi-circle around my bed. He, Luke and Gemma take a seat. There's not enough room to swing a cat, I suddenly feel very claustrophobic. Who are these people?

The older woman is still holding my hand and says, ‘Your dad and I have been so worried. You haven’t half given us a fright. We love you so much darling.’

I have a mother, father, best friend and husband? And they all love me? The feeling of claustrophobia lessens and the warmth from the woman’s hand exudes love. Something I’m not accustomed to. Having these strangers by my bedside, caring about me, wishing me well, acting like family is intensely alien. I know they’re not my family, they are Aisha’s but I’m not going to lie, it feels surprisingly comforting having them here, loving me.

6

My welcome-back-to-the-land-of-the-living party of strangers have finally left for the day. For a brief moment, I enjoyed the feeling of being loved and cared for. However, it was short lived. That feeling of claustrophobia soon came back, and I felt smothered, like I couldn't breathe. I eventually snapped and asked them all to leave, Luke included. I said I was tired and needed to be alone to get rest and all this talking was starting to hurt my head.

In all the time they were by my bedside, I kept as quiet as I could until I snapped. They asked me a few questions to which I nodded or shook my head, dependent on the correct response to each question. If they asked me a question that required more than a yes or no answer, I just looked at Luke and he answered for me. That worked out perfectly.

They had no idea that I wasn't their Aisha. I played the part well, I think. Played the victim, the disorientated lost girl so that they didn't pressurise me too much or probe too deeply with their conversation. They didn't seem surprised when I asked them to leave, instead they graciously acknowledged my wishes and made a swift exit.

Even though they all suffocated me with their love and concern, it did feel strangely nice to be appreciated and worried about. I know that Tom would have been concerned about me, well technically he is concerned, he just doesn't know he's worrying about the wrong person.

It's obvious that Aisha has grown up in a loving family, with close friends around her and a loving husband. I resent her for it. I bet she didn't appreciate what she had before the accident. But now that it's gone, I reckon she must be longing for it back. That's the thing, so many people on this earth are ungrateful little bastards, not appreciating what they have in front of them. But as soon as something is taken away from them, they mourn and grieve and cry. Do they have a right to grieve over something they lost but never appreciated in the first place? No, I don't believe they do.

My parents were useless at showing affection or nurture. They used money to show their love if that's what you call it. Not only did they both have high-flying careers, they also inherited two houses when my grandparents on both sides passed away which they rented out for additional income, plus they inherited a shed load of money and investments from them.

If we fell over as children and grazed a knee, we'd be treated to the biggest and best toy from the big toy store in town. But we never received a kiss to make it better or a hug to sooth away the pain. Yet, when it came to the big stuff, like when I was hospitalised due to my eating disorder and was being fed from a drip, they did nothing. They buried their heads in the sand, wanting me to 'suck it up'. They failed to understand why I was so upset about the way I looked, how I had let the bullies affect me so badly and why I tried to starve myself. They just thought I was attention seeking.

My dad passed away three years ago and my mother the following year. Father's cancer finally got the better of him and he gave up and lost his battle. So much for sorting it out, making it right and sucking it up. Mother then stupidly drove her car into a streetlamp, drunk. She hit the bottle after my father died so the drink finally killed her in the end.

In my mother's will, she left me everything. Nothing was left for Mel, not one penny. Mel thought it was because I was their favourite. Their favourite? Really? If anyone was the favourite, it was Mel with her perfect looks, her perfect relationship and her perfect life.

I didn't think Mel deserved any of the inheritance. My parents left it to me for a reason, guilt money no doubt. But she was insistent that she should receive some of the money. Tom got involved and fought in her corner, saying she deserved something, that we didn't need all of it and that there was plenty to share around.

She wanted some money to start up a small business. A small dent in the whole inheritance so I reluctantly agreed to give her just enough to set up the business and not a penny more.

Lying in my hospital bed, I start to compare my upbringing with what I imagine Aisha had. It doesn't seem like she's that well off. Perhaps she has money but judging by how her family present themselves, I very much doubt it.

I bet she was loved unconditionally even though she's fat. I never measured up, not to the kids in school or to my parents. It was only when I lost the weight that I started to gain confidence in my appearance. Some people may call this arrogance. To be fair, I probably would too but then I have every right to be arrogant. I worked hard for this body and these looks.

Luke's quite a catch really. I'm impressed Aisha managed to pull him. I haven't had a proper look at myself yet in a mirror, but I've had a good look under the bed clothes and I'm not impressed. Each to their own I guess, but Aisha's definitely punching above her weight. And, judging by how much she must weigh, that's a lot.

Her body's shorter than mine, her skin is freckly all over and pale. She needs some vitamin D injected into her. Her breasts are big and droop to the sides whilst lying down. Possibly a size 42 E at a guess. And, she's got a peculiar scar in her left breast, it almost looks like a bite mark. Perhaps she's into some weird kinky bedroom stuff, who knows?

I know she has brown hair; I saw that when I was being sucked towards her on the operating table. But whilst lying in bed, exploring her body, I pulled strands of her hair in front of my face, horrified to find a multitude of split ends.

Her toenails reveal the chipped remnants of a turquoise varnish and her fingernails are all jagged and un-loved. Her wedding finger sports two thin bands of silver metal with subtle crystals embedded within. Another tell-tale sign that she doesn't have the wealth that I do.

She obviously doesn't take much pride in her appearance. I'm not overly surprised, I mean who would take pride in this body?

I'm snapped away from my thoughts as the curtain to my enclosure billows and a male doctor strides into my room.

'Hello Aisha,' he says whilst holding his clipboard and clicking his pen. 'And how are we doing?'

He starts checking the machines and examining me.

Hmmm … how am I? Well, I'm not quite sure how to answer that one. Pissed off is probably the most accurate answer, but I'm not going to let on. I need to continue to appear sane.

'Um … not sure,' I reply. 'How do you think I am?'

'Well, you're recovering well. So far, I'm very pleased with your recovery.'

He continues, 'But I'd like to do a few memory tests with you please. Nothing major, just a few questions. Standard procedure after this kind of operation.'

Memory tests? Oh God, how am I going to get through this without him doubting my sanity.

'Memory tests?' I say. 'I can remember most things fine. I don't think a test is needed. Plus, I am very tired and …'

'Nothing to worry about Aisha. Just standard practice like I said, I won't keep you long,' he says. 'Right, easy one first … what's your full name?'

'Um, Aisha Brown?' I say, knowing full well Luke is called Luke Brown.

'Very good. Any middle names?'

Shit. No idea. I frown and realise I'm scrunching my face up trying to answer. I must be honest. 'Um … I don't know.'

'OK,' he says, scribbling something on his pad. 'Next one, your date of birth?'

Oh God, my cover will be blown for sure now. How can anyone forget their date of birth? I sigh and reluctantly say the only date I can think of, which is my own date of birth. 'January the first, nineteen-eighty-three.'

'Perfect,' he says.

What? Wait … no … we share the same birthday? That's insane! Hah! Excellent! Have that Dr. Whatever-your-name! In your face! Put that in your memory test pipe and smoke it.

'And finally, your full address and postcode.'

Dammit.

He asks me a couple of other questions, including who the Prime Minister is and explains I may be suffering from mild memory loss. It shouldn't be anything to worry about and will hopefully come back soon, once I move back home and back to normality.

Once he's left and I'm on my own again, I reflect on his words. Back to normality. What's that then? Nothing about this situation screams normality. I may have fooled the doctor into thinking I only had mild memory loss rather than him hearing the truth and deeming me insane. But I am still faced with this ridiculous, horrifying situation where I have switched bodies with a complete stranger.

I reach down to the flab covering my abdomen and my blood starts to boil. How could this have happened to me? She's down the corridor, with *my* husband, *my* body and *my* money. Whereas I'm here, looking frightful and with a pauper's wallet. She's also carrying my baby and she doesn't even know.

She needs to get rid of it for me. I didn't get to the abortion clinic in time and that's all because of her crashing into me. If she doesn't find out soon, it'll be too late. That *thing* can never be born, never.

I need to calm down. Keep a level head and think. I can't go anywhere right now and even if I could physically get out of bed, if I go marching in there, demanding this, that and the other, I will look as crazy as she sounded when she was shouting out, 'I'm not Zoe'.

No, I have time on my hands, I cannot afford to panic. I need to sort everything out and make it right, but to do that I need to come up with a plan of action. I'll get my life and my money back some way or another even if it kills me in the process.

7

Sitting in a pokey kitchen of a tiny terraced house, I wonder what the hell I'm doing. I should be fighting for what's mine. I should be doing everything I can to get my house back, my money back and my body back.

I've been out of hospital for a day now. Luke brought me back here, to *their* house but I have to pretend it's mine and that I love it. I also have to pretend that I love him. It's hard work. But I know I have to try my hardest to not draw attention to myself. I can't let anyone think I'm a fruit loop. Even though I'm out of hospital now with a clean bill of health, it wouldn't take much for Luke to pack me off to rehab or whatever it is they force you to do nowadays.

However, it's easier said than done. Luke keeps talking about things I have no idea about, so I have to just nod or change the subject. He's getting more and more suspicious every day.

Last night, my first night in this strange hobbit house, I made Luke sleep on the sofa. There's no way I'm having a strange man cuddling up to me every night and no way I should be the one to sleep in discomfort. After all, I'm the one who needs time to properly recover in the comfort of my own home, as the doctors recommended. In the comfort of my own home … pah! There's nothing comfortable about this place and it's most certainly not home. Luke didn't kick up a fuss, in fact, he didn't seem that bothered about sharing a bed with me. He just agreed, said he understood that I'd be more comfortable by myself in my own bed.

Halfway through the night, I wished he were closer though. I woke up, unable to breathe. It was as if someone had closed my airways, choking me in my sleep. Utterly terrifying. Luke heard me gasping and coughing and ran upstairs with an inhaler. I have to say, he was rather great. He comforted me by smoothing my hair and reassuring me it'd pass with every inhalation. He told me off a bit too though, saying that I should know better and that I should always have my inhaler to hand. First time I'd heard about my asthma. Another thing to despise about this body.

Looking around me now, I stare at the photos and pictures plastered around the walls. Sickening photos of Luke and Aisha, all cosy and in love. Irritating wall hangings of quotes saying things like, 'Home, Where Our Story Begins' and 'What I Love Most About My Home Is Who I Share It With'. The most cringe-worthy quote by far, is the one hanging straight in front of me, goading me. It reads, 'You Aren't Wealthy Until You Have Something Money Can't Buy … Love.' Whatever.

There's a pile of letters Luke's left for me to open on the table. This is the reason why I sat down in the first place, to open them. I mean, I'm not supposed to because they're not strictly for me but who really gives a shit. I'll have a pry into Aisha's life and see if I can learn anything about her.

Most of them are bills, junk and bank statements which are utterly horrifying. That girl needs to curb her spending, especially when it comes to takeaways. No wonder I'm trapped in this overweight body if that's how much she spends on junk food a month. There is, however, one letter that grabs my interest. It clearly states, 'Private and Confidential' on the front. I tear it open and have a good read:

Dear Mrs Brown … blah blah blah ***… Following our appointment on July 22, I enclose a leaflet on Premature Ovarian Failure. I was unable to provide you with this during our meeting due to you being clearly distressed and leaving the surgery before completion of our consultation. I trust that this***

finds you well and please contact the surgery if you wish to discuss this further or require any additional support …

Interesting. So, she was told she couldn't have children, was clearly emotional and then got back behind the wheel of a car. And here's me thinking I might have caused the crash by reaching for my phone. I knew I wasn't at fault! She probably crashed into me when her hysterical tears blurred her vision.

And now she's pregnant. Does she know that she's got a bun in *my* oven? Well if she doesn't know, she soon will and then what? She's going to want to mother it, raise it, bring it up as her own. There's no way she's going to raise a child who most probably is the spawn of a rapist, no way at all. I need to find a way to switch back before it's too late to abort the mite.

*

I am so bored. It's only been a day and I am so unbelievably bored. There is nothing to do in this house other than watch TV and stare at stupid quotes. My ribs still hurt so I can't exercise yet. But once the pain goes, I'll start running again, may even sign Aisha up to a gym.

Luke's making dinner whilst I'm watching crappy soaps on the television. Not something I ever do, but apparently Aisha loves her soaps and of course, I have to pretend to be her and love what she loves. He knows I'm veggie now, meat's one thing I couldn't pretend to love. I just said I wanted to try something new. Luke laughed when I told him, he thought I was crazy. I can't imagine Aisha ever giving up meat so it must be even harder for Luke to imagine her going meat-free.

Luke serves up dinner and plonks a plate of food on my lap. Great, so they don't even use a table to eat from, the slobs.

With his mouth full, Luke says, 'Well then Aish, how are you feeling now you've been home for a day? You feeling a bit more rested?'

I finish chewing my mouthful and purposefully swallow to try and make a point before answering. 'Yeah, I'm OK cheers. Just a bit bored.'

'Bored?' he scoffs, whilst spitting little specs of food onto the carpet in front of him. 'You, bored? I'd have thought you'd have loved this. Being waited on by hand and foot, being made to watch day-time TV all day and not having to work!'

I say nothing, just raise my eyebrows and continue eating.

'Well if you're that bored,' he continues, 'Why don't you invite Gemma over? Or perhaps go and visit Mrs Wyatt? I know you're not working but I'm sure she'd love an informal visit. You know, you *are* able to get up and about. You don't have to stay in the house doing nothing if you don't want. As long as you take it steady.'

I shrug my shoulders and let out a nonchalant grumble. I'm not in the slightest bit interested in seeing Gemma or whoever this Mrs Wyatt is.

'OK well what do you want?' He starts to get irritated now.

'Not to be here!' I lash out. I've had enough of the pretence. 'Not to be sat here with a man who eats food like a washing machine on a spin cycle.'

'Woah!' His voice is raised, so are his arms in a defensive stance. 'Chill out Aish. Look I don't know what's got into you, but ever since the accident, you just don't seem to care about anything and I'm getting a bit sick of it now. What's happened to you?'

What's happened to me? Where to bloody begin mate. I can feel the frustration within me bubbling to rage.

'I can't remember a bloody thing, that's what's got into me. I don't know anything about me, about this life everyone keeps saying is mine and I don't know you.'

Bugger, I've said it. I've ruined the pretence. The cat's out of the bag which could prove to be a massive mistake, but I needed that outburst. It's been bubbling away inside me for days now.

'What?' His volume lowers and he looks confused. 'But the doctors said you had *minor* memory loss?'

I sigh. 'I lied Luke. I passed his stupid test because I knew my date of birth and my name. I didn't want to fess up because I was worried that I'd end up staying in hospital for weeks on end. I just want to get my life back.'

'So you don't remember anything?' he says.

He's really grating on me now. 'That's what I said, yeah. I don't remember anything. You make it so hard to pretend everything's fine. All your questions, your annoying habits, this shit-hole of a house!'

'Really?' He spits the word. 'After everything I've done for you, given up for you, that's how you talk to me?'

I'm done. I'm not talking anymore. I don't need this. I throw the plate of half-eaten food on the floor and storm upstairs. Toss open the duvet, dive into bed, shaking with rage and lie there until I calm down.

*

I've been lying here for about fifteen minutes trying to hold my bladder, but it's no use, I desperately need a wee.

On my way back to the bedroom from the bathroom, I hear Luke talking downstairs on the phone. He seems agitated but I can't quite make out what he's saying. I bet he's talking about me though. I creep to the top of the stairs to listen in.

'… She's just so unreasonable Gem. She says she remembers nothing, nothing at all …'

'… Yeah, yeah I know. I wish that too. But she needs me. You and me, it can't happen again Gem …'

'… I still love you too. But, like I said before, we can't keep doing this. I told you before that we needed to stop so that I could build a family with Aish, I chose her then and I have to choose her now. She needs me …'

'… Oh, don't be like that. If things were different, perhaps it would work …'

'… Yeah, OK things *are* different because she can't remember, but does that make it right for us to keep seeing each other behind her back? …'

'… No, I can't tell her. Not now. One day we can be together, maybe. Oh God. What a mess. I'm so sorry Gem …'

So dear, sweet, loving Luke is really a cheating bastard. If Aisha were to ever find that out, she'll never want this life back. I'll have to make him want me, love me, choose me. He'll have to end this affair for good if I have any hope in switching back with Aisha.

8

It's been almost six weeks since the accident. I've been out of hospital for about a month now. If I said time had flown by, I'd most certainly be lying.

The last few weeks, since I found out about Luke having it away with Aisha's best friend, have been tedious and a true test of my inner strength. I'm undoubtedly a strong person, after what I've been through in my life. I don't easily let things get to me or have control over me and I can effortlessly manage my emotions, an ability that I've finely tuned over the years. However, trying to convince a man, who irritates me to high Heaven, to love me is hard work.

Luke isn't a bad looking bloke; I'll give him that. But he has some extremely annoying habits. Like the whole speaking with his mouth full issue. I mean, that is enough to put anyone off their food. I lose my appetite every time he scoops up a forkful of mashed potato or whatever else he's eating and shovels it into his mouth. How Aisha was the size she was is beyond me, I'm surprised seeing that every day wasn't enough for her to shed a few pounds at the very least.

Not only does he eat like a trout but he's also very messy. He leaves his dirty clothes on the floor by the washing machine door. I mean, why? When he can simply open the door and put them inside. He leaves the toilet seat up after every visit, he never washes up and he picks his nose. Yes, that's right, he picks his nose and God knows what he does with his pickings after. In fact, I don't want to know. And the farting, I'm not even going to get started on that.

Some people may say he's a bloke and that's what blokes do. Some people may call me a prude. But I have standards and to see someone slob around like him makes me so annoyed. He could be a decent guy if he took a little more care of himself and smartened his act up a bit. He's good looking but my God, he's a tramp.

What hasn't made things easier is that it's school holidays. Luke's a teacher, so this has meant he's been off work and in my face, every single day. He starts back at work in three days and I cannot wait.

I really miss Steve. I miss our meetings, our cuddles and kisses and the way he makes me feel. I haven't spoken to him in weeks now, not since we arranged to meet up after the gym, when Pete did what he did to me.

Pete. He's still roaming around, possibly preying on other women, maybe trying to hunt me down. Well good luck to him now. He wouldn't have a clue who I was if he bumped into me and I very much doubt he'd want any part of me, looking as I do now. I guess that's one positive thing about the switch. I expect he's moved on to his new target, anyway, probably bored of waiting for me to go back to the gym.

It's been hard to keep up the pretence with Luke. I've had to adopt the role of wifey by cleaning up after him, washing his clothes, scrubbing the toilet every time I want to have a pee. All while plastering a fake smile on my face in order to convince him to stay with me and not pursue Gemma. I can't have Aisha finding out about this and wanting to stay living my life. No way, no how.

He's still sleeping on the sofa though, that's one line I cannot cross, but Luke seems to be understanding, at the minute. Although, I can imagine he's going to start getting agitated soon, I mean men have needs and all that and the sofa isn't exactly comfy. Hopefully, it won't be long before I get my body and life back, so I just have to keep up with this act until then.

The doorbell rings.

'Can you get that please Aish?' Luke hollers down the stairs. He's having his morning crap.

Dammit. I was just listening to David Dickinson coercing someone into selling an ornate, pocket watch for fifty quid. Yes, this is what my life has become.

I open the door to Carol, Aisha's mum. My first visit from her since hospital. I've been ignoring her on purpose as I just don't know what to say to her.

'Aisha, darling,' she says with a beaming, kind smile. 'How have you been? Can I come in for a cuppa?'

Well, I can't exactly say no. I can't afford for anyone to get too suspicious of me, so I smile, nod and open the door welcoming her into the house.

She's very graceful and well presented. Quite timid looking, almost mouse-like. 'What can I get you?' I ask.

'No, no,' she says. 'I'll make the tea; you sit yourself down as you must still be resting. I must say you look a lot better since the last time I saw you darling.'

Before I know it, she's darted into the kitchen, popped the kettle on and is preparing our drinks. I stay in the lounge waiting for her return.

'You're very quiet sweetheart,' she shouts through the kitchen door over the sound of the boiling kettle.

I have nothing to say, that's why.

'Is Luke home? Shall I make him one too?'

'Yeah,' I shout back. 'He's upstairs in the bathroom. Probably be down soon.'

She brings three mugs of steaming drink into the living room; her right hand's fingers are delicately wrapped around the handles of two mugs and her left hand carries a third. She hands me the one from her left and sits herself down in the armchair.

It's tea. I hate tea unless it's green or nettle. I try to hide the grimace forming on my face, say thank you and take a sip.

'Urgh!' I can't help but exclaim. 'It's got sugar in it.'

Carol's eyebrows furrow in what I assume is confusion.

'I thought you'd like a little 'taste', as my treat,' she says.

'Taste?' I ask, confused by this expression.

‘Well, yes darling. Sugar in your tea, how you like it sometimes,’ Carol continues looking baffled.

‘I don’t have sug …’ Realising I may have almost slipped up then, I try to regain my cover. ‘Sorry, it just took me by surprise. There’s quite a bit I’ve forgotten. Ever since the accident I’ve grown to prefer green tea actually. It’s a good antioxidant. Just trying to look after myself a bit more you know?’

‘Oh, yes, OK. Luke said you had forgotten a lot more than we first suspected.’ She still seems a little puzzled by my response. ‘So, have you managed to get out and about a bit recently? You know, fresh air is good for you. You can’t be cooped up in here every day.’

‘Nah, not really.’ I shrug my shoulders. ‘I’ve been resting mostly but I’m thinking of taking up running actually.’

Carol almost chokes on her tea. ‘Running? You? Goodness me, what has gotten into you darling? I mean, it’s great you want to exercise but nothing too strenuous too soon OK? Perhaps, Luke could take you shopping or something, something small to start with.’

To be honest, it doesn't surprise me in the slightest that she thinks it ludicrous that her daughter should want to start running. I don't think this body's ever worn trainers let alone run in them.

'Hiya Carol,' Luke says as he bounds down the stairs. 'Sorry, I was just in the little boy's room. Ooo … thank you for my cuppa.'

He plants a kiss on her cheek and sits himself down on the sofa next to me. 'How are you Carol?'

Carol smiles, she obviously thinks highly of Luke.

'I'm alright thanks Luke, just worried about this one,' she says, looking in my direction.

She continues, 'We were just talking about you taking Aisha shopping or something, get her out the house for a bit.'

Luke looks at me, sees my look of disinterest, ignores it and looks back at Carol saying, 'I think that sounds a great idea.'

I'd much rather go and do something on my own, but without a car I'm a little limited. There's nothing I can say to get out of it. Not if I want to continue this pretence. I have to try to convince Luke that I'm remembering him and doing everything I can to make our relationship work.

‘You’ll have to come with Dad and I to church on Sunday darling,’ Carol adds. ‘That’ll get you out the house and hopefully put a smile back on that face.’

Eh? Church? Besides my wedding to Tom, I haven’t been to church since I was made to attend a Harvest Festival with school. My eyes widen involuntarily.

Carol can sense I’m not enthralled by the idea. The confused expression reappearing on her face.

‘Um … yeah OK. We could do that,’ I say with absolutely no intention of following through.

We make some more idle chit chat and Carol finally leaves after an hour or so.

‘I think she’s right,’ Luke says once she’s left. ‘I think a trip out will do you some good. Something small to start with and we do need some groceries before I go back to school. So, we’ll go to the supermarket tomorrow.’

I’m not bothered about going out with Luke or going shopping for that matter. But a few hours away from day-time TV and a break from these four walls will be greatly appreciated.

*

Luke is a nightmare to shop with. I'm the kind of person who knows exactly what I need to buy, I always shop with a list prepared and I get the job done, without delay. In and out as quickly as possible is my motto. There's no need to dawdle, not when it comes to food shopping. Luke, however, is the opposite. We have no list prepared and I'm made to walk down every aisle in sequence, browsing each section looking for deals. All prices are carefully studied before selecting the best bargain for our money.

I hate this. Previously, I would have had no concerns about voicing my annoyance to Tom about anything and everything. Now, I have to be on my 'best behaviour' which is so unbelievably arduous.

Down aisle number nine, not even halfway through, and Luke is staring at biscuits. I think we must have been here for at least six minutes, just staring at the prices of biscuits. Luke keeps asking me what I fancy. When we first arrived in the supermarket, I'd reply reasonably and politely with potential suggestions but at this point I really don't care. I just want him to get a move on and make a decision. I'm getting so frustrated and I know my face is showing it. But seriously, how long does it take a man to decide if he wants custard creams or bourbons?

'I just can't decide Aish, which do you prefer?' he asks me.

'Oh my God,' I snap. 'Here, take these. Decision made. Now let's move on … please!'

As I grab the custard creams, a whole bunch of the bloody things come crashing to the floor.

'Alright Aish, keep your hair on!' Luke exclaims.

Really? I have every right to be getting annoyed right now. 'Just get a move on Luke. Start on the pasta aisle and I'll catch you up once I've sorted this mess out. It's not like you'll get far from me in a hurry!'

In a sulk, Luke drives the trolley around into the next aisle away from me.

Crouched down, I start to pick the multiple biscuit packets up off the floor. A wrinkly, sun-spotted hand reaches out to help.

'Here, let me help you, my love,' the owner of the hand says. 'Although, I can't bend quite as well as I used to.'

I look up to see an old woman, possibly in her seventies, with little glasses perched on the end of her nose looking down at me.

'No, you're alright, thanks,' I say.

'Oh, it's not a bother,' she replies as she insists on struggling to bend down to help.

She starts jabbering away about this and that. I zone out, still fuming about Luke and how highly irritating he is.

Then, she says, 'I get a feeling about you, you know. Let me give you some advice, you can never ignore good advice. You take that there man's hand, and you accept the path you've been forced to walk down. You never know what you'll find.'

Oh God, I've attracted the local weirdo. What the hell is she going on about? She's got 'a feeling about me'. She hasn't got a bloody clue!

'Um, thanks for the help and all,' I say. 'But you can keep your advice and stick it. You don't know me. The sandwich aisle is near the exit, seems you're a few short of your picnic love.'

'I know you're not who you used to be love,' she says. 'Everyone's on a journey through life but sometimes you can be so focussed on both the road behind you and the road ahead, that you forget to explore side roads. You don't want to let them pass you …'

'Alright,' I say. 'I've had enough of this bullshit. I've thanked you for your help, not much use it was and now I'm off.'

I turn to walk away and hear her shout behind me, 'You need to leave the supermarket right now if you've any hope of finding yourself. Leave now, before it's too late. *She* needs you.'

What the hell is the old bag talking about? I don't turn around, instead I hurriedly look for Luke. He's miraculously covered three aisles in the time the woman was talking to me. As I approach him, I can't help but think about what she said, 'Leave now if you've any hope of finding yourself, before it's too late. She needs you.'

There's a big part of me that thinks she's off her rocker. But another part of me is actually a bit taken aback by some of the things she was saying. She's right, I'm not who I used to be, and I need to find myself. Besides, who supposedly needs me?

Before I know it, I grab Luke's hand and pull him away from his trolley load of food and say quietly but sternly, 'We need to leave now.'

I don't know why I've let her get to me like this, this isn't like me but she's definitely given me the creeps.

'What's going on?' Luke asks, concern plastered across his face.

I don't respond. Instead, I continue to march him towards the exit.

As we reach the flower aisle, with the exit within my sights, I stop in my tracks. There *she* is, Aisha, walking in the direction of the automatic doors. Close on her trail is Pete the Perve.

I gasp. My heart races and I involuntarily squeeze Luke's hand. No, no, no. She doesn't know him; she won't know to run. I can't let him abuse my body again. He took me once; he won't take me again.

I tighten my grip on Luke's hand and drag him closer to the exit. I don't know how, but I need to stop him.

'Aish, what the hell's the matter with you?' Luke cries pulling me back.

'I can't explain right now Luke, but we need to leave now ... Please. Trust me.'

As we approach the exit, Aisha turns around for whatever reason and crashes full pelt into Luke. I see Pete skulk off into the car park, glancing sporadically back towards us until he is out of sight.

Part 2

9

Look at her, just look at her. It's so bizarre looking at yourself in three-dimensional form without the need for a mirror. She's there, right in front of me and she is beautiful. Obviously, I know she's me. I always knew I was beautiful, just not *that* stunning. She could do with flaunting it a bit more though, standing there in sweats and trainers, her hair all a mess. Come on love, you've been given a chance at owning my body for however long and this is how you embrace it?

She's standing there, in front of us, mouth wide, face pale. She's going to blow my cover and make us both look like fruit loops in a minute if she says anything. Even though I want her to want her life back as much as I want mine back, I haven't had enough time to finalise a plan of action yet. Don't say anything, please don't say anything. Not here anyway. I don't feel as though I have control over this situation at all. I can't say anything to stop her, I can't take any action. All I can do is stare, eyes wide and hope she can read my mind.

I can feel my face flush. That's new. This bloody, stupid body. Why am I blushing? Is it anger or panic? It's suddenly very hot in here. This wasn't my intention, I wanted to make her hold her tongue with my expression, not appear scared or embarrassed. I look away to try and hide it from her.

'Are you OK, miss?' Luke says, breaking the deafening silence.

'No, I'm not OK,' she replies. Oh God, here goes. She's going to say something stupid; I just know it.

'I'm sorry … sorry,' she continues pitifully. And then the daft mare faints.

What a drama queen. But at least this keeps her quiet for a bit, I guess. Although perhaps it would have been better to just rip the plaster off, find out if she'll say anything sooner rather than later.

'Bless her heart,' Luke says turning to me. 'She's obviously not well. I'll stay here with her if you can go and get some help?'

I'm not going anywhere. If she wakes up whilst Luke's here alone with her, she could say anything. I haven't planned for any of this. She could tell him what's happened to both of us, make Luke believe her story, he could then cast both of us away, settle down with Gemma and then she'll never want to switch back. Not if her precious Luke turns his back on her. If anyone's going to be here when she wakes up, it's me so that I can handle this situation myself. I need my body back but on my terms.

'Probably best I stay with her Luke, you go get help,' I say. 'She might prefer a woman to be here when she wakes rather than a strange man. No offence.'

'Yeah, I guess,' he says. 'Won't be long.'

I stay standing, hovering over her uncomfortably. I'm not going to sit by her or soothe her, that's way too awkward. I'll just keep my eye on her from up here.

Although now I'm here with her, I wonder what I would say if she were to wake up. I mean, I can't exactly say you're pregnant with potentially a rapist's child and you need to abort it. Firstly, I don't want anyone to know about what happened to me for fear of losing my money to Tom or casting guilt onto Steve. Secondly, she discovered she couldn't have children before the accident. If she found out she was pregnant now, would she really care that I was raped, and that she could possibly be carrying the offspring of a complete sicko? She'd want to keep it for sure. She might already know that she's pregnant, made her decision already to keep it. She wouldn't want to switch back, not at the risk of losing her hopes of motherhood once again. This is a nightmare. I need to find a way to get my body back, as soon as possible. Who cares if Luke leaves her for Gemma? I don't. She doesn't have to *want* to switch back, I just need to make it happen, somehow.

A greying couple rush over to ask if she's alright. I usher them away, telling them that help is on the way and they needn't worry. The fewer people who are around when she wakes up the better. They hover for a few seconds, the nosy pair, and finally exit.

As my eyes are on the exit doors, the strange old lady from before wanders out after the couple. She turns to look at me, she smiles a crooked smile and nods before making her final exit through the supermarket doors.

I'm not going to lie, that woman gives me the heebie-jeebies. Did she know this would happen? That I'd see Aisha being followed by Pete and then see her bump into Luke like she did. Was this all part of some old psychic crone's plan? Perhaps, she's a witch of some kind that needs to be burnt at the stake or drowned at sea. Don't be stupid Zoe. You don't believe in any of that tosh. She probably smiled at me and nodded as she left because she got lucky with her bullshit for a change.

Hopefully, Pete's long gone now. That's one perk about Aisha pathetically fainting. He wouldn't risk hanging around for long out in public I doubt. Although, he could still be watching from a distance. A shiver travels down my spine. What would have happened if Aisha didn't turn around to come back into the supermarket? Would he have followed her home, followed her down some quiet roads or maybe the canal path? If she was planning to walk home, then he would easily find a couple of deserted, country spots for him to have his evil way with her. The horrific memories bounce back into my head of Pete pinning me down, his hot breath blowing in my face as he thrusted over and over again. I'll never let him do that to my body, ever again.

Then a realisation hits me, an epiphany. I'll never let him do that to *me* ever again. Do I really care if he does it again to my body, if it no longer belongs to me? While I'm in Aisha's body, I don't have to keep looking over my shoulder, wondering if he's lurking in the shadows somewhere, waiting to pounce. All along, I've been wanting to switch back and get my body back. But, without my body, the odds of Pete raping me again are a hell of a lot slimmer.

Aisha lets out a groan which snaps me out of my thoughts. She's waking up, what do I do?

'Don't just stand there Zoe,' I hear Luke shouting at me as he runs to her with a glass of water. He's followed by a young, spotty shop assistant carrying a chair. She looks like she'd much rather be at home watching trashy reality TV than be at work, helping a stupid woman who just fainted. Great help you've sourced there Luke.

He crouches down next to Aisha on the floor and helps raise her head to drink some water.

'You've just fainted,' he says to her. 'Do you think you can stand? There's a chair just in front of you.'

Watching her dramatically scramble to her feet, groaning and moaning, clutching onto Luke's arm, feeling around for the edge of the seat makes me squirm. How pathetic is she? She's only fainted, not done ten rounds with Mike Tyson for God's sake.

The shop assistant stands there, slowly playing with the gum that's wrapped around her tongue, staring at her.

'Do you want us to call an ambulance or do you think you'll be OK?' she asks in monotone. Like she really gives a rat's ass. 'You gave us all a bit of a fright then.'

She gave you a fright love, did she? Really? You've done nothing useful since being here other than bring a chair over for her to sit in and stare gormlessly at her. If that's you after being given a fright, you've not lived my friend.

As for an ambulance, is this girl for real? She's fainted. She doesn't need paramedics to be diverted from people who are dying just to give her water and slap her around the face a few times.

Thankfully, Aisha declines the ambulance. I just want to leave now, get away from this awkwardness so that I can think about what I want. Do I want to switch back for my money and, let's be honest, boring life? But be worried about Pete stalking me and wanting to have his way with me again. Or do I want to stay in this abysmal body and live without fear of Pete ever raping me again? But likely lose my money and beauty.

It's taken me years of hard work and dedication to maintain my figure. After being bullied at school for being fat and subsequently refusing to eat, I promised myself I would never pile on the pounds again and eat responsibly.

There is a big part of me that blames my father for my eating disorder. As a teenager, I felt like my father sided with the bullies. 'No wonder you're bullied, you're too overweight, sort yourself out and that way they'd have nothing to pick on you for,' he'd say.

On his death bed, he told me he felt guilty. He thought he was responsible for my eating disorder and how controlling and regimented I had become. He knew I was a stickler for time, just like him. He also knew I was unable to love, not properly, just like him. For the first time I could remember, he apologised and sobbed. I never thought I'd ever see my father cry and yet, on the verge of death, he felt it necessary to seek forgiveness. Perhaps that's why the money was left to me once mother passed away. The guilt was too much for them. I certainly wasn't their favourite like Mel thought.

He was right, it was his fault and also my mother's. They gave me nothing but money and discipline throughout my life. No love, care, affection. So, when I inherited the whole sum of money from them after they died, it hit me like a tonne of bricks.

I never wanted their money, I only ever wanted them to love me. For the first time since I was a bullied child, I sobbed uncontrollably for near enough a week. It was like the final kick in the teeth. My parents gave me everything they could think of once they'd left this Earth, knowing that they were too late to give me what I really wanted, love. Tom was the most supportive he'd ever been at this point. I inadvertently leant on him to get me through that time, which I hated. I was weak and he loved it.

My inheritance is guilt money and at the time, I didn't want anything to do with it. Now, however, I believe it was the least they could do. It was compensation for the loveless childhood I was brought up in.

Do I really want to give up my money so that I can live in a fat girl's body once again? It sounds so stupid. Why on Earth would I want to give it up and not just give it up, give it to a stranger to enjoy and spend? Also, I would have to be strong enough to lose weight properly again. I won't be able to stay in this overweight lump of a body without dieting and exercising. Would it be possible for me to go down that path again, starve myself again? No. No, I'm stronger than that now. If I decide to pass up my money and settle in this body for the sake of escaping Pete and his stalking, I will make sure I diet appropriately.

We've been in the supermarket for over two hours now, what with Luke's inability to choose which cheap food is the best and now this rigmarole. Time's getting on and this was not what was agreed when I said I'd get out of the house for a bit.

'I think we can go now Luke, she's in safe hands,' I say sternly and a bit sharply. I can't help it. If I don't make a point about leaving now, I fear we'll be here for eternity. Although, I'm not sure what safe hands they are, I wouldn't want to be left with a gum-chewing juvenile looking after me.

Yet he continues, making sure she's OK, asking if there's anyone he can call for her. I mean, it's nice of him, it shows his caring side and it's quite admirable really but at this moment in time, I have no patience for niceties.

'Come on then love,' I say tapping at my watch. 'Time's ticking.'

As we walk out of the supermarket, I purposefully turn around one last time, look her square in the face, and want to somehow let her know that I'm not hiding, I know who she is and what's happened and I'm the one who will decide our fate. I'm not finished with her and I need to decide if I want to switch back or not. She doesn't get to decide. It's up to me and will always be up to me. This is my life, my destiny and no-one will decide my path for me.

I think back to what my counsellor suggested I do if I feel anxious about control slipping away from me. But instead of letting my index finger absorb the tension and anxiety of not being in control and casting it out into the atmosphere, I move my finger to my forehead, feel the control pervade the digit and point it firmly in her direction. I'm not losing control, I have control, of me *and* of her and I want her to know it.

10

The sun is setting on what has been a rather draining day. I have some serious thinking to do. Do I stay as I am or do I fight to return to my previous life?

Legs crossed beneath me in the big armchair, a cup of green tea in one hand and my phone in the other, I decide to log into Facebook. I rarely use social media. I've not got many friends and those who have added me on Facebook are merely acquaintances. Ever since Tom found out about me and Steve, I deleted a lot of friends, including Steve and Mel. Tom became very untrusting, which is understandable, but it became very boring very quickly. In a rage one night, I deleted all the male friends I was associated with from my account, right in front of him to try and make a point. He said that I was being ridiculous, but I knew he was happy. Happy that I had allowed my friend-count to dwindle down to fifteen and he was the only remaining male friend.

The phone is automatically logged into Aisha's profile. I have a little gander, but nothing really interests me. She's a typical Facebooker. Her wall is filled with cute pictures of her and Luke, her and Gemma, unfunny cat memes and game invites. Both Gemma and Carol have posted on her wall, moaning about how distant Aisha's been since the accident. What a fake Gemma is. She's having it away with Aisha's husband one minute, then playing the caring best friend the other. I know the game she's playing, after all, I've played it myself. However, if I'm to stay in this body, I ought to try to make a bit of an effort to get to know her a bit. See how fake she is to my face.

I sign her out and enter my email address and password for my account. As I click, 'Sign In', a pop up appears on my screen, saying, 'Incorrect password'.

That's definitely the correct password, unless I've typed it in incorrectly. I try again. 'Incorrect password.'

How very odd. I've used Facebook recently to write a couple of posts. Nothing of major importance, I just had a moment a while ago when I was feeling a bit lonely, so I stupidly put a message on there to see if anyone responded. No-one bothered to even acknowledge it. I'll delete it once I get access as what's the point? It's only *me* who cares about me, and that's the way it's always been.

I also posted something about loving my life and loving my husband. At the time, I thought I missed my life with Tom and wanted to put a little message out there. Again, no-one commented or even 'liked' it, not even Tom. So that's something I'll be deleting too.

The last post was written only two days ago, and I could log in then. I wrote something about contemplating a new life and a new start. I just wanted to write something to explain to people why I'm not going to the gym, why I may be acting a bit different and see what attention I'd receive. That one can stay. As I *am* now contemplating a new life and a new start, as Aisha.

I wonder if she's somehow cracked into my account and changed my password, the crafty bitch. I'll log into my email and see if there are any messages in there from Facebook advising me of a password change. I load up UKIntermail and enter my email address and password and click 'Sign In'. Unsuccessful, a new pop up appears saying, 'Your Password Has Been Entered Incorrectly, Please Try Again'.

I attempt access another three times, each time 'Sign In' is clicked, my rage heightens. She's locked me out of email and

Facebook, how dare she! So, she's decided to take over my life then has she? Or maybe, she wants to find out a little more about the person who's taken her body and life. I don't blame her; most people are fascinated by me and want to be me. I wouldn't be surprised if she was starting to like living my life and looking like me.

Well, you best get used to it Aisha, as I'm not going to try to get my life back. I've decided. I'm going to try and work with the hand that I've been dealt. I mean, I've now got loving parents which I never had before, even if they are suffocating, but that's a bonus. Luke's annoying but not unattractive. And most importantly, I don't have to worry about psycho Pete stalking me or maybe even telling Tom about me continuing my affair with Steve. Pete can crack on, tell him if he wants, it won't be me having to face Tom's anger and being hung, drawn and quartered. It will be Aisha.

The downsides to staying in this body are: losing my money, seeing that little sproglet being born and wondering who the father is, having to lose weight again when I never thought I'd have to do that again in my whole lifetime and the worst thing, Steve not knowing who I am.

However, if I can convince Steve I am who I say I am, we can be together, properly. Tom won't be any the wiser, Luke means nothing to me anyway and he can scuttle off to be with Gemma and I'll be able to happily live my new life with Steve. I don't know how I'll explain all of this to him, but somehow, I will.

Whilst I'm online, I decide to write a blog. A way to let Aisha know that I'm going to stay in this life. I want her to think that I'm happy living her life, that I'm not going to give it up easily. Not now. She needs to know that I'm the one in control and I always will be. I start with the title, 'RE-BORN'.

*

It's eleven thirty on Saturday morning and I'm majorly out of breath from my first morning jog in this body. I hate being unfit and having to suck on this God-awful inhaler. Luke's due to go back to work on Monday but I needed to get out of the house this morning. I'd been up quite late writing last night and needed some fresh air as soon as I woke up. Normally a morning jog sets me off for a good day, it clears my head and makes me feel alive. However, now I'm inhaling medicine into my crippled lungs whilst wiping away the tears streaming down my face from choking. I am far from feeling alive.

Staggering up to the front door, I unlock it and practically fall into the house gasping and gagging, I must sound horrendous.

'Woah, you ok Aish?' Luke greets me in the hallway. I can tell he's fighting back the laughter. 'See, running is NOT good for anyone!'

'Piss … off!' I say through chokes, bending over, clutching my stomach.

Luke takes my arm to help me to the kitchen. I can feel his shoulders twitching while he tries to contain his laughter.

'Go on … laugh, why don't you?' I say, still out of breath.

With that, Luke lets out an almighty guffaw, 'I'm sorry … I'm so sorry, it's just … look at you!'

He's laughing uncontrollably now. I try to fight it but, he's right, I am ludicrous. So, I surrender and laugh along with him.

'Stop it …' I say laughing and gasping for air all at the same time. 'You're going to kill me!'

It feels really good to laugh. It's been a long time.

Sat at the kitchen table, my breathing starts to stabilise, and Luke gives me a cool glass of water. He sits next to me and says, 'You'll never guess what happened while you were out.'

'Go on,' I say. I hate guessing games. He's going to tell me regardless so why should I start guessing? It just wastes time.

'We had a visitor,' Luke says. 'You know that girl who fainted in the supermarket yesterday. Well, she only went and turned up at our doorstep this morning saying that she was Aisha and that she'd switched bodies, or something, with someone called Zoe. Like what the actual?'

What? She can't do that. What an absolute idiot. She's going to make us both look insane. I want to start living my new life and if she keeps sounding off like this to everyone, I won't be able to. She should be happy living my life, I've got it all. She'll have money and a decent husband, providing he doesn't bore her to death.

'Are you kidding me?' I say. 'What else did she say?'

'Oh, I don't know, something about thinking her memories were confused with dreams but then when she saw me, she knew it had actually happened. That she had actually switched, and I was real. I'm just pleased Gemma was here …' he cuts himself off, realising what he'd said.

'Gemma was here? She still here?' I ask. Knowing full well she'd have scarpered. Meeting Luke in secret the dirty cow.

'Oh, no … no, she left about twenty minutes ago. She popped by to see you, stayed for a coffee waiting for you to come home, but she couldn't wait any longer and had to leave. Something about a hair appointment. But she heard it all too.'

He's a good liar, I'll give him that. I guess he's had a lot of practice.

'That's a shame, I'd have liked to see her,' I am equally a good liar. 'Well, it sounds like that woman is a complete fruit-loop. I'm definitely Aisha, no need to worry there!'

'Gemma said she'd pop back round after getting her hair done, so you'll see her soon,' Luke smiles at me.

Great, I was hoping to get away with not seeing her. I haven't seen her since hospital. I don't have any aspiration to form a friendship with her. If she thinks she can sleep with Luke right under my nose and still be my best friend, she's got another think coming! She's messing with the wrong woman.

*

Sunday morning and the September sun is beating down. Gemma never came round again yesterday. She's obviously got better things to do than check in on her best friend.

The landline rings. Luke answers it.

'Hello?' he says. 'Oh, hello Carol. How are you? …'

'… Yes, yes she's here. One sec.'

I am not in the mood for chatting to Carol. I thrash my arms back and forth in front of me and whisper, 'Tell her I'm not in, I don't want to talk to her.'

Luke gives me a quizzical look. 'Actually Carol, she's just popped out. Can I pass on a message? …'

'… OK, yes, I'll ask her … OK take care. Bye.'

'Well that was awkward!' he says. 'She just wanted to know if you wanted to go to church with them this morning. They'll be leaving in half an hour.'

Well, obviously the answer is no. I'm not remotely religious, I guess I'm open to the idea of religion but I'm certainly not a churchgoer. Besides, I don't want to be spending more time with them than is necessary. I'm not used to parents *wanting* to spend time with me and this keenness to see me puts me off.

'Um … nah, I don't think so,' I say. 'I'm going to chill out today and enjoy the nut roast you have planned for us I think.'

I'm not overly keen to spend yet another day bored, in this house with Luke, but I'd rather do that than go to church.

We spend the day eating and having a few drinks out on the patio, enjoying the sun. I try to engage in conversation as much as possible, asking him how he feels about returning to work, asking him about my work as a care worker, talking about past holidays and how we met. He wants to tell me these things as he wants me to remember. I want him to talk about these things as I want to know more about the life I'm living so that I'm more able to dupe him and Aisha's parents into thinking I'm regaining my memories. And be able to live the pretence that I am who I look like I am.

It's nearing seven-thirty and my phone rings. It's Gemma. Do I answer it or don't I? I'm too intrigued to hear what she has to say.

'Hiya Aish,' she starts. 'I think I've done something stupid.'

No apology for not coming round yesterday. But then again, why would she? She would think Luke kept her visit quiet. I doubt there was ever any intention for her to visit later in the day.

'OK, what am *I* supposed to do about it?' I ask. I'm not used to playing the best friend role and to be honest, I really don't give a shit about her doing something stupid.

'I just need to speak to you Aish, I miss having you to talk to and I …' she stops herself short and then continues. 'I popped round yesterday, but you were out, and Luke told me he had a visitor. Did he tell you?'

Yeah, he did, but he also said you were there when Aisha turned up, you lying scum.

'Yes, he did.' I reply.

'Well, did he show you the note too?' She asks.

The note? What note?

'Um, no? What note?' I ask, feeling anger re-surface yet again.

'She left her number and …' she hesitates. 'I just called her and am supposed to be meeting up with her in twenty minutes. I'm so sorry …'

Well, this will not do. I can't have Gemma starting to believe Aisha. No way. She needs to call it off. However, she knows exactly where Aisha will be and at what time. I could use this to my advantage, go and see her myself, get her to back off a bit.

'Don't go,' I blurt out. 'You obviously changed your mind because you're calling me. I'll go and find out what this crazy woman is on about. Leave it to me.'

'No, it's OK. I'll just call it off. I'm sorry Aish, curiosity just got the better of …'

'No don't call it off.' I interrupt her. 'I want to find out why this woman is saying all this rubbish. Where were you supposed to meet?'

She gives me the address, apologises again and asks me to let her know how it goes. She shouldn't apologise, this is perfect. A perfect opportunity for me to finally speak to Aisha face to face and tell her that she will never get her life back.

11

When I used Gemma as my excuse for rushing out of the house so quickly, Luke seemed positive about it. He agreed when I said I needed to see my best friend, as I felt I hadn't really made a lot of time for her since the accident. It's a bare-faced lie and I feel no guilt about lying to him. Gemma means nothing to me but I'll let him think I'm trying to rebuild mine and Gemma's friendship and regain my memories. He wants me to try to remember things and go back to how things were, back to 'normality'. I want him to think that I'm doing everything I can to remember my past. Although spending time with her is the last thing I would want to do.

Thank God Gemma called me, worried about the mistake she'd made in making that phone call. If she'd have gone along to the bar to meet her, who knows what would have happened. Aisha, I'm sure, would be very convincing, she'd have turned on the water works and made Gemma believe her story.

My taxi pulls up outside The Pitcher and Piano, I pay the fare with the small shrapnel I have. I hate having so few pennies to my name. The big wooden door to the bar that once housed thousands of library books is open. I march inside.

She's sat on a table by a window, self-consciously holding and staring at a menu, with her back to me. On the table are two drinks. They both look suspiciously alcoholic. Perhaps she doesn't know she's carrying a child then. That's going to be a revelation for her!

'Aisha,' I whisper in her ear.

She jumps, the menu falls to the table, she turns to me with a great big, bloody stupid grin on her face which soon fades when she sees *me* stood there as bold as brass. I can't help but sneer back at her, I flick my eyebrows and sit in the chair opposite.

She's sat there, open mouthed, flabbergasted. I love that I have this affect on her. She looks an absolute state, her hair is un-straightened, she has no make-up on and looks like she hasn't properly slept in weeks. Why isn't she enjoying looking like me? She should be revelling in the beauty of the body she's been gifted.

There's an awkward silence so I wait for her to say something first and take a sip of the drink that's in front of me, Gemma's drink I assume. I scowl, it's Martini and Lemonade. Gemma has exceptionally poor taste in alcoholic drinks.

I impatiently look at her from under my brow. Come on, grow a pair and say something to me.

Finally, the woman speaks, 'What are you doing here?'

She starts to stutter, 'I … was expecting Gemma.'

Well, yeah, of course you were. Surprise! I scoff and take another sip of the god-awful drink. I mean, I may as well as it's paid for with *my* money.

'How dare you turn up like this,' she growls. There are those kahunas, I knew she'd grow them eventually.

She continues, 'If I'd wanted to see you, I'd have asked to see you. Gemma will be here in a bit, we're going to try and sort things out, and so I suggest you leave now.'

Blimey, she doesn't get it. Obviously, I have to spell it out to her. 'Gemma's not coming. She told me she was coming to meet you. Let's just say, I reassured her that you were fresh out of the loony bin and couldn't be trusted.'

I'm sure I can see her quivering, tears pooling in her eyes. She doesn't know what to say. I have her exactly where I want her, under my control.

She then asks me if I know why we crashed. Really? She can't remember. It's her freaking fault we crashed. I tell her about the letter I found from her doctor. I can see her pathetically trying to beat back the tears pooling even heavier in her eyes when I tell her she found out that she had premature ovarian failure. She was a mess that day and shouldn't have been driving. I make sure to tell her that she caused the accident. It was her to blame for this whole situation.

She tries to hide an escaped tear that started to roll down her cheek, by wiping it away. 'Why Zoe? Why are you doing this?' She whines at me.

This is ridiculous, she's an absolute state! She should be happy living my life, spending my money. What a waste.

She thinks I'm happy living her pathetic life. I'm not happy about any of this, but I'm forced to choose which life is going to be easier in the long run and I have to choose hers. She continues her whining, asking me why I'm so happy living her life and why I don't want to go back to how things were, before the accident.

I lie by telling her I was unhappy in my life with no friends and no family. All I had was Tom and my bank balance. I tell her that I now have Luke who's a decent catch, not that I mean it. I also rub it in, that I have her loving parents and her best friend. I need her to think that I have no desire to go back to that life. She won't know the real reason why I need to stay in her body and her life, so I need to convince her some other way.

She's getting so wound up, it's hilarious to see. I'm pushing all the right buttons. She needs to stop fighting to get her life back and start appreciating what she has now. What I've technically given her.

She unsuccessfully tries to threaten me by saying that she will find a way to switch us back and that she'll convince everyone about what happened. She's not going to give up on her life easily. I have no idea why she's clinging on so hard to a man who cheats on her and clearly doesn't love her as much as she thinks. Nor do I have a clue why she is so keen to give up the money she's just gained and a body and face to die for.

'What about the money?' she asks. 'Luke and I don't have half the money you have in savings. You'll get bored and …'

I want to wind her up some more, it's just too easy. I interrupt her with another lie, saying that I have plans underway to get my money back. I don't but she doesn't need to know that. I'm sure I will find a way of getting everything back somehow. But first of all, I tell her, I need to focus on losing all of *her* weight.

Then I remember the alcohol sat in her glass. There is another way I can convince her to stay with Tom and stop all this melodramatic nonsense. She needs to find out she's pregnant. She'll never give up on a child, not when she knows she can't have children in her own body.

'Talking of bodies,' I say. 'Should you really be drinking that?'

Suddenly I feel ice-cold liquid hit my face. The rest of the martini has been thrown all down me. I lose my train of thought and miss my chance to tell her.

'I will find a way Zoe, with or without my body,' she cries as she storms towards the exit.

I'm not going to let her have the last say, no way. I'm the one in control, not her. She won't succeed in getting people to believe her and she won't get her life back. I want to show her that I have the upper hand, that she is out of control. That I'm the one in charge, I need her to turn around.

'Best get a move on then Aisha, time's ticking!' I shout back at her, taunting her. I want her to feel threatened by me, that I've got some kind of plan up my sleeve. Mess with her mind.

Sure enough, as predicted, she turns around and sees me raise my finger to my forehead, slowly point it in her direction and show her that I'm the one in control and always will be.

She'll find out soon enough that she's pregnant. It won't take long for her to realise that she will want to continue living my life. Then, Pete can be a distant memory.

*

Over the course of the last two months, since meeting with Aisha, there's been no contact made by her. Hopefully, she's got the message at long last.

I've been trying so hard with Luke. Trying to convince him that I'm slowly regaining memories and feelings for him. The gullible idiot. But as time goes on, it just gets harder and harder and I've given up. What's the point when he's clearly in love with someone else. He's a cheating scum bag and I know he's still seeing Gemma. I check his phone regularly without him knowing and the text messages I found told me everything I needed to know.

Only last week, I found a receipt in his coat pocket for baby clothes and toys. So, when he went for a bath one evening, I checked his phone and saw a picture message of a positive pregnancy test from Gemma, with a caption saying, 'You're going to be a dad!'.

Aisha really doesn't have a clue what an idiot she's married to. I mean, she's an idiot herself but even I have to have a little sympathy for her. She couldn't conceive with her husband, yet her husband has managed to get her best friend up the duff. The irony is unfathomable.

Out of spite, I used all of Luke and Aisha's savings to get laser eye surgery. I paid privately and was seen almost straight away. If Luke's going to be spending money on his pregnant mistress, why shouldn't I spend a bit of his hard earned cash on me? Plus, it stops me from having to put these bloody annoying lenses in each day, just to try to look a bit less hideous.

I have to question, where does this leave me? Why have I been wasting my time, trying to get him to love me just to prevent Aisha from wanting her life back. I'm also an idiot.

There have been a number of times over the last few weeks where I have really missed Steve. It's been over four months now since I last saw him, last spoke to him and last kissed him.

He must be wondering why he's being ghosted by me. What if he's tried to contact me? Aisha would have got the messages or phone calls. Could Tom know?

I have to speak to him. I have to see him. Not just because I miss him, but also to check he hasn't given the game away and unwittingly told Tom about our continued affair.

Seeing how deceitful Luke has been in his marriage confirms to me how weak Tom was to take me back. He shouldn't have forgiven me. I was pleased he did at the time as it prevented us divorcing.

However, now that I've lost my money anyway, there's a bitterness deep within me. If Tom hadn't forgiven me, I could have been living with Steve, happily. I wouldn't have had to sneak around, meeting him in secret. In turn, Pete wouldn't have been able to do what he did because I wouldn't have been stupidly walking along the canal desperate for another secret meeting with Steve. I wouldn't have then fallen pregnant with potentially a rapist's child and I wouldn't have been driving to the abortion clinic. Which means, I wouldn't have crashed my car and all this chaos would never have happened. Oh, how my life could have been different if Tom just couldn't have found it in his heart to forgive me.

Steve is the only man I believe I've loved. He makes me feel wonderful and we're cut from the same cloth. That's close enough to love, I think.

I have absolutely no idea how to convince Steve about what's happened. But, I will. I'll make him believe me. By Christmas, I will happily be living with Steve. Failure is not an option, not for me.

12

It's early November and I can't believe I've wasted so much time with Luke. For such a time-focused person, I'm a dick. I should have contacted Steve long ago. I place a fist on his front door, and confidently knock five times in the same rhythm I always knock.

'Hello?' Steve says as he opens the door, a bemused expression plastered across his face.

My God, he's so handsome even with his face all skewed in curiosity. His broad, toned shoulders loom over me. He's shaved his head, but it suits him, it makes him look rugged and even more macho. How I just want to pounce on him, right here, right now.

'Hi Steve,' I smile and maintain control of the situation. 'May I come in, it's about Zoe?'

He looks panicked. He looks left and right as if expecting to find Tom lurking in the bushes or something.

'It's nothing bad,' I say trying to reassure him. 'I have a message from her for you. She wants to explain why she hasn't been in contact with you for months. There's a good reason.'

'Um … you'd best come in before someone hears you, I guess.' He reluctantly opens the door further, letting me in before him.

'You can go through into the living …' Before he finishes his sentence, I've already walked ahead of him, straight through to the living room and I take a seat on his sofa.

He looks even more confused now especially seeing how comfortable I am in his home. He'd be expecting a stranger to wait for him to show them through to the living room, but I've been here tons of times before. I know this place inside and out.

'Um … make yourself at home?' he says sarcastically.

'Yeah, will do!' I say, oblivious to his sarcastic tone.

He hovers, standing in the living room doorway, looking inquisitively toward me.

'Sorry … what's this about?' He's starting to sound impatient. 'You've barged your way in, I don't know you from

Adam and yet you're sat there, all cool calm and collected. Am I missing something?'

'I get it, I'll explain everything,' I say. 'Probably best you sit yourself down … Stephanie.'

'What did you call me?' he asks.

'You heard me,' I say. 'Stephanie … my cover name for you.'

'There's only one person who calls me that,' he says. His eyes are fixated on me and he slowly lowers himself into the armchair, looking all the more tense. 'Start talking.'

I'm just going to come out and say it. I've been too long without seeing him. He'll believe me, I'll make sure of it.

'Steve, it's me … Zoe.' I say.

I can see his agitation escalate. 'What the … who the hell do you think you …'

I interrupt him. 'I know, I know. It's hard to believe and I get it. But it's me. It's so good to see you Steve. It's been too long.'

'Look … This has got to be a wind up!' he says. 'You've been talking to someone but whatever you've heard, it's not true!'

I can tell he's freaking out. He probably thinks I'm a troublemaker, here to blackmail him or something.

'No, it's not like that. It's *me*. Honestly …' I start to explain but he interrupts me.

'You're crazy!' he says. 'I don't have to listen to this bull …'

I interrupt him again. 'It's not bullshit Steve. Stop interrupting me and let me explain. Three months ago, I crashed my car, died and was resuscitated. But I didn't wake up in *my* body, I woke up looking like this. I switched with a girl named Aisha Brown.'

I continue before he gets the chance to speak over me again. 'You must have read the news articles about the crash. I haven't been able to come and see you up until now, because I didn't know how to tell you. I missed you so much, so I just had to come …'

'I'm not having this,' he says, voice volume increased. 'I don't know who you are, but you are NOT Zoe. I need you to leave now.'

He stands up and walks back to the living room door, holding it open, waiting for me to walk out. Obviously, I'm not going anywhere.

'Steve,' I say, quickening my speech. 'You have to believe me. I have no-one right now. Tom is happily living with a woman posing as me. I've got a new husband called Luke who's been having an affair behind the woman-I-switched-with's back and got another woman pregnant. As I was resuscitated, I got zapped into the wrong body. I can't switch back, I don't know how … Oh God, I sound insane. I know I do. But it's true. It's a load of shit and I need you. I've never needed anyone before, not really. But I really do need you now. I miss you.'

'Look, you're not my Zoe,' he says. 'I mean, look at you! Now, I don't like to get violent, especially not with women. So, I suggest you make your own way out of my house before I have to resort to throwing you out.'

I need to think of something that will convince him quickly. 'Your tattoo!' I say. 'The woman, pushing weights, close to your heart. That's me!'

I can see his face softens a little but he's still twitchy, pacing left and right. 'How did you know about that?'

Oh my God, he just doesn't get it. 'Because … it's me you idiot!'

'But … it's impossible.' he says. 'You can't have. You look … you're …'

'Fat and ugly,' I interrupt. 'I know, but it's still me. Just think about it.'

'I don't need to think about it,' his softened expression has now vanished once more. 'You're not my beautiful Zoe. I know your game. You found out information about me and Zoe and now you're here to blackmail me. Well, it won't work. You need to leave… I won't ask you again. Get out of my house … now!'

Control of this situation is slipping away from me. I can't let it. Without thinking, I use my counsellor's coping technique, the way she intended me to use it. I raise my index finger to my forehead and press as hard as I can, try to absorb the tension of not having control into the finger and point it out into the atmosphere. Just like she advised me to do.

'What the hell did you do that for?' he asks. 'You have absolutely no right to try and threaten me. It won't work.'

'I'm not threatening you, you moron!' I say. 'How could I threaten you? You're the love of my life. That stupid counsellor, the one that Tom made me see, suggested I do that when I feel out of control, out of my depth. It's supposed to help me release tension; it's supposed to help ground me …'

His shoulders lower, his breath starts to steady and his eyes warm. He slowly moves back toward the armchair, takes a seat and says, 'Your counsellor? Zoe told me she was seeing a counsellor. What you're saying … it just can't be true.'

'It is,' I say point blank. 'If you ever felt anything for me Steve, you'll help me.'

He sighs, slumps in the chair and lowers his head. I take this as an opportunity to reach out to him. Slowly, after raising myself from the sofa, I walk towards him and kneel on the floor in front of his chair and place my hand on his knee.

'Steve, I love you,' I say softly. 'You believe me, don't you?'

He raises his head to look into my eyes. 'It just sounds too crazy. You're not *my* Zoe. I can't believe I'm actually listening to this … What you're saying is impossible, but you do seem to know things that you shouldn't. I dunno … maybe I need more proof? What am I saying? This is ridiculous, you can't be Zoe, it's impossible …'

'You want proof?' I ask. I start to rattle on with as much information as I can possibly think of, to try and convince him. 'More proof other than our cover-name and the tattoo? OK, here's your proof. You married my sister Mel yet you loved me. You loved me since I was bullied in school and you protected me. You stood up to the bullies who tormented me. I had an eating disorder when I was a teenager and you held my hand in hospital in secret and told me that I was beautiful and didn't need to starve myself. We meet up at The White Tavern close to my gym to avoid Tom finding us. I have a birth mark on my collarbone.'

Steve's staring intently at me, I can see he's gradually starting to believe what I'm saying. At least I hope he is.

I continue to rabbit on. 'You served in the army until you got hit by shrapnel in your leg. You have a scar on your left leg. It's shaped like a boot, we call it your 'Italian scar' because it resembles the shape of the country. I always tell you off for being late so you purposely turn up late for things just to get on my nerves. You love it when I sing. You call me your 'Nightingale' …'

'OK, OK,' he cuts in, stopping my ramble. I can see in his face he doesn't want to believe me but he's starting to.

'So, do you still think I'm lying and totally insane or is there some part of you that's starting to believe me?' I ask him.

'It *is* impossible, but … I can't believe I'm going to say this, but yeah … I think I am starting to believe you. You know too much. But it's just so insane, this kind of thing doesn't happen.'

'Well, it did. It happened to me, Steve,' I say. 'All I need is for you to believe me. Thank you.'

That's exactly what I needed to hear. He believes me. Finally, I'll get Steve back in my life, we can finally be together without fear of Tom finding out and without Steve discovering how Pete violated me.

'I love you Steve,' I say.

I raise one foot so that I'm now kneeling on one knee, push myself up, lean in towards his lips and seize my first chance in months to kiss him.

His hands press hard against my chest, pushing me away.

'What are you doing?' he asks. 'I said I think that I believe you, but things are different now. I mean, look at you!'

'It's still me Steve, I'm Zoe.' I feel so rejected. How dare he push me away.

'Well yeah,' he says. 'Looking like that … I mean … sorry, but you may be Zoe, but you're not *my* Zoe. There's just no … attraction there. I'm sorry … When you look like my Zoe again, then you come back here, and I'll snog your face off. But, not until then. Sorry … but I just can't bring myself to kiss you or do anything else. And, if I'm honest, I'm not sure I ever will.'

Oh my God. The shallow, selfish prick! I know I'm not exactly attractive, but I honestly thought I wasn't *completely* repulsive.

'There's more to me than just my looks, Steve,' I shout at him. 'I thought what we had was worth more than that! You always stood by me, even at school. You saying that's just because you 'fancied' me?'

'Well, it helped,' he says. 'I'm sorry … just being honest.'

'Well screw you!' I bellow at him. 'It's over Steve. You'll never find anyone as good as me. You'll die a lonely, miserable man. When I get my body back, and by God I will, you'll never touch me again. You hear me?'

'Whatever,' he says smugly. 'You'll come running back to me one day, you always do. I'm like a drug to you. When you're *my* Zoe again, you can knock on my door again, but not before then.'

'Not this time Steve,' I continue to yell. 'You either love me for *me* or not at all. You push me away now; you'll never see me again. Never!'

'Close the door on the way out, yeah?' he says with utter contempt etched across his face.

'With pleasure!' I scream back at him.

I march towards the front door and slam it as hard as I possibly can behind me.

*

What a complete and utter arsehole. To think I've wasted so much of my time and energy on that useless example of the male species. The one man I thought I loved, the one man who I thought really, genuinely loved me, *for me*. What a shallow, ignorant waste of oxygen.

I honestly thought he would believe me. That he'd support me and love me. Of course, he wouldn't. I was a prize trophy to him. Someone beautiful who'd look good hanging off of his arm. Someone he could bed whenever he felt like it. Now I'm average looking, he wants nothing to do with me.

Am I heartbroken? Is this what it feels like? I'm so angry and feel so rejected. He was the one consistent good thing in my life, or so I thought. He was always there, showering me with affection, stabilizing me. Now he's gone. I'm alone and have nothing.

But I don't need to be alone. *She's* living *my* life, sharing a bed with *my* husband, spending *my* money, abusing *my* body. What is the point in wanting to stay in this body now? I have nothing but I could have it all once again. Tom isn't shallow like Steve. Tom loves me for who I am, he always has done.

She's not going to keep living my life. I thought I wanted to stay in this body, hide away from Pete and the sproglet that could be his. Well I'm not going to hide anymore. I'll never let Pete abuse me again. I'm strong. I'm in control. No-one and nothing will stand in the way of me getting what is rightfully mine back.

First things first, I need to tell Tom the truth about the accident. It should have been Tom I told all along, not Steve. As much of a boring drip that he is, Tom's loyal, loving and will stand by me, no matter what.

I know Tom's phone number off by heart so compile a lengthy text message. Rather than a phone call, Tom can re-read a message. I've learnt my lesson from visiting Steve. It's too easy for someone to push you away when you speak to them face-to-face but it's not so easy to reject it when it's in writing.

Hi Tom! You won't recognise this number. However, you do know me. Very well! Zoe's been acting different, right? She can't remember a thing about her life before the accident and may even have said things like 'I remember a different life' or 'I look completely different' or even 'I don't know who you are but you're not the husband I remember' yeah? Well that's because she's NOT Zoe.

Please keep reading as it's important …

When we crashed into each other on the 22nd July, we both died and were resuscitated AT THE SAME TIME but somehow, we switched bodies. Crazy hey? But it's true.

I am YOUR WIFE. You are living with someone called Aisha Brown and I am being forced to live with her cheating husband. But not anymore. I need you to know the truth. It's taken me a while to summon the courage to message you. I need you to trust me when I say that I am Zoe.

She obviously hasn't told you yet, otherwise I'm sure you'd have tried to find me and contact me. I met up with her a while ago and she told me then that she wanted her life back. It's going to be hard for you to believe me, I get that. But, just

think about it. She's so different and she blatantly doesn't love you. Just ask her yourself. I'm sure she'll tell you the truth if you just ask.

Please consider this crazy revelation to be true. I miss you and want you back. Call me or text me. I'll be waiting. But, time is of the essence Tom so please don't make me wait too long.

Z x

I purposely sign it 'Z x' because that's how I end every message I ever send to Tom. It's my signature, a way of helping to convince him. I hit send and wait patiently for a response from Tom. Two hours pass by and finally my phone springs to life, the screen flashes the words, 'Tom Calling'. I answer it.

13

The last couple of weeks have been intense to say the least. The initial phone call from Tom was short and to the point. He didn't believe me. He told me to leave him and his wife alone and to not cause any unnecessary distress when they'd been through enough over the last six months. They'd been through shit, well so had I. I certainly wasn't going to leave it there.

I sent him text after text, faking my love for him, trying to prove my authenticity and attempting to convince him that I had changed. I'd told him that the accident had changed me and that I had never appreciated him but I did now.

Eventually, after a few further phone calls from him telling me to stop harassing him, I finally made a breakthrough. I was not going to let this go and he reluctantly agreed to meet with me.

Four days ago, we met at The Cosy Club, a bar and restaurant in the centre of Taunton. It's our favourite place to go for bevvies and meals out when we feel like having pub grub instead of wining and dining.

It took a lot of convincing him over multiple Margaritas, but I thought he walked away believing me. We talked about our wedding, holidays, my upbringing and parents and even talked about the day of the accident. I told him that I remembered him ringing me when Aisha's car slammed into me. It took a lot, but I apologised for trying to get rid of our baby even though I didn't mean it. His eyes pooled with tears at that point and that's when he revealed that the scan had shown twins.

Oh, how I wish that I didn't crash and could have gotten to the abortion clinic. Not only is *she* pregnant but potentially she has *two* rapist's children growing inside her. That means that as they grow, it will be two faces that I'll be constantly inspecting to see if they start showing any resemblances to Pete, or even Steve.

Of course, I didn't let on to Tom that I was shocked and disappointed by this revelation. Instead, I told him that I would raise them with him if he just let me. I pretended that I regretted trying to abort them and that all I wanted was to be a mother. Of course, this wasn't true in the slightest. I'd never love them. They'd have to live with my hatred towards them, but if it meant I got my life back, I could cope with that. I didn't have the best childhood, yet I survived. They will too. I'll pack them off to boarding school and let Tom raise them in the school holidays.

We said our goodbyes, he agreed that he would speak to Aisha for her to confirm that what I'd told him was true and I really thought he believed me.

I sent him a message after we met. I thanked him for meeting with him and attempted one more plea for him to believe me. However, I haven't heard anything from him since then. Not a text or a phone call, nothing. I even tried sexting him to try and get some sort of response but, yet again, nothing.

I hate Christmas but still, I made the extra effort to send him a Christmas card, confirming one final time that I hoped we'd be together again once the New Year came. But no response. Not even a thank you.

There's only one thing for it. I have to go and see him. I need this whole thing to be resolved before Christmas. Luke is barely at home anymore, probably cooing over Gemma's baby bump and playing happy families with her. I'm living in someone else's house without a penny to my name and I've had enough. I need to sort this once and for all. I've had enough of waiting around, I'm the one in control of this and they need to know it.

*

'What are you doing here?' Tom asks as he opens the door to me. 'She'll be back in a minute and I can't have you here when she returns.'

'We need to talk Tom,' I say. 'I thought you believed me, but it's been four days and no contact. Four days! You can't just keep me hanging …'

'OK, come in,' he says impatiently. 'But you can't stay long. I don't know where she's gone so I have no idea how long she'll be.'

As I walk through to the lounge, I say, 'How can you not know where she's gone? You used to keep track of me and my whereabouts all the time since, you know, Steve and all that.'

'Well, she's *not* you, is she. She can do what she likes, I'm not constantly worrying if she's cheating on me. I know she's faithful. It's called 'trust' Zoe. Besides, I was in the bath and when I came out, she was just gone. I don't need to keep tracks of her whereabouts as I don't think for one second, she's a cheat like you.'

Woah. Are they playing happy families? Has she managed to get her claws into him? By the sounds of things, he's grown feelings for her. Well that needs to be nipped in the bud! Tom's my husband not hers.

'Sounds like you've been getting rather cosy with Aisha. Well, when we switch back, which we will do, you won't be so interested then. Not when she looks like this.' I say and gesture to my body.

'Keep your voice down,' Tom says. 'Like I said, she'll be back soon, and I don't want her catching you here. Aisha's kind, caring, loving and not a bit selfish or self-obsessed like you are.'

Oh my God. He's fallen for her. How the hell has he done that? If I don't have Tom or Steve, I really do have nothing.

'Tom, you don't love her,' I say. 'You probably love the idea of her and the fact that she looks like me. But she's *not* me. This is *us* we're talking about. You and me, together forever. What about our vows?'

'Our vows?' he says, getting annoyed but still maintaining a low volume. 'You're a fine one to talk about vows. I forgave you time and time again. Well, now I've seen what it's like, felt what it's like to be with someone who truly loves and respects me. I should have finished things with you a long time ago, Zoe.'

Shit, this is bad. It's getting out of control, I'm out of control. I need him back; I need to be back living *my* life.

'I love you, you believe me, don't you?' I have no choice but to pathetically start to beg. 'Please, just give me a chance. I've changed since the accident. I never appreciated you, not as much as I should have. You know me, inside and out, come on and give me another chance.'

Under his breath, Tom mutters, 'She needs me. I love her.'

He loves her. How dare she make him fall for her. He's an idiot if he believes she loves him and not her darling Luke. How the hell has this happened? The last thing I knew, Aisha wanted nothing more than to have her sad, pathetic life back. Now she's seen how wonderful my life is and is doing everything she can to keep it, even make *my* husband fall in love with her.

'Just kick her out!' I snap. 'She doesn't belong here anyway. It's not her house, it's mine! She can piss off back to her drip of a husband. I don't give a shit about her I just want to be back here with you.'

The lounge door swings open, and there she is. All red faced with anger and pure hatred towards me. She's visibly shaking and my God, her stomach is huge! She already looks ready to burst and she's put on weight. Baby weight and some.

'What the hell's going on?' Aisha blurts. 'What do you think you're doing coming here, shouting the odds, marking your territory? You lost your right to do that when you abandoned your husband to shack up with mine!'

Is this woman for real? Of course, I'm going to come here and fight for what is mine. She really thinks I want to stay with that cheating slob of a husband.

'You're welcome to that wimp of a man, go back to him, back to where you belong. I want my house back, all my lovely things back, my money back and my husband back. Go on, go, time's ticking Aisha!' I tap on my wrist.

Then she surprises me. Out of nowhere, she shouts, 'Enough of this *time's ticking* Zoe! You don't need to threaten me, I'll go. I'll leave you to your happy lives together.'

And with that she scarpers upstairs, and I hear bangs and thuds from the bedroom above my head. She's finally got the message. She's finally accepted that I'm the one in control, not her.

Tom runs up after her.

'Tom ...' I shout after him, but he completely ignores me.

I walk to the bottom of the stairs, trying to listen into the conversation coming from above but I can't hear anything clearly. As I'm about to start climbing myself, Aisha comes blubbering down the stairs, bags in hand, snot streaming from her nose.

I stop her. I've not finished with her yet. She's now realised how dire her life was before the accident. That's why she's so distraught to be giving up the life she stole from me. 'You really think you could have my life? I feel so sorry for you. Your life was so pathetic that you had to steal mine?'

She tells me I'm bored living her life and that's the only reason why I'm back, to claim *my* life back.

'Bored? Bored? Oh, you really have no idea, do you?' I say. The poor, pathetic woman hasn't got a clue what her 'darling' husband Luke, has been up to with her 'dear' best friend.

Tom then dramatically hurls himself down the stairs and stands between us, arms outstretched, like a lion protecting his pride.

'Leave it Zoe,' he says. 'Look at her, she's pregnant and doesn't need this added stress.'

There was a time when Tom would be protecting me, sticking up for me. Now he's there, guarding *her.* Well I'm not having it. He's *my* husband, not hers. He should be with me, wanting me back and kicking her out, the tramp.

'Are you actually sticking up for her?' I just can't believe Tom is that stupid. 'She's been fooling you since the accident, pretending to be me. She's carrying *our* children!'

I look down at her disgusting bulging baby-bump. 'I've a right mind to stab her in the stomach, get rid of the little shits. I never wanted them. Well, I was going to get rid of them before the accident, perhaps I need to keep trying!'

Tom loses it. 'That's enough Zoe!'

I can't believe he's actually choosing *her* over me and willing to throw years of marriage away to be with that pathetic lump. Well, if he does choose her then there's no way that I'm going to let them keep my money. No chance. They have absolutely no entitlement to my inheritance, my parents' guilt money. I earned that money, and I will get it back.

'If you'd really prefer to shack up with that pregnant bitch, then do it,' I shout at Tom. 'But I tell you now, if you choose her then you lose my money. That's right, it's *her* or the money.'

I can see Aisha trembling. I love having this control over her. Yeah, you'd better worry love. I won't let you take *everything* from me. No chance. Then she theatrically loses her balance and pathetically clutches at the banister to support her.

What a drama queen. She thinks I'm bored of living her life and that all I want is my money back. I'll tell her exactly what her sad, ridiculous life means to me.

'Oh, that's right!' I say. Feeling such resentment towards this pitiful woman. 'Playing the vulnerable-pregnant-woman card, are we? You think the only reason why I'm back here is because I'm bored and sick of being skint? Well there's more. Your darling husband, the one you think you love and that *loves* you back, has been cheating on you for two years and you haven't got a clue!'

'Just because you're a cheat it doesn't mean everyone is. Besides, who is he supposed to be cheating on me with?' she whimpers.

I take great joy in telling her the magnificent news. It's been a long time coming and I want to hurt her. I want to hurt her so badly. She's taken everything away from me.

'Your best friend,' I smile. I love revealing this to her, kicking her while she's down. She deserves it. Stealing Tom from me and trying to steal everything else.

She rocks, grabs her head and looks into Tom's eyes. Hilariously, she's about to faint. Again. She fainted in the supermarket and now, yet again, she's losing control and consciousness. She's got as much inner strength as a Rich Tea dunked in coffee.

Tom turns to me and begs, 'Zoe, call for an ambulance! Now!'

For God's sake. What a wuss she is. I just stand there, staring at how ridiculous she is, lying there on the floor. And equally, how ludicrous Tom is for comforting her.

'Zoe!' he yells. 'Ambulance! You happy now? You did this, you selfish evil cow!'

My eyebrows raise and I stare at Tom in disbelief. 'I'm the selfish and evil one, yeah? Wow. I'm not the one poisoning you against your own wife! I'll call an ambulance, for you. Because

I love you. But, as far as *she's* concerned, she deserves anything coming to her.'

The ambulance turns up fifteen minutes later. I spent that time trying, yet again, to convince Tom that he was making a mistake. That I was the one he loved and wanted to be with. But it was no use. She has her claws well and truly dug deep into him.

As he hurries himself into the ambulance next to her, he doesn't even cast a look in my direction. His eyes remain fixated on her and her hand is grasped firmly in his. The love he has for her sickens me to the core. She'll pay for this. I'll make sure of it.

14

God how I hate Christmas. This year, it was the worst. I just knew that *she* and Tom would have been all cosied up together, playing happy families, welcoming the New Year in. Tom always loved Christmas which irritated me to high Heaven. I mean, what's the point in it? I'm not religious, I don't give a shit about presents and it's ridiculously over-commercialised. Everywhere you go, you see fairy lights, hear the same irritating sounds of *Wizard* and *Slade* blaring in shops and people looking miserable. They're miserable because they're fighting crowds, panicking about getting the best turkey for Christmas dinner and going into debt, once again, in order to buy presents for their ungrateful families. All for one day of the year, one pointless day.

Growing up, we never celebrated Christmas like other families did. Mel and I normally had one super expensive present from our parents each and a stocking consisting of 'necessities', like socks and shower wash. There is so much sympathy shown towards poor families, kids not getting a visit from Santa or parents not having enough money for a decent meal. Charles Dickens has a lot to answer for, for showing far too much empathy for the less-wealthy. Well, it's the same for those with money. Sometimes it's even worse. In my experience, often with money comes less love and doing things for the sake of doing them. No-one says, 'Aww, the poor *rich* kids' or 'We must look out for those rich children in need of *love* at this time of year'.

We never went to Carol Services or Christmas markets or had our own family traditions like making Christmas puddings. Christmas Day was like any other. My parents would be there physically but not in mind. My mother would have her laptop open, working and my father would be barking orders at us as normal whilst Nanny Jane bustled around in the kitchen, making us something to eat. Certainly not a roast with all the trimmings and crackers were unheard of in my house. The table was for eating at, not for wearing stupid hats and reading nonsense jokes.

Every Christmas Eve, father would get the poxy little 'tinsel' tree down from the attic and come Boxing Day morning, it would be boxed up and returned to its residing place, under the dusty rafters. We didn't celebrate Christmas, we tolerated it.

This year, I never thought I could hate Christmas even more than I had done previously. But I did. I longed to be with Tom. Surprisingly, I missed seeing him so excited to open presents and agonise over the roasting of the potatoes. I missed my house and would have even agreed to hanging tinsel on the bannister, something I never would have endured previously. I also miss Steve. Even though he was a complete prick, I miss our kisses and our secret meetings. Why the hell did this have to happen to me? Why has my life turned to absolute shit?

Luke and I shared Christmas dinner in pretty much silence. He bought me a heart necklace which I refuse to wear. The fact he's buying romantic gifts for his wife yet cheating on her behind her back is unbelievably disrespectful. Some people may call me a hypocrite. Well, I guess I am. I couldn't help falling in love with Steve, but I'm starting to realise what it would feel like if the shoe were on the other foot. I didn't buy anything for Luke, and he was pissed right off. Well, he should have thought about that before getting his end away. Why would I buy anything for a man who means absolute jack to me?

He left Christmas Day afternoon. He packed his bags and left. Probably to move in with Gemma. I don't care. I still have a roof over my head, granted it's not *my* roof, but it's still a house so I'm not homeless just yet.

Between Christmas and New Year, I reached out to Mel. It took a lot to make that call, considering I'd previously said that I would never answer the phone to her again if she told Tom about the abortion. She did tell him, which is why he was trying to call me when I crashed.

However, I need someone. I need someone to have my back. I convinced her to meet with me and told her my story. She believed me, eventually. I've got the hang of convincing people now, sharing memories that only she and I would have known. It was a last-ditch attempt at trying to get someone to support me, to be on my side. But it epically failed. She never had my back growing up, why did I expect her to suddenly support me now?

She wanted me to apologise again for trying to get rid of Tom's baby without him knowing. If anyone needed to apologise, it was her. She shouldn't have called Tom to tell him I was driving to the clinic. She betrayed me. I can't remember the accident fully, and I know Aisha was to blame, but if Tom weren't trying to call me, perhaps I wouldn't have been distracted and would have been able to stop in time. Mel is also partly to blame for causing this whole caboodle. Our meeting ended with a blazing row and her telling me that she wanted nothing more to do with me, she'd had enough, I was dead to her.

New Year's was even more miserable than Christmas. For the first time in my life, I felt truly alone. Growing up, I felt alone but for different reasons. I felt lonely because I had no love shown towards me and my parents weren't like other people's parents. I was jealous of the families who were *actually* families. But at least I had people around me. Now I have no-one, not Tom, not Steve, not even Mel. I comforted myself over a few bottles of prosecco that I found in the fridge and watched Jools Holland bring in the New Year. Everyone cheering, watching the London fireworks, singing Auld Lang Syne. The tossers.

I could have fought for Tom more. I could have fought for my house back and made sure that Aisha was kicked out at Christmas. The truth is, I needed time to figure out how I was going to do just that. I've realised, the only way I stand a chance at getting my life back is to switch back and the only way I can do that is to try and die again. This means, I also have to try to kill Aisha in the process. Am I really a murderer? I know I'm a cold-hearted bitch, but have I really got it in me to try and kill another human being? I guess it wouldn't be classed as murder if we were both resuscitated, would it?

I have to do something though. To be left, without even a Christmas text from Tom or a 'Happy New Year' phone call, I'm reeling. It's time for me to come back out from the shadows and claim my life back. They may be all cosy and comfortable with each other, but not for long. I have nothing, *she* has everything. It's not fair and it's not right. If I can find a way of switching back without risking my life in the process, I will. But if not, then Aisha needs to watch out because I'll get everything back one way or another.

*

The taxi drops me off outside the big gateway. How I hate not being able to drive, bloody stupid accident meaning I had to surrender my licence. Getting taxis all the time costs a bomb. I'm so sick of having to scrimp and save for just the basic things in life.

Walking up the long driveway towards *my* home, the anger boils inside me. I bought this place, with my money. I let Tom live there. I could have ditched him and shacked up with Steve back along, but no, I stupidly stayed to avoid losing my money. I could have hired the top lawyer and managed to send Tom packing but realistically, he would have walked away with buckets of cash due to me being the adulterer. At the time, that was something I couldn't risk. I should have. Things would have been so different.

Now, to avoid the risk of having nothing to my name, I need to convince Tom to take me back. I need to get rid of Aisha once and for all. How many times now have I given him an olive branch, apologised, told him that I love him. Yet, his focus is still on her and not me. The only way I can get everything back, Tom included is by getting rid of *her*.

I pound on the door. No response. I ring the doorbell impatiently and shout for Tom to answer. Nothing. They're out. I reach in my pocket and pull out the silver key, twiddling it between my fingers.

When Aisha collapsed in the house a few weeks ago, Tom stupidly left me alone. I took the spare key and called him to say I'd locked up. I pretended that I cared and that I was doing them a favour. He thanked me, but there was no sincerity there. This just riled me even more.

I'll go inside and wait for them. That will be a nice surprise for them to get home to.

Thankfully, Tom hasn't changed the alarm code, so I deactivate it and walk through to the lounge. There, in pride of place above the fireplace is a collage of photos. Photos that I don't recognise of Tom and *her*. There is a picture of them chinking champagne glasses together, presumably on Christmas Day judging by the garish tree in the background. Another of them outside the caves at Cheddar Gorge, a few others taken in beer gardens and on Weston Super Mare beach and one large photo, slap bang in the middle of the rest of the photos, of a three-dimensional scan of the twins. One big happy freaking family.

She must be due around March time. I bet they've already started planning and buying things for the little shits. That can only mean one thing, they must have a nursery somewhere. And I know exactly the room they would have chosen. I stomp up the stairs, crash open the door to the room I used to use as a gym. Sure enough, the walls are now covered in hideous teddy-bear wallpaper, cuddly toys are neatly laid out atop an ottoman and two wooden cots stand at the heart of the nursery.

They're excited about raising *my* children. The children I wanted to get rid of. The children that could have been conceived from the most appalling moment of my life. I feel bitter resentment, hostility and utter rage. My face feels like it's on fire and my hands start to shake. The realisation that these children will be born hits me like a thousand blades embedding themselves in my heart.

This room needs to be destroyed. These children should never have had the chance to grow and be born, let alone be loved. I let out a long, screeching howl. My nails embed into the wallpaper. I claw away, tearing shards off it in rage, screaming, 'Fuck you' over, and over again. I can't stop, I won't stop. It's stuck so fast though that it doesn't tear as much as I need it to right now, but I keep digging my nails in, ripping pieces of teddy-bear paper off the wall so they fall around my feet.

It feels as though the cots are staring at me, mocking me behind my back. I swing around and kick the cot behind me so hard I whimper, grabbing my toe in pain, rubbing and soothing it. The pain eases and I try to push the cot over, wanting to crush it with my bare hands. It doesn't budge. I lift it up by its rails and try slamming it to the ground, but it stands firm. If cots could talk, it would be teasing me saying, 'You can't break me!'.

Without any further hesitation, I run back downstairs, out through the back door, all the way down to the bottom of the garden to where the garden shed stands. I manically search for something I can use that will demolish the goading cribs. I pick up a hand saw but cast that to one side, it would take too long. I find a hammer but that wouldn't even make a dent. Then I remember. The axe Tom uses to chop wood for the fire is placed just behind the open shed door. I grab it and race back to the house and back up to the nursery, the axe slung over my shoulder. I'm so out of breath it hurts but the adrenaline pushes me through.

I hammer the axe down on the first cot. Crash! The side rail breaks in two, but it's not enough. I swing again at the base this time and the cot crumples and smashes to the floor. I do the same to the other cot and slam the axe down repeatedly until my arms can't swing anymore.

'You think you can mock me?' I scream as the final blow shatters the remainder of the second cot to the floor.

I feel hot tears rolling down my cheeks. They mix with the stream of sweat pouring from my forehead. The nightmare of the last year finally takes hold of me and I inadvertently collapse to the floor, sobbing uncontrollably.

The mobiles above the cots spring into life, singing their tunes, tormenting me. I need to get out of here now. I throw the axe to the corner of the room, slam the nursery door behind me and run as fast as my overweight body permits down the long driveway, the gravel crunching under each step, until I crash to my knees gasping for air.

Breathe, for God's sake woman, breathe! I grab the inhaler from my pocket and heavily suck in the cool, comforting medication. My breathing slows and I wipe away the sweat or tears, I can't tell which, from my face. I need to compose myself; I need to regain control.

I turn my face back toward the house, the front door wide open. I need to close it, lock it up. Hide what I've done. They'll know soon enough, once they open the nursery door, but I can't risk them calling the police if they return to see the front door open. They'll know it's me once they see the damage I've caused, but I know Tom won't call the police. No matter how he feels about me now, he won't want to see me behind bars. I stand back up; my jeans are shredded from when my knees hit the sharp stones. I brush bloody gravel away from my grazed knees and walk back to the house, set the alarm with still shaking hands and fumble with the key in the lock.

What the hell just happened? I never lose it like I lost it then. But then again, I've never been in a horrendous situation like this before. I can no longer run, but I hurry back down the long drive. I need to get out of here before they return. Who knows how long they'll be out for? Sod waiting for them to get home, I can't let them see me like this, all tear stained, weak and out of control.

As I walk out of the driveway, onto the main road, I look behind me and their car appears from around a bend. Shit! They can't see me. I quickly pull the hood of my coat up over my head, covering my face to avoid being noticed. Holding the side of my hood, I peer back behind me and see them turn into the driveway. That was a close call, too close.

I take my phone out of my pocket and call for a taxi to collect me from the country pub around the corner. Back to the house that I will never call home, back to the life I will never call mine.

15

The first thing I do, once I return to the house, is lock the front door. I know they won't just roll over and forget what I've just done. I mean, how could they? I've just destroyed their wonderful, happy nursery, turning it into a scrap yard. I completely lost it and I hate myself for it. I don't hate myself for smashing the cots to smithereens, neither to I hate myself for tearing at the walls. But I do hate myself for losing control.

Just seeing the room, consumed in such devotion, ruined me. If I don't switch back soon, they're going to raise those children with so much love, love that I couldn't possibly give them. Perhaps that's what they deserve, they're only innocent children after all. Perhaps I've been too emotional about the whole matter. I've allowed my emotions to consume me, make me break. The fact of the matter is, though, I hate them. They aren't even born yet, and I hate the little blighters. I can't help it. I never wanted them and now, I fear all too much, that they will be born, loved and no-one other than me will know the truth.

I haven't even taken my coat off when there are several loud bangs, hammered onto the front door. I freeze, heart racing. They're here. It didn't take them long to see the room, figure out it was me and hunt me down. The door is locked, they can't come in. I'll stay quiet in the hope they leave.

The door bangs again with such force, I almost imagine them to crash through, shattering the wood to shreds. The canvas print of Luke and Aisha's wedding on the hallway wall clatters to the floor.

'I know you're in there!' Tom's roar sounds through the letter box. 'Come on Zoe, come out!'

Shittin' hell. I've never heard Tom *this* angry before, not even when he found out about my affair with Steve. My heart is pounding more and more now. Calm down, woman! Keep control.

'We're not going anywhere until you open this door!' he continues.

I believe him. I mean, I wouldn't let something like this lie if someone did it to me. I can't blame him for being angry with me. If he knew the real reason why I demolished their beloved nursery, he might react differently. But then again, probably not, as he'd then know about my secret meetings with Steve and who knows, he could be even angrier. Judging by how he sounds now, I doubt it though.

I try to silently pick up the fallen print and put it back on the wall, but it slips through my fingers making a small clatter once again. Shit, they know I'm here now. He bangs again.

'Go away!' I shout. It's an uncontrollable response after hearing yet another threatening knock. 'You're not coming in!'

Well, they definitely know I'm here now. I wait for the next bang and another shout from Tom. Instead, a small, timid voice sounds.

'Zoe, please open the door.' It's Aisha. 'We just want our key back and then we'll leave you alone.'

I think about posting the key through the letterbox. If that's all they want, they can have it. However, I know that's not the truth. They want answers and they're not going to leave until they get them.

What the hell am I doing, cowering in here? My husband is outside, livid granted, but he wouldn't actually hurt me. Would he?

At some point I'm going to have to face the music. I'm going to have to let them in and see what happens. Perhaps we can amicably work things out. It doesn't *have* to get heated does it? I want to avoid having to stage another accident, killing both of us in the process just in the vain hope that we'll be resuscitated again and switch back to our rightful bodies. It doesn't have to be that way. Tom just needs to realise he doesn't love her, that he loves me no matter what I look like and then we can work things out. I can live with this body, just about. Once I've lost more weight.

Slowly and cautiously, I turn the key in the lock. As soon as the lock clicks open, the door is flung open. Bad choice Zoe. I shouldn't have opened it. Who was I kidding? We can't possibly work this out amicably, I've gone too far this time and I know it. I try to push the door back, stop him from entering, but he's too strong. His foot is wedged in the doorway and with one forceful push, I have no choice but to jump back and watch him stomp down the hallway.

'How dare you just barge in here!' I shout behind him. 'Get out!'

I shouldn't have let them in, in the first place. What a stupid thing to shout, 'get out'. Like they'd listen to that now that they're inside. But I don't know what else to say.

'Not until this is finished! Once and for all,' he bellows as he strides into the kitchen.

From the hallway, I see him grab the kitchen table and fling it over in sheer rage. There's an almighty clatter as Luke's pile of schoolbooks that he left here, on that table, fall to the floor. Aisha pushes past me into the kitchen as Tom flings one of his arms across the kitchen drainer, sending the dried plates and cutlery to the floor. Broken crockery everywhere.

There's a pile of plates on the shelf above the sink. I see him grab them. He turns to look at me with such fury, I fear he's going to throw them at me.

'Stop!' Aisha yells at him. 'Enough is enough! This isn't the Tom I know.'

Isn't the Tom she knows? Oh, so she knows him so well now does she? I know him a hell of a lot better than you do, love. Although, he's never ever threatened to hurt me before.

Aisha swings round to look directly at me. I can't believe what she says. 'Look! Look at what you're doing to him, what you've already done to him. This has to stop now!'

Woah … hang on one cotton picking minute love. What *I've* done to him? He's the one who's come barging in here, shouting the odds, putting me at risk. Yeah, OK so I smashed some things up, some special things to you. But, what about me? Look at what's happened to me, what *you've* done to me! You've taken everything from me, everything!

My blood starts to boil, my nostrils flare, my jaw clenches. I barge past Aisha. 'Go on then!' I scream in Tom's face. 'Do it! If you hate me so much, go on, throw them at me!'

He can't think that I'm scared of him. There's a part of me that worries that he actually might throw them at me. But there's the other part that thinks, if he were going to throw them at me, he wouldn't have hesitated like he is doing and would have thrown them already.

I can see his grip on the plates tighten, his eyes redden. Oh God, he actually might throw them. Suddenly, I'm pushed to one side and Aisha stupidly throws herself into the kitchen's no-man-land. What a freaking martyr she is, my hero. That'll be the day.

'This is not right Tom,' she whimpers at him. Trying to calm him down. Good luck with that love. 'Put the plates down! Otherwise, it's not just Zoe who'll get hurt.'

Sure enough, the fear of him hurting *her* stops him in his tracks. His grip loosens on the plates and she ushers him to a seat she'd rescued from the debris. So, it took her risking herself for him to stop. Of course, he wouldn't want to hurt precious Aisha, the one carrying *my* children. No, he couldn't possibly hurt *her*. WHAT ABOUT ME?

'I wouldn't have done it, I wouldn't have. I wouldn't want to hurt her. I just feel so angry!' he pathetically says, his breath slowing and tears pooling.

I can't help but laugh at this ridiculous situation. He looks so pathetic, so lost, so … typical Tom. We used to row and then I'd laugh, and he'd laugh. We'd make up, rip each other's clothes off and take it up to the bedroom. That's how we worked. I wait for him to start laughing, but nothing.

Instead, *she* speaks. 'What the bloody hell is so funny?'

What's so funny? You, thinking his love for you is genuine. That's what's so funny. He still loves me, I know it. We've been through too much for him to just stop loving me. He's confused because she looks like me, that's all. Well, I'll help him remember his love for me.

'Don't you miss this love?' I say to Tom. 'This passion? You used to love it! This is what we're about. If we were still together, we'd probably be ripping each other's clothes off by now and racing up to the bedroom.'

'Well, we still could!' I continue. I turn to face Aisha. Her face is hilarious, eyes wide and all a to-do. I'll rub it in some more, see if she gets the point. 'Run along Aisha, Tom and I want to play.'

With that, Tom's rage returns, he tries to stand, probably to come at me again, but she lunges herself at him. She wraps her arms around him, smothering him, mollycoddling him.

'Look at you,' I smirk. 'You're pathetic!'

He truly is. He needs a heavily pregnant woman to protect him. Protect him from me.

'I wouldn't touch you again with a barge-pole,' Tom says spitefully.

That hurt. That really hurt. To think a short while ago I was hoping we could be amicable about all of this, that Tom would realise his love for me and push Aisha to one side. That he'd forget her forever and Tom and I would live happily ever after. Bollocks to it. It would never be that simple, nothing in my life has a happy ending. I should know that by now. He'll never love me again, looking like this.

'Of course, you wouldn't! Look at me!' I shout at Tom. 'I'm not exactly God's gift to mankind. No wonder you wouldn't, no man would, including Aisha's so-called husband.'

Yeah, that's right love. Not even Luke, your darling, slob of a husband put up with you. Even he had to stray in order to get satisfaction.

'I've tried to sort this body out, lost a bit of weight, styled my hair. But it's useless. I can't make shit look good! The only way to get you back is if I get my body back with or without the horrendous bump. That's the only reason you 'love' Aisha,' I hold my hands up to the side of my head and make a quotation gesture with my fingers, as I say 'love'. 'Because she looks like me!'

'She's twice the woman you'll ever be,' Tom snarls at me. In size maybe but that's it. She wishes she were me. 'She's the mother of my children, not you! She's kind, funny, loving. Everything I searched for from you but could never find.'

Wow. He's obsessed, she's turned him against me, completely. How do I compete with that? I know I'm not loving; he knew that when he married me. I can be kind, I think, sometimes if they deserve it. And, I thought I was funny, in my own way. I mean, I like to laugh at people and that's funny.

He's not going to leave her easily, maybe I need her to leave him. Stir the shit a bit and make her think he's not the loyal, loving husband she thinks he is.

'You really think that?' I direct at Tom. 'That's not what you were saying a few weeks back when you made love to me, right here in Aisha's bed!'

That'll get her thinking. It's working, I see her face go pale as she unwraps her arms from around him. She stares at him, tears forming in her eyes.

Tom tries his hardest to convince her that I'm lying, and he tells her he loves her. It makes me sick.

'You'll pay for this,' he yells at me inches from my face. 'It's a fantasy in your head. I don't want you. I haven't for a long time.'

He really doesn't love me anymore does he? I don't stand a chance of making things go back to how they were, not as I am now. I can feel the self-control slipping away from me. Hold it together for fuck's sake. Don't lose your shit now.

He continues, 'I love Aisha get it through your head. Please!'

'Get out!' My mouth shouts the words that my mind is screaming at me not to. 'Get out, get out, get *out*!

Tom speaks sickeningly kindly to Aisha, telling her that he'll protect her, they'll get new locks rather than push to get the key back from me. He says that he won't let me bother them again and that they should just leave. Yeah, leave. Get out and stay out. But I can't let them have the last word. They won't get away with taking everything from me. They won't have the last laugh. I'll claim everything back, one way or another. I have nothing left to lose. They've made sure of it. Well, more fool them.

'You know what, Aisha? I found out the other day that we both died and were resuscitated at exactly the same time that day.' I knew all along, from the moment I saw the light and felt the paddles pull me back to her God-awful body. But she doesn't need to know that. 'Our souls must have floated around that hospital for a moment, only to be sucked back into the wrong bodies. It can't be too difficult to re-enact that!'

Tom grabs Aisha's hand and pushes me to one side, pulling her towards the door. As she passes me, I want her to know my thoughts. I want her to know how serious I am about getting my life back. I want her to know that she won't get away with this, with stealing *my* husband, *my* body and *my* money.

I whisper in her ear, clear enough for her to hear but not loud enough for Tom to acknowledge it. 'I will get my body back, even if it means killing you in the process.'

They've left me no choice. I have nothing left to lose. To think I'd started to soften, to think there could be another way. She's got her claws too deeply into Tom, that there's only one way left. Only one way to resolve this whole rotten mess. I need to kill us both.

16

It's been six months since we crashed on the twenty-second-of-July. Six months of living a lie, six months of living alone and six months of waiting to switch back to my rightful body. Well, the time has come. No more waiting around. The clock's been ticking for far too long now. It's time to get my body back, no matter what it takes.

If I kill her and we don't switch, I'll be convicted for murder. A prison sentence wouldn't be any harder to handle than the life sentence I currently feel I'm serving, so bring it on. If I die and she survives, then so be it. I can't keep living as I am anyway so what difference does it make? At least I wouldn't be alive to see those little bastards grow up. The best outcome is that we both die, get resuscitated and switch back. It would be a flaming miracle. But it's possible. We switched once before, if fate allows, we can switch again.

I shouldn't have just let them leave. I should have chased them away. I need to get to my car, get to them before they get home, drive into them and cause them to crash.

Aisha's car is parked on the side of the road, the wing mirrors starting to grow moss. It's been six months since I last drove a car. Sod not having a licence. I have bigger things to worry about, the police will soon have bigger things to worry about too, rather than me driving without a valid licence.

As I run out of the house, down the garden path onto the street, I see Tom's convertible, still parked by the side of the road, engine on, roof down. Even in January, he's got the roof down. Typical Tom. He used to say, 'What's the point in having a convertible if you have the roof up? Just stick the heating on and wrap up!'

Have I got time to speak to them one last time before they drive off? One last time to prevent what I'm about to do. One last time to talk some sense into Tom. No, I do not. Their car revs then reverses in order to make room for them to pull out into the road, around another parked car. They pull away before I've managed to reach them.

As they head off, the car they were parked behind appears, replacing my view of Tom's car. It's blue. I gulp, a lump forming in my throat. I freeze in my tracks, a cold shiver travels down my spine.

It's an all too familiar SEAT Ibiza, sporting white racer stripes from front bumper to rear. Pete. What the actual fuck is he doing here? My stomach drops, bile rising to my throat. Why would he be parked outside this house? How did he know where I live? Does he know I've switched bodies, is he waiting for me, stalking me?

Shit. It's not me he's watching, it's *her*. Of course. I saw him at the supermarket, following her. Now he's obviously stalked her here to my doorstep. If that's the case, he knows she's pregnant. He'll think the children are his. They could well be his, but he'll assume they are for definite.

He's not pulling off behind them though. He's not following them. Why? What's his game? I'm stood here, on the pavement staring at the rear bumper of his car. I hesitantly step a little closer to the SEAT, then turn it into a casual stroll. As casual as I can muster under the circumstances. I can't look too suspicious. I'll just walk past his car, have a sneak peek through the window then turn around pretending I've left something in the house or something. I dunno, but I need to see for sure it's him.

As I walk closer to his car, I can't see anyone sat in the driving seat. The closer I get, the clearer I can see an empty seat behind the wheel. Where is he? I walk up to the passenger window and look inside. There's Pete's stinking gym bag wedged in the footwell, surrounded by empty burger wrappers, scrunched up cigarette packets and crumpled lager cans. Well, it's definitely his car, but, where is he?

I look left, I look right, no sign of him. I look back toward the house, nothing. Where the hell … then I watch the convertible driving away in the distance. No, surely not … could he be? He wouldn't have jumped in the back seat whilst they were in the house, would he? He wouldn't stand a chance against Tom so why would he even try? Unless he's going to attempt to tell Tom about my affair and make Tom believe *he's* the father. Or does he have other plans for Tom. Tom will have the disadvantage as he doesn't know what Pete did to me. Pete could jump him when he's least expecting it. From my own experience, I know how heavy Pete is. Even though Tom is exceptionally strong, anyone is weak when sprung upon out of nowhere.

I need to stop this, now. I scramble with my car keys, this shitty car doesn't even have automatic locks it's so ancient, I doubt it even starts. What on earth possessed Luke to get it repaired is beyond me. The insurance company wouldn't pay out for repairs, but he insisted on getting the body work restored as we couldn't afford a new car apparently. He knew someone who could do it for cheap. It's probably not even the same car. It's probably two different cars welded together. Apparently, Aisha loved this car so much that Luke couldn't bear the thought of having to send it to the scrap heap. Where it evidently belongs.

After battling with the lock, I finally sit inside. My God it stinks, like old man socks. Well, here goes nothing, I turn the key in the ignition. The engine cranks and groans, then dies. Fantastic. Come on, you useless lump of shitty metal, start! I try again, it chugs away, but nothing. I slam my hands on the steering wheel. The one time I really need to be somewhere before it's too late and I'm sat in a rusty car that isn't even a car because it doesn't bloody drive!

Right calm down. Be rational and take your time. Don't flood the engine, it just needs warming up. I turn the key for the third time, as gently as I can under this pressure. I keep it turned while the car chokes away until it finally starts spluttering into action. Yes, at long bloody last!

I hurtle down the road as quickly as I can to try and catch Tom and Aisha up. I have to get across town to my house and every light turns red. Of course, they bloody do. I'm so tempted to run the fourth red light I'm forced to stop at, but I don't. I can't run the risk of being stopped or having an accident now. I need to get home before Pete has a chance to speak to Tom.

Finally, I see my driveway in the far distance. As I approach, I see the convertible heading away from the house, down the driveway, back to the main road ahead of me. I slow down, waiting for them to notice me and stop. But they don't. Instead, they pull out into the road, and drive straight past me hurriedly. I catch a glimpse of Aisha in the passenger seat, her face is all scrunched up as if she's in a world of pain. She sees me.

Fuck's sake, now I have to try and stop them. Why the hell are they back on the road? Originally, I wanted this, I wanted to be chasing them, I wanted to cause another accident. But now Pete's gone and ruined that plan. Now, I have to try and stop Pete from doing whatever *he's* planning. Whether that be to tell Tom that Pete could be the father, or if it's to try and bump Tom off and rape my body, pregnant or not, again. Who knows?

Whatever the reason, I'm not waiting to find out. I have to stop him.

I turn around in the driveway, seeing them in the distance. I put my foot down as hard as I can on the accelerator and drive as fast as this junk-mobile permits. Soon, I am back on their trail.

They've seen me. Tom accelerates. He's going too fast; I'm struggling to get this car to move quickly enough. Drive faster! He takes the bends more cautiously than I do. He's not as brave and I'm on a mission. His cowardice means I can catch up with them and stay hot on their heels.

I'm right behind them now. I sound the horn. I sound the horn again, and again. PULL OVER! I need you to pull over! I hold my hand on the horn for as long as I can whilst driving one handed. Yet, Tom continues his flight away from me. I need to overtake them, slow them down.

There are too many cars coming from the opposite direction and too many bends. I keep moving the car out to the middle of the road to look past Tom's car, but every time I do, a car comes towards me sounding its own angry horn, causing me to swerve back into my lane.

Finally, I see a chance to over-take, and I take it. I accelerate as hard as I possibly can which is bloody difficult when up against Tom's car. And draw parallel to theirs. I try to get their attention by frantically waving my hands, trying to signal them to stop.

'Stop the car!' I shout, but they can't hear me. 'There's a maniac in your back seat!

Surprisingly this lump of junk on wheels has automatic windows. I lower the passenger window.

'Pull over! This isn't the time; I'm not coming for you!' Tom's window winds down as I yell these final words. Perhaps they heard that, I don't know. I hear Tom shout something back but can't quite hear it, something about me trying to kill us all. I don't think they heard me properly as they continue to drive.

A loud horn sounds and flashing headlights grab my attention back to the road ahead. Shit! There's a car heading straight for me. I accelerate even faster, the car rattling and revving. Tom slows, allowing me to swerve in front of him. The other car wooshes past us, its horn bellowing into the distance.

Bloody hell, that was close … Oh shit … shiiiiiit. I see a give way sign and an all too familiar T-junction approaching.

An elderly woman, with glasses perched on the front of her nose walks across the road, without even looking.

I can't brake, I can't brake! The car is slowing, but not enough. I pump the pedal as much as I possibly can, my foot to the floor, pedal wedged in between.

The woman makes it to the other side before I've reached the junction, she turns around to stare at me. My God it's *her* the crazy, spooky, supermarket witch. Why won't this car stop? STOP! Suddenly, there's an immense bang, straight into the back of the car. My body is thrown forward, glass pierces my skin, I crumple to the tarmac below.

*

The sound of sirens in the distance gets louder and louder until it's right by my side. Is this it? Is this when I die? Did Aisha die? I try to move, try to look at Tom's car but it's not where I expect it to be. It's in the bushes on the other side of the road, upside down. My breathing slows. I want to die; I want to be resuscitated.

A gentle male voice, says, 'Hello. You're OK. Can you tell me your name?'

I can't speak, I let out a groan, but no words form. I can taste blood in my mouth.

'Hello? Can you hear me?' the same man asks me.

I feel him place his fingers on my neck. 'We're losing this one over here!'

A familiar feeling of calm and tranquillity runs through my veins. The bright, white light looms above my head. My body lightens, I'm weightless, the tarmac underneath me moves further away. This is it, the moment of truth, am I dying? I crave the white light, it's calling me. I need to reach it … NO! Not yet … not yet. I'm not ready to go, I'm not ready to die, not yet. I have to switch back; I need someone to restart my heart. Please, bring me back.

But there's no sound of a defibrillator, there's no electrical charge, I'm still floating.

No, I don't want to go, I don't want to die. I want my body back and my life back. Please, don't tempt me anymore with the bright light, I need to find my body.

I'm still floating, hovering between the ground and the light. I'm not being pulled further toward the light, neither am I being pulled back to *my* body or *any* body for that matter. Shit! This is it. I have finally died. No-one can bring me back.

Suddenly, horrifically I'm pulled rapidly back towards the ground. The pull is more intense than last time. I'm hurtling towards a bush, far from the scene of the crash, far from both crumpled cars, faster and faster. There's no paramedic below. There's no defibrillator that I can see. Instead, there's familiar grey hair bobbing up and down below me. She's pressing her sun-spotted hands rhythmically deep into a rib cage. A rib cage of a man. A tall man. A balding, overweight man of similar age to me. A man that I loathe. No, no, no, no, nooooo!

A gargling, low, choking splutter is released from my new tired lungs. You have got to be fucking kidding me!

Part 3

17

Karma is a bitch; we all know that. Bad things happen to bad people. They may not get their comeuppance straight away, but eventually they get what they deserve, they get what's coming to them. However, what the hell did I do to deserve this horrific punishment?

There are murderers, paedophiles, terrorists who deserve to rot in jail or worse, be tortured and made to suffer like they made other people suffer. There are rapists. By God, how they deserve to suffer. But not in my case. Oh no. My rapist got to die or switch or whatever the hell he's gone and done. Where is the suffering in that?

Instead, I died and was brought back into the body of this fucking beast of a man, by one hell of a crazy bint.

What did I do that was *so* wrong? OK, so I was a cheat. Yeah, I know I was a cheat and it was wrong of me. But no-one got badly hurt, did they? Well, maybe Tom did. And Mel. But they have lived on, they're happy, they're not dwelling on the past. They've cut me off from their lives, so they can't be hurting that much.

Yeah, so I threatened Aisha. A bit. I mean, who wouldn't if they were in my shoes? She had everything. She didn't suffer. I wanted her to, but she didn't. It was me who was suffering, me who lost everything I'd ever known, me who gained no positive outcome from our switch.

I was the one who was bullied in school. I was the one who was raised in a loveless family. I was the one who was hideously violated. I was the one who lost out. Me. Yet, here I am, staring up at the old crone who stupidly tried to revive a rapist, only to pull me into his body. Where is the justice? Where is the karma?

'What … the … hell have you done?' My voice is weak. I try to shout it at the old woman, but I can't. I can't catch my breath. The heavy cigarette tar lodged in my lungs prevents me. I cough hard and long until my chest aches. 'Get … the hell … away from me!'

Staring into her tired, wrinkly eyes, I catch a sparkle. She smiles, winks and says, 'You'll thank me one day. Best get you to hospital.'

I'm going nowhere with her. She's crouched down, tugging at my arm, trying to help me to my feet. Well I don't need her help. I don't want her help. She's done enough damage already.

'Get … your wrinkly hands … off me!' I force, still through rasps. 'Leave me. I just want … to die.'

'Not today,' she says quietly, still smiling and feebly trying to lift my arm. 'Your heart gave up, probably from the shock. It must have been a heart attack. But miraculously the soft grass protected your head, there doesn't seem to be any major damage. Still, best get you checked out for any internal bleeding and get that heart seen to. You never can be too careful.'

Her tugs on my left arm cause a pain to surge through my right arm, from my lower neck, down to my fingers. What have I done? I've broken my arm or something. It bloody hurts!

'You're hurting me! Get … off!' I raise my leg to kick her away, but this sends further waves of pain through my arm, so I drop it back to the bushy undergrowth beneath me.

I raise my left arm and manage to push her chest away from me, fighting back the pain as I push. Her chest feels so weak and frail beneath my fingers. Yet, she was powerful enough to complete compressions and revive Pete's body, with me now trapped in it. How did she know how to do CPR anyway?

'You should have just … let me die! I'd rather … be dead,' I continue. I'd rather be dead than live in this body of all bodies.

Her smile has faded, she shakes her head disapprovingly. 'You're ungrateful now, but one day you won't be. One day, you'll thank me. I saved your life when I didn't have to. I saw a man being tossed from his hiding place in the back of their convertible. I had to run to his aid. No-one else would have. I'm the only one who could have helped you, so I did.'

'Well … I wish you … hadn't!' If only I could clear my throat to make my words stronger, louder and more threatening. Yet these lungs just won't allow it. 'You didn't … help me, you've … ruined me.'

'Let me give you some advice …' she starts. Here we go again, I've heard this bollocks before. 'Some things in life just happen. You need to follow your path through life and look out for side roads. I've given you a side road, so I suggest you take it. You never know where it may take you …'

'Enough!' I interrupt her, voice still coarse. 'I've heard all … that bullshit before. There is … no path. There's no … destiny. None of that … crap. Leave me … now! Or I swear to God … I'll hunt you down … and …'

'Right, yes,' she interrupts me, surprisingly calmly. 'I've done my bit. Now the rest is up to you. If you're fast enough, you may catch the last ambulance before it leaves. They don't know you're here, but I can signal them for you?'

'No!' I croak through gasps. 'No … no ambulance. I don't … need help. No-one can help me … now.'

'Your choice. I respect that,' she says. 'I'll leave you be. But you're wrong. There *is* someone who can help you. Someone who knows you the most … One last thing before I leave you. Remember, don't let *this* side road pass you by.'

Craning my neck, I watch her scuttle off, through the bushes and back onto the pavement, further down the road, hidden from the view of anyone other than me. The sudden chorus of sirens startles me, the sound of engines roaring and driving off. Then there is silence. I strain my neck around to see if any paramedics are still there, but there is no-one. I am alone, stuck in this undergrowth and trapped in this body.

Lying here, I can't bring myself to look at who I have become. Has this really happened? This must be a nightmare that I'll wake up from. The past six months have to have been in my head, my subconscious playing tricks on me. I'll wake up soon and be back with Tom, back in *my* house, excitedly planning my next secret date with Steve. Nothing that's happened seems real. It's unfathomable. How on Earth can someone switch bodies in the first place, let alone switch again into someone else … someone like Pete. If I just close my eyes and fall asleep, perhaps I'll wake, and everything will be back to how it was and how it should be.

With my eyes now closed, I try to drift. But my lungs hurt, my arm throbs and the stale stench of cigarettes wafting from my clothes penetrates my nostrils. This is not a dream. This is reality. This is one hell of a fucked-up mess.

There is nothing more that I want right now, other than to die. Please God, if you *are* real, take me! I look up to dusky, icy sky. Come on, if you can hear me, take me! I want to die. Please! There is nothing left for me. Nothing. You hear me? If I am forced to live inside this body, I want to die!

Warm tears start rolling down my cheeks. I wipe them away with my working arm and feel the stubble scrape my skin. I let out a blood-curdling scream, my lungs clearing of vile tasting phlegm.

I don't deserve this. I don't. Please don't torment me by making me live in this body. I know I've done wrong. I know

I've not been the kindest person in the world but please! Please … help me.

But there is no response. God is either not real as I always suspected, or He's sat there, laughing at me, mocking me. I've never asked anything of Him before. Now the one time I'm begging Him to help me, nothing. No 'sign', no inkling that He exists. Nothing. I am truly alone.

If God won't help me die, I'll freeze myself to death. It'll be slow and painful, but I don't care. The sun is already starting to set, and the temperature is lowering. Clouds of vapour appear in front of me with every exhale breath that leaves my body. I start to tremble, and my teeth begin to chatter. All I have covering me is a jumper and a thin hooded coat. I pull the hood up and slide the coat sleeves gently over my hands.

This will take a lot of inner strength and perseverance but it's my only option. A true test of my personal strength, the strength I've always boasted about, the strength I've lived my life by.

*

Moonlight now fills the clear January sky; my body is shaking violently. I try to control it by holding my breath, then swallowing and forcing myself to relax. But I can't. I can't control it. It's overwhelming. I exhale, breathe in, then out again, trying to slow down the shivers. But it's no use.

I've been lying here for what, an hour? Two maybe. I'm not sure. This isn't the way to go. My new body is obviously in shock, along with the fact that frost is starting to coat it. I've tried to die a slow and painful death, but I can't do it. I've failed. I've failed myself. Evidently, I'm not as strong as I make myself out to be, not when push comes to shove. I hear my father's voice in my head, 'Suck it up Zoe. Make it right.' How can I make this right? How can I suck this shit of a situation up? I'm trapped here in this evil body, alone, freezing. It's no use, I need to get up. I need to go to hospital, at least I'll be warm there.

Pressing down on the frosty grass blanket beneath me with my good hand, I try to push myself up into a sitting position. The pain soars through my body, acid forms in my throat. I lean to one side and violently throw up. Every retch sends more ripples of pain through my torso. Trembling, I'm determined to move. Come on, woman. You need to sit up.

My legs are numb. Frozen into the ground beneath me. I wiggle my toes, trying to bring life back into them. I hear cars whizzing past on the main road. If I can just make it there, perhaps I can flag one down and hitch-hike my way to the hospital.

With one almighty, painful push, I clamber to my feet, blood rushing to my head. Stay standing Zoe, don't fall back down now, not after you've put in all this effort now. Clutching my right arm with my left, I put one foot in front of the other. Slowly but surely, I begin to walk.

Every step sends unbearable pins and needles through my legs. Nausea travels from my stomach to my chest once more. I bring up bile and mucus, there's nothing else left to throw up. I wipe my mouth, yet again feeling the prickly chin against my palm. Come on, stop arsing around and get to the road!

Shit! I need a pee, desperately. My bladder is no longer numb and it's crying to be released of urine. Hold it. You can hold it. You don't want to go there, you don't want to see what's inside these trousers, again. I try to avoid the desperate urge, I can't. I'm going to burst. But I'm not ready to hold this penis in my hand. This penis that once exploited me. I'm not ready to face the awful truth of who I am now. Shamefully, I let the hot urine trickle down the inside of my trouser leg.

I need someone to hold me, tell me everything will be OK. I've not felt so alone and frightened before. I need to get to the road.

Finally, body convulsing, I reach the kerb and stick my thumb up in the air. The first car that speeds past, blares his horn and continues his journey. I count another five cars that drive past, ignoring my plea for help. If I were a woman, alone, I almost certainly wouldn't be made to wait for help like this.

I alternate the transfer of my weight across each foot, trying to keep the blood flowing to them. Another three cars whoosh past, 'Bastards!' I shout after each one of them.

It's no use, no-one will stop for me. My legs give way causing me to fall to the kerb-side. The pain from my arm is lessened now, perhaps it's too numb for me to feel pain anymore. Or perhaps, *I'm* now numb to the pain. I curl up into a ball on my side, losing any remnant of hope I still had.

18

Crunching footsteps grow louder towards my closed eyes. I passed out, for how long I have no idea. It could have been hours or maybe only a couple of minutes. But, now that I'm conscious, I wish I were still sleeping. At least then I wouldn't remember how cold and in pain I am. The word cold is an understatement. The word freezing is an understatement. There is no word icy enough to describe how unbelievably cold I am right now.

'Ye alrigh' mate?' The Somerset drawl sounds from a male voice above my head.

Why do people insist on asking such a stupid question, when the person they are asking is clearly not all right? But I have little to no energy to argue or get arsey. To be fair, this man is offering to help me when so many others wouldn't even stop to check if I was OK.

Through chattering teeth, I manage to say, ‘Hospital … please?’

‘Yer, ye don’t look great mate, I have to be honest,’ he continues. ‘Righ’ then. See if ye can put yer arm round me shoulder and I’ll try helpin’ ye to me truck.’

Even though it’s stiff, I wiggle the fingers of my left hand. I still have life in it, so I raise it slowly to avoid causing pain, up towards his direction.

‘Got ye, mate,’ he says. ‘Right then, with a heave-ho, let’s go!’

Agony courses through my body once again. I thought I was numb to the pain. My body tells me otherwise. I can’t stay here. If I do, I’ll certainly die, eventually but not without experiencing a whole world of pain first. This pain I’m feeling is nothing in comparison to what I’ll feel if I stay put and don’t suck it up and make it to the hospital. This man is my saviour, I need to make the most of it. Leaning into the man, I pull myself up, swallowing back the pain.

‘There we go,’ he says. ‘Right, let’s get ye in me truck and get ye to some doctors yer?’

Once I'm in his truck, he puts the heating on full blast. Little needles prick into my skin, all over my body as I slowly, but surely start to warm up. He had a blanket in the back of the truck, so gratefully I accepted it and wrapped myself up within the soft fabric.

'What 'appened to ye then mate?' he asks. 'How did you get in the state yer in? Not being funny, but ye stink to high Heaven.'

Where would I begin. I can't tell him the truth, even if I wanted to. I can't tell anyone the truth. Never. It's too mortifying for words. I can't even think of what to say, so I ignore his question and fire my own one back at him.

'What time is it?' I managed to ask without gasping for air or my teeth chattering. The heat and the blanket are doing their job.

'Nearin' nine pm, mate,' he replies. 'Yer lucky I were passin' as me missus wanted me home by nine, but I wanted an 'alf a cider before gettin' home. Bin a long day, mate. I tell ye.'

''Ere you weren't involved in that car acciden' earlier on were ye?' he continues. 'A righ' corker of a smash-up it were. So I heard on the radio.'

My eyes widen and I glance over at him. I shake my head hoping I'd hidden my expression. His eyes were fixed on the road ahead, so I think it went un-noticed. Although, he also wouldn't have seen me shake my head.

'No,' I say calmly. 'Why, what happened?'

'Big smash-up, big indeed,' he says. 'Two cars, one female dead. That's what they be sayin'. I mean, what a way to go. Don't bear thinkin' about do it?'

One female dead? So, either Pete or Aisha are dead, one of them didn't switch. Bloody hell. I hope to God it's Pete who's dead. I may be roaming around in his God-awful body, but I hope his spirit has gone to Hell where it belongs.

He continues babbling on. 'It were a total tradegy … no … um … tradgery …'

'Tragedy?' I interrupt. I can't listen to him struggle any longer.

'That's the badger!' he says. 'Tragedy. Yer, a total tragedy. I heard the woman who died was preggers. I mean, it brings a tear to me eye. Dunno if the babber survived though. I'm hopin' so.'

My heart thuds to my stomach. My body is dead? There's no way I'll be able to switch back now. Not ever. Am I destined to live out the rest of my days, trapped in this body? I should have persevered with the cold; I should have found the strength to die out there. But I didn't. I'm weak. The fact of the matter is, I don't want to feel pain or suffer.

Did the twins survive? Only this morning, I was wishing them dead. But now, knowing that it's a possibility, how do I feel? If they are Pete's offspring, then technically they are still mine. I'm forced to now live every day with a constant reminder of the horrific ordeal I endured at the hands of Pete. I'll never be able to move on, not with this new reflection I've been 'gifted'. I always feared the twins would be that constant reminder, but now I see them solely as innocent children. It wasn't their fault this happened to me. I'll never *love* them, but I think I can now accept them. That's if, they're still alive.

'Was anyone else hurt do you know?' I ask the man, suddenly thinking of Tom. I so hope he wasn't hurt. I can't say I love the man, but I've always cared for him. I wouldn't wish pain onto him.

'No idea mate,' he says. 'All's I knows is the one woman who were preggers. That be it.'

They're probably all in hospital themselves. Well, apart from my body. That'll be in the morgue. Tom will be there and maybe even Pete. Shit, I don't know Pete's address. The hospital reception staff are almost certainly going to ask for my address. I can't rightly turn up and say that I don't remember where I live or give the details of someone else entirely. They'll take me for unnecessary tests, waste time. No, I can't do that. What can I do? Looking out of the window, I notice The White Tavern. That means we're about a ten-minute drive from the gym. We'll have Pete's record there and I can find out his address that way.

'Can we make a slight detour please?' I ask. This will undoubtedly cause me more pain, I'm finally comfortable in the warmth of the truck. But, it's the only way to avoid too much questioning once I get to hospital. 'I own a gym, not far from here. I need to just pop in and get something. I won't be long.'

'Um … mate,' the truck driver says. 'Not bein' funny but you think that be a good idea? I mean, look at the state of ye.'

Probably not a good idea at all, but it's my only choice. Plus, I'll need somewhere to sleep once I get out of hospital. I live in his body already so I may as well live in his house too.

'Probably not,' I say. 'But I have to.'

'I think it be a daft idea mate if you ask me,' he says. 'What be so important that it can't wait till yer better?'

'Drop me off here then and I'll walk. You've done enough already in all honesty,' I say. I need to get to the gym, then the hospital. I can't explain why to him. I'd much rather he drive me there as I can't imagine being able to walk all the way by myself, in this pain. But I can't force him to. He's been surprisingly kind already; his patience must be wearing thin.

'Well, seems like it be important to ye and I ain't prepared to feel guilt for the rest of me life if ye end up in the canal. I'll take ye there, no probs mate. I can go in there for ye, if you like?' the man says.

'No, no. I'll go in. I'll have to unset the alarm so it's best that I go in, just in case something happens. I feel a lot better now that I'm warm again. I'll just hold my arm, I'll be fine. Thank you.'

I'm actually shellshocked. This man knows nothing about me, not even my name. And yet, here he is, willing to help me, save me. There *are* some kind people in the world after all.

'Alright mate, if you insist, you direct me there then,' the man says.

There are no lights on, everyone has left for the day. The gym stays open until eight o'clock most evenings for different classes and for those who go for a workout after work.

I don't have a key. Shit! I can't see the truck driver from here, so that means he can't see me. There's a camera above my head, but I also know it doesn't work. It hasn't worked for a while. Something I used to get so wound up about, trying to chase the maintenance manager to get sorted. Even though it's now six months since I last worked here, I can't imagine they'd have actually got it working. I look up and can't see a light flashing on the camera so I'm confident that it's safe for me to proceed.

Pete must have something on him that I can use to pick the lock. I've never actually picked a lock before, but my father showed me once. He said it was a good skill to learn in case I was ever held hostage, locked up and needed to escape. Ideally, I need a paperclip. Like Pete would have one of those in his pockets.

Rummaging in my coat pockets, I pull out a wallet, some keys, a half-full packet of cigarettes, a lighter and some used tissues. I swallow down the acid forming in my throat at the thought of touching one of Pete's used tissues and cram everything back into my pockets. Well, nothing of use there. I pat down my chest one-handed and feel something protruding out of my coat, to the left of my heart. A name badge. That could do it.

I unclip the name badge and have a quick glance at it. 'Peter Wright, Supervisor', it reads. Peter Wright. I scoff to myself, what an ironic name. There is *nothing* right about Peter Wright.

Inserting the pin into the top of the lock, I twiddle the pin back and forth, just like my father showed me. It's hard to grip the pin end with my left hand and with the name badge flopping everywhere. Nothing. Come on, open up! I keep twiddling. Is the pin too short? It's so hard to do this when I'm not using my dominant hand. I'm not sure but I persevere, moving the pin back and forth until finally, click! The door finally opens. My father would be so proud. Pah! My father wouldn't be the least bit proud of the person I've become.

The alarm starts bleeping impatiently. I input my code to calm it down and silence it. Perfect, right, just need to get this address and get the hell out of here.

Behind the reception desk is a computer. I type in my credentials. My right arm twinges, I grimace for a second then carry on. Please work, please don't have expired. It logs me in, thank God. I worried for a second that my password would have expired and then all of this would have been for nothing.

In the search bar, I type in Peter Wright. Bingo! His address appears on the screen. His medical card also shows that he was referred to the gym by his GP. I tear a piece of paper from the notepad next to the computer and scribble both his address down and his GP's. I'll spend the rest of the journey to the hospital memorising them.

'Hello?' I hear a male voice shout. It's the truck driver. For God's sake, why the hell didn't he wait in the car. That scared the shit out of me.

I head back to the main door and see him standing there, looking impatient.

'Sorry,' I say. 'All good, let's go.'

'Good,' he says. 'Course, you know I wanna help ye out an' all, but I do have a missus to get home to.'

'Yeah, sorry, I know,' I say. 'Thank you.'

Clutching my arm, I hobble back to the truck, the driver closely following me.

We don't speak for the rest of the journey. I think he's pissed off with me for wasting time. To be fair, if the shoe were on the other foot, I'd be steaming by now. I could do without his jabbering anyway, so I can concentrate on memorising this address.

'Right, we're 'ere now mate. Time to get yer help. Hope ye get a gurt lush nurse lookin' after ye,' the truck driver says as we pull up in the 'drop off' parking bay.

The hospital looks intimidating in the dark of night. Its grey walls towering over me. The last time I was here, I switched into a body I loathed. A fat, unattractive woman. Or so I thought. I didn't have a clue back then. I'd take Aisha's body over this one any day.

I reach into my coat pocket to take out Pete's wallet, see if he has any money in there that I can give the man. Opening it up, I see a photo of a pretty-ish blonde woman, in her twenties with a boy who couldn't be older than three. She's sat on a stone wall, with a field behind her, wearing a blue and white summery dress. Her arms are wrapped around the young boy who sits on her knee. Both are grinning widely at the camera. Could Pete have a family? Is this woman his wife? Does she know who he is and what he does to women? She can't possibly know. And the boy. Is this Pete's son? My God, if he is Pete's son, he'll be destroyed if he finds out his father's dark secret.

'You alrigh' there mate?' the man asks, obviously getting impatient.

'Oh yeah, sorry,' I say. I take out a ten-pound-note and hand it to him. 'Thank you. You didn't have to stop, but you did. I really appreciate it.'

He beams a massive smile, takes the note and says in delight, 'Proper job! What a beaut! That'll be me cider for tomorrow. Thank ye and look after yerself.'

It occurs to me that I don't even know the man's name. 'Can I ask your name?'

'Course mate, it's Donald, Don for short.'

'Well, thank you Don. Honestly, thank you so much.' I say, forcing a smile to form across my face. I leave the truck and head inside the A and E department.

19

Why are receptionists always so miserable? You'd think, working in a hospital, you'd show compassion and be overly friendly to patients in need. I'm sure not *all* receptionists are obnoxious but the few I've had the misfortune to meet have been anything but pleasant.

'Name?' the woman, nearing middle age says nonchalantly from behind her desk. Her face is glued to her computer screen, no eye contact made with me at all.

'Um … Peter Wright,' I hate having to say the name out loud, confessing to being the owner of this name, and this body.

'Address?' she asks, again, no eye contact, not even a glance in my direction. She just sits there, staring at the screen, tapping away on her keyboard. It's just pure rudeness and I can't stand it. There is no excuse for poor people skills, especially working in a role such as this where empathy and kindness are key.

I rattle off the address I'd memorised in the car.

'GP?' This woman is unreal, still tapping away on her keyboard. Not even a thank you for the information I've provided already, not even a look of acknowledgement in my direction.

My politeness is rapidly diminishing. I give her the GP information and I can't bite my tongue any longer. 'A bit of acknowledgement wouldn't go amiss you know. How rude are you? Very, that's how rude you are. Show a little compassion and actually gain some people skills yeah?'

She finally tilts her head up to look at me, a look of disgust sweeping across her face. She points to a sign that reads: *Any aggression or inappropriate behaviour shown to our staff, will not be tolerated.* 'I don't expect to be spoken to like that sir. So, I suggest you calm down, or I will need to call security.'

Wow! She's the one who's rude and yet I'm the one who is now out of order? You've got to be kidding me!

'Seriously? You're the one who's shown aggression and inappropriate behaviour to me, ever since I walked through those doors,' I can't help myself; she needs to be told. 'How dare you put this on me, that I'm the one at fault. You should at least greet people with a smile. Can you actually smile love?'

Her eyes widen, she looks frightened her words have a slight tremor to them. 'I won't be threatened sir. So, I suggest if you want to be seen by a doctor today, you calm down, take a seat and say nothing else. Otherwise, I will have no choice but to call security.'

Threatened? She's the one threatening me with security. However, I can see she's scared of me. She's quaking in her boots. I mean, I get it. Just look at me. I *am* intimidating. I'm no longer a slim, attractive blonde with a big gob. I'm now a massive, thug of a man who's angry beyond measure. Maybe she should have been kinder, maybe she'll learn from this. Or maybe she'll continue to be a miserable bitch through to retirement regardless of who stands up to her in the future. I can't afford for security to be contacted; I can't be the centre of attention. I need to get fixed and get out of here as quickly as possible without drawing attention to myself.

Raising my left arm to my head in a gesture that implies I'm backing down, I say, 'OK, OK. I'm calm. I'll just take a seat, no need to get security. You won't hear another peep from me.'

There are delays as per normal in A and E. I've been forced to wait here for over an hour already. Thank goodness I warmed myself up in Don's truck. It's almost eleven o'clock now and there are only three other people in the waiting area. You'd think at this time of night, the wait times would be reduced, but no. I can feel angry impatience starting to bubble away inside me. Keep it together. Hold your tongue and bite your lip.

Then a woman, in her twenties, who's clearly pissed as a fart, staggers in through the automatic doors, trips over the first row of chairs knocking the end chair over. She hurls some abuse at the chair as she fumbles around, trying to pick it back up. After re-gaining her composure, somewhat, she zigzags her way to the reception desk. Let's see how Bitch-Face on reception deals with this class act hey!

The receptionist greets the woman with a kind smile, looking directly at her and says, 'You alright love? How can I help you?'

She's having a laugh, right? So, she's as nice as pie to a complete pisshead but is ignorant and rude to me, a polite citizen in need.

The drunk spits and swears at the woman behind the desk, about complete nonsense. Yet the receptionist continues to smile and empathise with her. Where is the justice in this? If anyone is displaying threatening behaviour, it's this drunk, yet not once does the receptionist respond with a threat of calling security. Just because I look like this, I'm deemed intimidating and a risk to the public.

The drunk takes a seat opposite me. She mutters and swears to herself, body swaying and eyes intermittently shutting. Then her eyes shoot open, staring at me.

'Whar … a …. fuck … you lookin' at?' she slurs in my direction.

'Nothing love,' I say. I'm not going to get involved in this. I turn my face away from hers. I can't face the risk of security getting involved.

'Fat … wanker!' she spits in my direction. I ignore her. I *am* a fat wanker. I can't agree with her more.

She quietens down once she's realised that she won't get a rise from me. If I were in my original body, I wouldn't hesitate to shout back at her, give her a piece of my mind. However, now I am a big burly bloke, I realise that if I speak my mind, it will come back to bite me on the arse.

A female doctor appears and calls a name. Not my name, no. The doctor calls the drunk through. How the hell is that fair? I've been waiting for over an hour-and-a-half now. She's been here all of fifteen minutes and gets called straight through. I can't even see anything physically wrong with her apart from the fact she's off her head. Control your anger woman. Don't start raging and sounding off. It's so hard to control it though. I stand up and march over to the reception desk.

As politely and calmly as I can manage, I ask, 'How come that lady got seen before any of us? We've all been waiting for ages, yet she's been seen first. Any idea how much longer I'll be waiting as I'm in a lot of pain.'

No longer is the receptionist the kind, empathetic employee she was with the drunk. Her smile has faded, and the fear crosses her face once more.

'Sir, I'll have to ask you to stay in your seat. We are busy at the moment, you will be seen as soon as possible,' she says, without any compassion for me or the other people waiting.

My rage is bubbling, I'm trying to keep it at a simmer, trying not to get to boiling point.

'I understand, you're busy,' I say through gritted teeth. 'However, I don't understand why she was seen before us? Surely, it's a first come, first served basis?'

'Actually, sir,' she replies. 'It's based on your own individual circumstances and the severity of our patients' conditions. She's evidently vulnerable so needs to be seen quickly.'

That drunk is deemed vulnerable? Wow. What, so the alcohol made its own way down her throat, did it? I would imagine those that are on the receiving end of her vile tongue are the vulnerable ones. But what do I know? She's a young woman, getting preferential treatment for being a dickhead as far as I can see.

Oh … bloody hell. A sudden realisation dawns on me. *I* was that woman once. OK, not a pisshead, but I spoke to people like that, minus some of the swearing. I spouted vile comments and used my looks and money to get me preferential treatment.

'Hmmm …' I say to the receptionist. 'I'm not sure she should be getting preferential treatment for being a drunk …'

I'm cut short. The swinging doors from reception to the intensive care unit swing open and Tom strides through reception and out through the automatic doors. His face was tear stained, he looked grey and troubled. He thinks I'm dead. Or he thinks Aisha is dead. He's grieving. Are the twins dead too?

'Excuse me,' I say to the receptionist and she glares back. 'I'm just going to get some fresh air. Call me if the doctor comes for me please.'

She scoffs and mutters something under her breath. I don't care, she can think what she likes about me. What I do care about, is the man stood outside, the man who's lost and staring into the dark night.

I leave reception, still hugging my arm. The pain is still there but not as excruciating as it once was. Perhaps I'm getting used to it now. Walking out into the night sky, I stand within a couple of metres of Tom and lean against the hospital wall. I want to talk to him, but what do I say?

What does anyone say in these kinds of situations, let alone a man like me? What would Pete do? Pete would spark up a cigarette most likely, well I'm not going to do that. But I will offer Tom one. I know he doesn't smoke, but it's a way of getting his attention, perhaps try to start a conversation.

Clasping Pete's cigarette packet with my left hand, I reach over to Tom, 'Cigarette?'

To my utmost surprise, Tom says, 'Thanks,' and takes one.

'Have you got a light?' he asks.

I have never seen Tom smoke before. He is always so health conscious, not as much as me but still. I never thought he'd take one. No way. If he wants to smoke, things must be bad. I am not in a position to lecture him now about his health, so I pass him the lighter.

'Cheers,' he says, pain in his eyes. He takes a drag, then he looks at me. Recognition casts across his face. 'Don't I know you? You're Pete, from the gym no? You hurt your arm?'

Shit! I forgot Tom knew Pete. Not well, as Pete would always come into the gym on my shift, but Tom had seen him in passing. I'd also told Tom that Pete was a sleazeball and that my reason for my sabbatical from work was due to him kicking off that day. What do I say?

'Um … yeah, I'm Pete. You're married to … um … Zoe I think the name is yeah?'

Tom's eyes fill with tears at just the mention of my name. He's not crying for me though; he's crying for Aisha. Is she really dead? I know my body's dead, but is she? Did she die and did Pete switch into her body? Or did she manage to switch back to her original body? This is all too much for me to try and fathom.

‘Sorry …’ I say.

‘For what?’ Tom asks, confused.

‘For kicking off with her that day. She must have told you about it.’ I can’t believe I’m apologising for Pete. But I have to say something for Tom to confide in me. I need to get him on side, I need to find out about the twins.

‘Don’t worry about it,’ Tom says. Don’t worry about it? Seriously? That’s how much I meant to you. If only you knew what this man, you see right before you did to your wife Tom.

He continues, ‘I’ve got bigger things to worry about right now.’

‘Why? What’s happened?’ I ask. Please tell me, please feel you can confide. ‘I mean, I don’t want to pry, but I can lend an ear?’

‘We lost her. She … um …,’ I can see Tom’s struggling to say the words. Tears stream down his face, he sniffs. ‘Didn’t make it.’

Well, I know that. I know my body’s dead but what about the twins?

'What, Zoe you mean?' I say, keeping up the act of surprise. 'Dead? Oh, I'm so sorry Tom.'

'Not Zoe … Aish … I mean, yes. Zoe was involved in a car accident and she … she didn't make it,' Tom says through heart wrenching sobs. It's confirmed, he's definitely grieving for her, not me.

'She was pregnant, wasn't she? So I heard. Please say the children are OK Tom?' I ask. I honestly don't know how I feel about the twins. I know I no longer wish them dead though.

'Yes … they survived,' Tom says. Then he lets out another gurgling sob. 'But they'll never know the kind, loving woman that brought them into the world.'

The kind, loving woman that brought them into the world? What about the woman that conceived them? Do you even care about her? I need to know if Aisha is still alive or if Pete now inhabits her body. Even if he does, he can't go around abusing women anymore without a penis, that's a bonus. Still, he deserves to be dead, more than Aisha does.

'Was there anyone else hurt?' I ask.

Tom's face darkens. 'There was another car, another woman. It was *her* fault. I wish she died instead. She caused this accident; she deserves to pay.'

With that, Tom throws his cigarette on the concrete pavement and storms back into the hospital.

Oh my God. Does Tom hate me that much to want me dead? Have I really gone too far this time? I really need to look at myself and how I've treated people in the past. I'm forced to now live in this body. Perhaps I do deserve this. Maybe I *am* evil, and this is karma for all the wrong things I've done to other people.

Tom thinks I'm still in Aisha's body. He has no idea anyone else was involved in the accident. He's going to take his grief out on whoever is now in Aisha's body, whether that be Aisha or Pete. If it's Aisha, will she convince Tom that she survived and switched back? If it's Pete, then this whole saga begins again for Tom, for Aisha's parents, for everyone. Would Tom be able to grieve properly for his loss or would Pete pretend to be Aisha. My head hurts. This is so confusing. I just need to know if Aisha survived. My God, I hope Pete's dead. No matter how much I despised Aisha for taking everything from me, she can't die. I want this whole switch-cycle to be over for everyone, forever.

20

The time is nearing three-thirty in the morning. I've not slept and feel exhausted. Finally, about thirty minutes ago, I was called through to get my arm examined. I've dislocated my shoulder. All this time, I thought it was my arm that I'd broken, but it was in fact my shoulder popped clean out of its socket. I just need to have it in a sling for a couple of weeks. Other than that, there were no broken bones, just a few bruises and scrapes. A miracle really considering Pete had been flung from a moving convertible.

Understandably, the doctor asked me questions. I lied in response to most of them. He asked me what happened, and I told him I'd fallen down the stairs. I considered saying that I'd been mugged and beaten up, that probably would have been more believable considering the injuries I'd sustained, until the police got involved and found out nothing had been stolen and I had no suspect to pin it on. My web of lies would have become so tangled that it just wasn't a lie that would hold up.

The doctor evidently didn't believe me. He kept probing me for more information, but I didn't let on. I was not going to tell him that I was involved in a car accident. I don't want anyone to know that I was there, at the scene. If I do, it will be released in the papers, Tom will find out and start to question things. He may even end up finding out that Pete was in their car through police investigations and DNA findings, which would open a door that I want kept firmly shut. No, no-one can know what happened.

Because the doctor didn't know the full story, he treated me for my dislocated shoulder, but I'll never know if I suffered any further injuries, internally. I mean, I died at the scene. My heart gave up. Was this because of Pete's underlying heart condition or was it something else entirely? The doctor didn't do any x-rays or ultrasounds because as far as he was concerned, there was no need. The thought wouldn't have even crossed his mind because I gave him no further information, other than the fact that my arm was in agony. It doesn't worry me though, if I die suddenly of a heart attack, who will really care? I certainly won't. I want to die, but I'm too chicken to do it myself.

The big downside to all of this is that the sun isn't even rising yet and I have no-where to go. I was hoping to be kept in hospital overnight at the very least. That way I would have been somewhere warm with a bed. But no.

'There you go,' the doctor had said. 'All patched up so you're free to get on home. Keep your arm elevated as much as possible to reduce the swelling. Keep rested and take advantage of people running around, helping you.'

Whatever Doc. You didn't have a clue about me and the fact that I have no-where to go. You've cast me back out into the freezing night and now what the hell do I do? I practically begged to stay the night but was told there weren't enough beds available and my injuries didn't warrant an overnight stay.

Standing outside the hospital's main entrance, looking out into the residential estate that the hospital was randomly built within, I have absolutely no idea what to do with myself or where to go. So, I pull my hood over my head and start to walk, the bitter breeze striking my face.

No lights are on in anyone's homes. They're all tucked up, warm in bed. Snuggled with loved ones or curled up next to their dog. Do they have central heating or open fires to keep them warm? Or do they have both? Maybe some of them even have electric blankets or hot water bottles, warming their sheets as they snooze away. What wouldn't I do for a hot water bottle right now to hug as I walk. I wouldn't ask for much, just something warm to hold. I keep walking as briskly as Pete's body allows, to try to keep my body temperature above dangerous.

Approaching the town centre, Taunton is a ghost town at this time in the morning. Not even the drunks are still out and about, even they've gone home. A place that is normally full of daily hustle and bustle is now eerily quiet. I imagine this is what the town would look like at the end of the world. No sign of life and no warmth or love. A barren landscape lost in time.

Walking down the High Street, shops are boarded up and litter blows softly in the icy breeze. Shop doorways have become home to sleeping bags, wrapping homeless people up tight, yet scarcely giving them any necessary warmth. They look warmer than me right now though. What I would give for a sleeping bag, for some company even. But I can't bring myself to approach any of them, scared of what they may say or do to me. I used to walk past homeless people and scoff at them, thinking 'druggies' or 'wastes of space'. I'd never give them money or food or anything. Thinking, they'd done this to themselves, they deserved to be out on the streets scrounging. Now, I feel different towards them. I too am now homeless. But I'm not a druggie or a waste of space. I didn't deserve to be in this horrendous situation. Perhaps, they got dealt some bad hands in life too.

What I do need right now is to find some form of shelter, so that I can try and get a bit of kip. Sleep will help me think more clearly come the morning. But where?

My left hand is in my pocket, my right in a sling. Feeling around in my pocket, the jingle of keys sounds. Pete's keys. Most probably house and car keys. No, don't even think about it. It's not an option. I'm desperate to get shelter, warmth and sleep. But I can't contemplate going to Pete's house. This is a man who I loathe, I hate everything there is to hate about him. What would I find there? I know he has a photo of a woman and child in his wallet. What if he was playing happy families but abused women as a pastime, in secret.

Or worse, what if I found a woman locked up in his cellar like you see in the films. A woman who'd been tortured, raped and abused. God knows what a man like Pete had been up to and what he was hiding. No, I can't find out, I can't go to his house. No chance.

The gold-plated, grand gates of Vivary Park emerge in the near distance. I know there is a pavilion inside those gates, and even some public toilets. A couple of places that would have a roof to keep the bitter winter wind off my skin. There's a band stand with a roof and even copious bushes which would give some shelter if the pavilion or toilets are locked. I'd have more hope of finding safe haven in there than I do out here with the homeless occupying most sheltered spots.

Pushing the gate to the park, I'm surprised to find it open. I always thought they locked the gates to the park in the evening. I was evidently wrong.

When I was at boarding school, I would often walk from school to the park in free periods, sometimes even skipping lessons and taking a wander on my own, weather permitting. It was only a fifteen-minute walk from school, so providing I could leave the school premises without being seen, I'd regularly use this place as a means of escape from the bullies. There was a children's area within the town park, and I used to love to sit on the swing, kicking my legs off the ground, swinging back and forth until my worries melted away.

There's a stream that runs through the greenery with ducks and swans using it as their home. When I was sick of swinging,

I'd take a walk to the stream, buy some duck feed from a kiosk and throw the food towards the flocking birds.

In Summer months, children would be playing football on the large green. Parents would be lining up at the ice-cream van, waiting patiently to get some iced treats for their kids, and most probably for themselves. And smaller children would be playing in the kids' area, parents laughing at them, pushing them on the swings and playing with them. I'd sit there, watching them, jealousy filling my body. I'd think to myself, why couldn't I have parents like that who loved me and wanted to play with me?

Walking around the park now, all these memories come flooding back. However, now, the ice-cream van is boarded up for winter, the ducks are no-where to be seen and the swings creak and squeak lonelily in the breeze.

I am desperate for the loo. I've been holding it for far too long now and I don't want to wet myself again. I stink to high Heaven already and the shame is unbearable. However, the thought of having to touch Pete's vile todger is unpalatable. But necessary. I don't know how long I will be forced to live in this atrocity of a body, so I need to 'suck it up' and whip it out. Get the whole ordeal over and done with. Surely after the first time, it'll get better, easier?

There's a bush to my left, hidden from all angles, not that there's anyone in the park that would see me, to my knowledge. Opening the fly, I feel revolting, there's no denying it. I don't even know how to do this. I'm a woman. It's not something I ever thought I would have to do, hold a penis and aim, let alone hold *this* rotten one in my hand. I can't face holding it; I can't bear the thought of it. So, I pull my trousers down entirely, squat and let the urine flow to the grass below.

All buildings are locked. Of course, they would be. So, I set up camp in the band stand. The low, metal walls and wooden roof offer little shelter from the freezing air but I feel hidden and safe here. Lying on the stone floor, huddled up to the metal edge, I tighten my hood under my chin and wrap my left arm in my right's sling, absorbing the little warmth the thin muslin offers and close my eyes.

I imagine a band playing *Tchaikovsky's 1812 Overture.* If I imagine hard enough, I can hear brass, string and wind instruments, working together to produce the stirring sounds conducted by a man waving a baton to the beat. A canon firing towards the end of the majestic piece. It's somewhat soothing and distracts me from the numbness travelling from my feet to my shoulders.

My mind starts to drift. How the hell have I ended up here, like this? What has become of me? Do I *really* deserve this? I think back to the homeless people I saw on my walk down the High Street. They must ask themselves the same questions daily. I can't say I've ever spared a thought for the homeless before, not even at winter. Sure, I know there are people living on the streets, I watch the news after all and ignore their begging for money regularly. But, not once have I ever thought, what if that happened to me? Perhaps, if I had known that I'd wind up homeless myself, I'd have shown them a bit more compassion. Perhaps even used some of my money for good, rather than spending it on myself. Perhaps I should have done this anyway, regardless of whether I knew I'd end up like this or not. Well … hindsight is a bitch.

I must have drifted off, as a blinding light shining in my face, jolts me awake.

'Excuse me Sir,' a male voice says. 'I'm going to have to ask you to move on please. No sleeping in the park.'

Squinting up at the location of the light, I can see the silhouette of a man, in uniform holding the blinding torch. Fucking great, it's the Police.

'How about getting that light out of my face?' I bluntly retaliate. He moves the torch away from my eyes but it's still on me. 'I've got no-where to go. What's the harm in me sleeping here? There's no-one about, I'm not disturbing anyone …'

He interrupts me and starts spouting shit about Section thirty-five of some Anti-Social Behaviour Crime Act bullshit and how failure to comply could end up with a fine or imprisonment. A fine? Pah! How can the homeless pay a fine? What ridiculous bollocks! Basically, what he's saying is that I'll end up in jail if I don't leave the park. Well at least I'd be warm in jail, I guess. But, looking like Pete does, I wouldn't have an easy ride in prison.

'OK, OK!' I shout. 'I'm leaving, OK, I'm leaving.'

The police officer escorts me out of the park. I mean, what crime have I committed exactly? I have no other option than to sleep outdoors. Does he really think I would *choose* to sleep here? I had no other choice and now he is happily chucking me out of the park to freeze to death in the gutter. I thought the Police were supposed to help people. No help being offered by this officer, not to me, when I need it. Can't he see I've got an arm in a sling and am in need?

He stands by the gate to the park, staring at me, waiting for me to walk away. Walk away where? Where is the compassion? Does anyone actually care about other people nowadays? I aimlessly put one foot in front of the other. I need to get away from this man before I say something I regret. What a complete arsehole.

Pete doesn't have a watch or even a phone on his body. Perhaps his phone got flung from the car. I have no idea what time it is. I can only guess it must be verging on five o'clock now. I've had literally a few minutes sleep, I'm freezing cold and I'm starving. I've got a little money on me, maybe forty pounds with change, fat lot of use that is when everywhere is closed. I can't even think what day it is. So much has happened to me that I have no idea. All I know right now is that I need to find somewhere. It's still going to be three hours or so before the sun rises. I can't stay outdoors a minute longer, let alone for three hours or more.

The menacing stone tower of Saint Mary Magdalene Church appears before me. I've wandered unwittingly through the gateway and the grassy yard, up the pathway and now stand outside the grand oak door. I haven't set foot in a church for years and I doubt it's even open, so why have I brought myself here? This would be the last place I'd think of to come. But, something inside me has brought me here, something is telling me to try it.

I turn the large, ring-shaped, brass handle, expecting the door to be locked fast. However, with a loud scrape and a decent push, the oak door opens. Suddenly, I freeze on the spot. If the door is open, who else has done the same as me and sought shelter from this old stone building? Do I dare find out? I have to, I have no other choice. It's either walk inside and face the unknown or freeze to death out here.

The church is empty, thank God. Shit, can you blaspheme in a church even if it's in your mind? Shit, can you think the word shit? Oh … crumbs. I can confidently say, you're allowed to say crumbs. The shadows casting off the furniture are eerie. The whole church is spooky as anything. There are people buried here aren't there? Oh … crumbs, there're dead bodies beneath my feet. A shiver travels down my spine, I'm cold already but this shiver is spine numbing. I don't exactly believe in ghosts, but right now I swear I just saw a monk walk across the stage or whatever you call it, at the front of the church. Stop being a dick, woman. There's no monk, no ghosts, no God. Chill the fuck out.

Sitting down in one of the pews, I take in my surroundings. Why do people find such solace in a cold, dank place like this? They do though. They come here regularly, pray to a man up in the clouds who they think will make everything better, and for what? They get nothing in return.

I raise my legs up on to the pew and settle down onto my back, closing my eyes. God, I think to myself. If God were real, where is He now? Where is He? He's not with me, He's not helping me. There is *no* man in the clouds, no man listening to people's prayers. No man … My thoughts are cut short. A feeling a warmth travels from my feet to my nose, I gasp and embrace it.

I fall fast asleep.

21

The winter sun beams through the stained glass windows, waking me from my not so peaceful sleep. The pew was not the most comfortable thing to sleep on, but I was so tired, I'd literally have slept on rocks. I could have slept better, but the main thing is that I caught a few winks. At least I was in from the cold with a shelter above my head. I certainly feel better for it. However, I am gasping for some water.

I've no idea what time it is or how much sleep I've actually had. I've no idea what day it is even. What was the day yesterday? Friday? Saturday? Yes, Saturday. So that makes today Sunday. Sunday! Shit. It's Sunday and I'm lying here, in a church looking like a complete druggie who's been dragged in from the streets. I need to move before people start turning up for a service.

As I'm walking down the aisle towards my escape, I hear the brass latch of the big oak door clatter and slowly, the door opens. What the hell do I do now? There's nowhere for me to run to and I can't exactly hide without them finding me. From behind the oak door, a woman aged in her forties appears wearing a dog collar.

'Oh!' she says, clearly taken aback by how hideous I look and probably smell. 'I wasn't expecting to see anyone here this early, can I help you?'

No-one can help me and certainly not a woman of the cloth, I'm beyond anyone's help.

'No,' I say, continuing my walk towards the front door. 'I was just leaving actually.'

'Well, you may as well stay for the morning service. It starts at ten o'clock, so you'd only be waiting forty minutes or so,' she says. God loves a trier, perhaps that's how she got her calling to do what she does.

'No, honestly,' I need to get out of here. She's stood in my path though. I don't want to be rude, not to another woman and certainly not a vicar. But I will if I have to.

'We'll be having tea and biscuits after the service. So, you sure I can't tempt you?' she says. She looks down at my arm. 'You seem a little … troubled. Perhaps we can help?'

'You can't help me,' I snap. It's no use, I need to get out and she's not taking no for an answer. I really don't want to be rude, not looking like this as I know how intimidating I can come across to others, but she's leaving me no choice. 'No-one can help me. Not even *your* God can help me. I can't even help myself. Now, if you could let me pass, that would be most appreciated.'

'Oh, yes, of course,' she says, moving to the side for me to pass her. 'Well, you know where we are if you ever want to talk. St. Mary Magdalene's always has their door open.'

Well, to be fair she's right about one thing, they did have their door open when I needed a sanctuary. But she's wrong on every other level. I am beyond help; this whole situation is completely out of control and I will never be able to talk to anyone about any of this. Ever.

I don't acknowledge her, I don't smile, I just keep my head down and walk out of the church. It's another crisp, sunny day. Thank God it's not raining, things could be worse. Not much worse, but all the same, I'd best be grateful for what little comforts are thrown my way.

Now what though? Where do I go from here? I need water, a shower and some clean clothes. I also need something to eat. Pete's body needs probably three times the amount of food to sustain it as my old body did. And I can feel the hunger pains striking my gut.

There's a little van back towards the High Street that sells healthy smoothies, that'll give me a boost. Looking at the menu, my mouth fills with saliva. I bet Pete never enjoyed anything half as healthy as these tasty treats. But how to choose. I could easily enjoy any of them.

There's a mother and child being served in front of me. I hear the little girl whisper to her mother, 'He smells mum!'

The little girl turns to stare at me. Her mother whispers in her ear whilst casting her own glance in my direction, 'It's rude to stare Sylvie. Come on, take your smoothie. Let's go.'

The little girl Sylvie, does as she's told. She takes her smoothie in one hand and holds her nose with the other. Her mother throws me one last look of disgust before they walk away.

I would have done the same a few days ago. In fact, I probably would have been worse and hurled some abuse at someone who looked and smelt as bad as I do right now. Probably saying something like, 'There's no excuse for you smelling like shit. Go take a freaking bath!'

'What can I get you?' a kind looking young woman smiles at me from inside the cart window.

The little girl had distracted me from the menu. I still haven't decided what I fancy but I need to get a move on, conscious of my lingering stench.

'The Island Breeze please and a bottle of water,' I say.

'Coming right up!' she says, still smiling and starting the blender. She doesn't bat an eyelid about my appearance. I am a human being to her, a customer, someone who just wants a smoothie. I am so grateful to her for just acting normal and treating me like anyone else. Would I have done the same? Probably not, no.

'There you go,' she says. 'Enjoy!'

I pass her the money and say, 'thank you', meaningfully. I really am thankful for her not casting judgement. I put the bottle of water under my arm and take the smoothie in my hand. Doing things one-handed is trickier than you'd imagine.

Oh … my … God. I've taken a sip of the coconut, banana and pineapple blend and I am in pure bliss. I can feel the antioxidants course through my body already. I bet Pete never even ate apples, let alone tried something as fruity and tasty as this. Already, I feel more alive.

There are benches scattered down the pedestrianised High Street. I take a seat to enjoy the remainder of my fruity remedy. I'm still hungry but the smoothie is starting to take the edge off a bit. Once I've finished this drink, where do I go from here? I can't roam the streets of Taunton forever and I certainly can't spend another night camped out in the church or worse, in a shop doorway. Fiddling with the keys in my pocket, I know that Pete's house is not an option. However, I am tempted. He's bound to have a shower and I'd be able to get fresh clothes. But no. I don't want to find out about his life, I know his dirty secret, that's enough for me.

'Oi, oiiiii!' I hear a male shout behind me. 'Who do we 'ave 'ere then!'

I turn around to see six teenage boys huddled in a group, evil grins plastered across their faces. One, wearing a baseball cap, kicks an empty cola can across the paving. Another, stocky boy has a mobile phone in his hands, the camera pointed purposefully in my direction. This isn't good, not good at all. My heart starts to race and beads of cold sweat form across my brow.

'Alrigh' mate?' the ringleader calls in my direction. 'Oi! Bum! Yeah, I'm talkin' to you mate, don't fuckin' ignore me!

Do I run or do I fight? It brings back memories of being bullied when I was young and when I was told that if I ignored them, they would eventually give up. Bullies never did give up though. Not if they were determined to make someone's life a living hell. I need to confront them. After all, I'm not a scrawny woman anymore, I'm a big burly bloke now.

'Why don't you just piss off, yeah?' I shout back at them. 'Just trying to have a drink in peace. That too much to ask?'

'Yeah, it *is* too much to ask mate,' he replies. 'You're scum. Look at you, you're pathetic. Hey boys … what you reckon? Reckon he belongs here or d'you think he should go crawl under a rock somewhere and die? Do the planet a favour?'

The other teens snigger. One short, fat lad shouts, 'Yeah, fuck him up!'

Another lankier one with half his teeth missing shouts, 'Do one, hobo!'

They're all huddled around my bench now, forming a circle around me, the camera still filming everything. Shit, what do I say? I've never been punched before; will it be as painful as it looks? I can feel panic rising within my chest, my useless heart pounding.

'OK boys just let me leave quietly no need for things to get nasty,' I say. I can hear my voice trembling as I say the words.

'Hah!' the ringleader says. 'Is already nasty mate, you're here! Nasty tramp! What, you a junkie or something?'

'Yeah,' the short, fat one says. 'Probably high as a kite right now. After his next fix! Probably broke his arm whilst he was pissed. Scum! Ptish!'

Warm, wet liquid lands below my eye. The fat one's saliva trickles down my cheek. I wipe it away with my sleeve. I don't know what to do. What does anyone do in this situation? The little bullied girl inside me just wants to run but I can't. I can't show signs of weakness. I need to regain control and the only way I can do that is to not rise to them. Let them have their laughs at my expense and hopefully they'll move on.

'Ha, ha, ha! Nice one Lardy!' the ringleader praises him for spitting on me.

I see a middle-aged couple walk past us. Both of them glance in my direction, yet they do nothing. He puts his arm around his wife's waist and hurries her along. Another bloke walks past in the opposite direction. He's probably in his thirties. Casts a brief look towards me then looks at his watch, pretending not to have seen what is unfolding. They've all turned a blind eye, no help or support shown. No compassion, no acting the Good Samaritan. I don't overly blame them; I would have done the same, I probably *have* done the same in the past, turned away from someone in need. But now that *I* am that someone in need receiving this torrent of abuse, I just want someone to come to my rescue. Anyone.

'Not saying much, now are you? You fat waster!' the ringleader exclaims. He moves his head inches from my face. 'Urgh! 'Ere boys, have a whiff of that? He fuckin' stinks man!'

'Enough!' I say, my mouth quivering, yet not taking orders from my brain to remain silent. No-one will come to my rescue; no-one will fight my battles for me. Only I can help myself right now. 'You've had your fun, now piss off, will you? Go back to mummy and daddy yeah?'

They all break down in hysterics. 'Got some balls ain't ya?' the ringleader says, holding his stomach whilst he laughs.

'Smelly ones!' the toothless one shouts, sniggering at his own joke.

'You getting scared mate? I can hear your voice shakin',' says the ringleader. 'We starting to scare you? I'll give you something to be scared about!'

He clenches his fist, raises his arm in the air and swings it towards my face. I scrunch my eyes, waiting for the impact. This is going to hurt! Nothing. I slowly peel them open again and his fist is hovering in front of my nose.

He starts laughing uncontrollably, lowering his fist to his thigh. 'You dick! You wet lump of lard. I ain't gonna hit you! … Or am I?'

He raises his fist again and I flinch. I can't help it even though I know I'm giving him what he wants. Giving him a show, something more to fuel his amusement at my expense.

'What a joke!' he jeers. 'Have this! This'll make you smell better!'

Instead of lowering his fist, he grabs the remainder of my smoothie, holds it above my head and I gasp as the freezing cold fluid drenches my bald head, soaking my coat, jumper and shirt, through to my skin beneath. I start spluttering and choking after inhaling some of the fruity drink.

'Hahaha,' he continues to laugh, his gang of followers laughing along with him.

He throws the empty carton at my head and says to his friends, 'Come on boys, let's leave the stinking hobo to it now. Oi, Moose, did you get it all on film yeah?'

'Got it all Boss!' the stocky one replies.

They leave and walk away in their group, sniggering together as they replay the last five, upsetting minutes recorded on film.

Sat on the bench I have never felt so alone and shaken. My whole body is trembling. I kept my calm throughout but now all I want to do is break down. My chin starts to wobble, and my eyes begin to fill with tears. No, don't get upset. Crying doesn't solve anything. I've cried far too much lately and what good has it done? None is what, none. This is a shit situation, made even shitter by wankers like that.

They don't know me, they judged me. They judged me by how I looked, how I smelt. They mocked me without knowing who I really am. If I were in *my* body, they wouldn't have done that. If I were in *my* body, I wouldn't have *let* them do that. But I'm not in *my* body, I never will be again. Now I'm a man. If I'd have stood up for myself more, who knows what would have happened. Perhaps, it would have been a lot worse, I'd have taken a beating almost certainly. As Pete, I'm strong but not strong enough to take on six of the bastards.

Oh God, is that what I've done my whole life? Have I judged people unfairly, made them feel shit, caused them unnecessary pain just because I was ignorant to who they really were? Did I do this to Aisha? Perhaps I did. Perhaps she didn't deserve some of the comments I made towards her or the judgements I made about her.

I think back to the people I've met so far whilst dressed in this body. The hospital receptionist, the police officer, the child and mother earlier and now this gang of thugs. All of them cast judgement upon me because of how I looked. Yet two people didn't. The vicar and the woman who served me my smoothie. They didn't judge me; they didn't bat an eyelid at my appearance. All they wanted to do was help me. What makes them different?

It's not safe for me to be roaming the streets. I can't defend myself properly. I'd be the one deemed in the wrong even if I did defend myself against those lads, just because of how I look. I realise that now. The police wouldn't think twice about arresting me if I got into a fight or kerfuffle. I'm the one who looks a threat, I'm the one who looks dangerous.

I take the ring of keys out of my pocket. I'm going to have to 'suck it up' and face the fact that I need somewhere to hide. I need a roof over my head and somewhere that is safe. There may be nasty surprises waiting for me there, but they can't be much worse than what I will most certainly face out here. I don't want to, but I need to go to Pete's house. First though, I need Pete's car.

22

To say the taxi driver was disgusted with my presence was an understatement. As soon as I got into the taxi and gave him the address for Aisha's house, his nose shrivelled, his jaw clenched, and he wound his window right down to get fresh air circulating around the small car. He wacked the heating up to compensate but I was still freezing, the ice-cold wind blowing in my face causing my nose to run uncontrollably. I don't blame him for being disgusted. I'm nose blind to my own stench, but I must properly hum. I've not showered for at least two days. God knows when Pete last took a shower. I am soddened with stale sweat, urine and now a festering banana-coconut-pineapple medley. I have no doubt that that concoction must smell utterly horrendous.

He dropped me off right outside Pete's car. He took my money without a single look in my direction and not one word of appreciation. I did not tip him. To be fair, I need what precious money I can get at the moment and I'm most certainly not going to be charitable to a rude taxi driver.

Standing outside Pete's car, I look at Aisha and Luke's house. That was technically my home for a while, but I hated it. I was fixated on getting my mansion back and wasn't at all grateful for the bricks and mortar I was gifted for a short while. Now, how I long for a roof over my head, I would give anything just to wonder into the house that stands in front of me and curl up in the bed I've known as mine for the last six months. But I can't. This house is no longer my home, neither is the mansion.

With a click of the key, Pete's car bleeps sending its indicators flashing and the doors unlock. My God it's a mess and it freaking stinks. I'm surprised I can smell it over my own stench, my nose may be blind to my own body odour, but unfortunately my sense of smell is still very much in working order. It hums of stale cigarette smoke, rotten food and something else … I don't even want to know what that smell is. I take a seat behind the wheel and wind down the window. I need to move the car away from this location, it's been parked here for too long, people will start to think it's been abandoned and then report it to the police.

However, how can I possibly drive with my arm in a sling? This might well hurt and possibly do me more damage, but I have to take this sling off temporarily. I hoop the sling over my neck and discard it on the seat next to me. I'm dosed up on painkillers but as I grip the steering wheel, pain soars through my arm. I swallow the pain and reach down for the gear stick. Hang on. It's not a normal gearstick. Instead of numbers, there are letters. This is an automatic car. Key in the ignition, I start the car and move the gearstick to 'D'. I loop the sling back over my neck, securing my arm within it and drive one-handed to a deserted canal carpark in the village of Creech St. Michael.

There's a number of empty carrier bags amongst all the rubbish in the car, so I start filling them with empty burger wrappers, beer cans and fag packets. There's even a random crusty sock which I pick up with my nails, trying not to gag as I put that in the bin bag too.

The more rubbish I clear, the more belongings of Pete's I find, namely a mobile phone. That could certainly come in handy. I put the phone to one side and continue stuffing the bags with Pete's trash.

Five bags filled with crap. I try to squeeze them into the tiny picnic bin in the car park. Two fill the bin, so I stuff the remaining bags between the bin and the stone wall behind it.

Back in the car, there's still a lingering smell, but thankfully it's much more manageable. Right then, let's have a look at Pete's phone, see if I can gain access somehow. I pick it up, ready to try to unlock it, but freeze. What if I find something on here that I really don't want to see? From what I know of Pete, he's a sadistic prick, God knows what he might be storing on his phone. Sod it. I need a phone. I have a phone. Just get on with it and open it, woman. Whatever you may find, you can deal with it, like you've dealt with everything thrown your way of late.

I try to turn it on. The battery's dead, of course it's dead. Now I've summoned the guts to finally turn the bloody thing on, it's out of battery. For God's sake. There must be a charger in here somewhere. Please, let there be a charger in this tip of a car. I scramble around in all the compartments surrounding the driver's seat, nothing. I look in the glovebox, nothing. I get out of the car, go round to the boot and have a look inside, not that this would be a logical place to keep a phone charger. What a surprise, nothing.

Sitting back behind the wheel, I throw the phone onto the passenger seat in anger. What's the flaming point? Perhaps this is a sign that I'm not supposed to open the phone, I'm not meant to find what's hidden within it. Then I notice the hidden compartment between the two front seats, just behind the hand break. Now that makes sense. That seems a much more logical place to keep a charger. Please let there be one in here. I open the leather covered compartment and lo and behold, a phone charger! I plug in the phone, turn on the engine and wait.

Come on you bloody stupid thing! Turn on! I try the 'On' button again, nothing. It needs more charge before it switches on. How much charge does it bloody well need before I can actually use the sodding thing? I try the 'On' button once more, nothing. Are you kidding me? I have little patience at the moment as it is, but this metal piece of junk is really testing what little patience I have remaining. Last time. I press the switch again, finally a loading icon. I have 'buffer-face'. Staring at the screen, watching and waiting for the screen to load, eyes glazed over, impatience on overload.

Finally, I'm in. Holding the phone to my face, I expect it to flash up requesting an unlock code. It does for a brief moment then a message saying 'Face ID' flashes up before it instantly unlocks. Without me doing anything. Facial recognition! Of course. Tech nowadays is insane. Whoever invented facial recognition didn't factor in the possibility that someone may switch bodies enabling access into someone else's device though, did they? Hah!

Perching the phone on the steering wheel, I hover my left index finger over 'Photos'. Do I really want to look at Pete's photos? What if he's got some sick fetish and stores porno pics on his phone or worse, he keeps photos of underage kids? I wouldn't put it past him. But I do need to know what I'm dealing with. I don't want to get to know Pete better, but I have to. I have to know if people will recognise me, how they will respond to me, what situations I may be walking into. I tap the 'Photos' icon.

All the pictures are surprisingly legit. There are many disgusting selfies of him grinning down the camera, making faces, blowing raspberries. God he is vile, evil and now I have *that* face. I brush off the shiver running down my spine and continue to swipe. There are pictures of the same pretty blonde and young boy as the photo I found in Pete's wallet. Photos of them at Christmas, at birthdays, some with Pete in them, some with just her or the boy. They must be his family, his happy, blissfully ignorant family. If only they knew what their darling husband or father was up to in secret. It doesn't bear thinking about.

I click on albums. Shitting hell! There's an album called 'Zoe'. No … no way. He'd been taking pictures of me? Or of Aisha as me. And the prat named the album 'Zoe'! Did he think he was invincible or something? That I would never report him, that the police would never ask for his phone, that they'd never find or even think to ask for this as evidence? Well, of course he didn't worry about any of that. He had me wrapped around his little finger. He knew I wouldn't report it. He knew I wouldn't tell anyone anything. He knew I had too much to lose. So, he brazenly carried on, storing photos under this album.

Dare I look? No. I can't bring myself to open the folder. He took so much from me. I can't face any shocking revelations. I close the 'Photos' app and launch 'Contacts'. Let's see if I can shed a little light on who Pete knows and who has the misfortune of knowing Pete.

Scrolling down the list of contacts, I can see he has many numbers stored. Maybe over two hundred. Nothing really jumps out at me. I don't recognise any of the numbers apart from the gym and a few pubs and restaurants. And then I get to Z. Are you actually shitting me? I have *never* given Pete my phone number. How the hell did he get it? I click on 'Zoe Young' and he has my landline stored but no mobile. So, he's gone to the trouble of finding out my landline but yet never called it. Or has he? Perhaps he has, perhaps he's dialled the number because he was tempted to tell Tom about my continued affair with Steve. What if he has told Tom about it? Maybe that's why Tom threw me to one side, thought he was in love with Aisha. Unless he's never dialled it but stored it there just in case he ever needed to blackmail me. So many ridiculous thoughts racing through my mind, the anxiety causing my heart to pump loudly.

I tap 'Recents' to see if he ever did dial the landline. I can't see my number in his 'Recents' list, but it doesn't mean to say he's never called. The list only goes back two months. I guess I'll never know. Scrolling back up, I look again at the list of recent calls. There is one recurring name. Sophie. Is this the woman in the photos? Is this his wife? His poor pathetic oblivious wife.

The last call made to Pete by Sophie, and evidently answered by Pete was three days ago and lasted four minutes. Hang on a sec. If Pete has a loving wife, why is she not concerned about Pete's whereabouts? At the end of the day, Pete's been technically missing overnight because I've been occupying his body. Is she not worried where he is? Pete's probably dead and she hasn't got a clue, doesn't even seem to give a shit! If Tom ever stayed out all night, not that he would have done without telling me, his phone would probably have crashed with the number of missed calls from me clogging its memory. So why hasn't she tried to call him?

I close the 'Contacts' app and re-open 'Photos'. Next to the album called 'Zoe', there's another album called 'Family'. I tap on it and view the most recent photo of Pete, Sophie (I assume) and their son taken a month ago. She and her son are smiling at the camera and Pete is smiling at her. I snarl at the look on Pete's face. How can a psycho like him love? Surely, it's impossible. I look at Sophie. What is your secret? Why don't you care where your husband is? What has he done to you?

Pressing the 'back' button, it takes me back to the albums again and *my* album screams out to me. It's telling me to open it.

'Go on, have a look, you know you want to,' it says, tempting me.

No, I *don't* want to. But I know I have to. I have to find out what Pete's been up to. I must know the truth. Was he infatuated with me? Or did he keep photos of me as some sort of a sick trophy. I hover over the album for a couple of seconds, swallow and tap.

There are over one-hundred-and-sixty photos. The photos date back over a year. There are photos of me in the gym that Pete evidently took from the carpark, looking in through the window. They're hazy and his reflection in the gym window distorts them, but they're definitely of me. Several taken at the same time from different angles, some portrait, some landscape and some zoomed in. There are photos taken on different days of me at the gym, I can tell because I'm wearing different clothes.

He's taken shots of me running. Running in the park, running around my neighbourhood, in the mornings, in the evenings. All different occasions, all different locations.

Moving on a month, and from all different angles, some distorted some clear as day, Pete took photos of me leaving the gym after my shift. He snapped me walking towards the canal path, photos of me along the canal, of me walking into the White Tavern and incriminating pictures of me kissing Steve taken through the pub window. All these photos taken over the course of a few months. He'd been following me for months, sussing out where I was going and when, working out my routine. All the while, plotting his violent attack on me. How the hell did I not notice him following me?

I continue swiping, addicted to what story the next pictures would tell. He snapped Aisha entering the supermarket that day. The day when I caught him following her out of the exit. The pictures are blurry and from a distance. I think he may have even taken them through his car window. There are photos taken of her meeting me at the café, the drink being thrown on my head. He had been watching us from outside the café, the creep. There are snapshots taken of her walking into the mansion, again blurry and zoomed in, he was possibly hiding at the end of the drive behind the gate pillars.

Horrifyingly, on a different date, Pete took pictures of Aisha undressing through the window of the upstairs bedroom. Hazy and yet again zoomed in but I can tell that it was dark outside, and the bedside lamp highlighted her shape. He was taking photos of her, thinking it was me. She didn't have a clue, neither did I. He didn't get enough of my body the day he abused it, he kept going back for more. Compiling his own sickening explicit camera roll. I feel vile, abused, violated but I must see more. I have to know the extent of his stalking.

The photos continue through October and November. I continue swiping and see images of Aisha issuing tea and coffee to people in some sort of a club. Again, taken through the window, unnoticed. How did he get away with not being seen? How come no-one noticed him with a camera clicking away taking shot upon shot of her. Of me. Of *my* body.

I clasp my mouth in my hand as I reach a picture that sickens me to the core. How the fuck? I didn't think this could get any worse, but it has. My stomach churns, my head pounds and the palpitations in my chest throb and take away what little breath I have left. I check the date, and I check again. No … this can't be right. How the hell has this happened? The date for this photo is undoubtedly December-the-thirteenth. Last year. Less than two months ago. This one isn't blurred. It isn't zoomed too far in and it's not in the least bit hazy. Clear as day, outside his house, in his doorway, I can see Aisha. She's in *my* body and she's talking to Steve.

23

What the hell was Aisha up to? Here, right in front of me is a photo of Aisha, speaking to Steve. *My* Steve. It's not me speaking to him, no. The picture was taken way after I last had a meeting with Steve, in my body at least. I wish this photo could talk, right now. What were they talking about? Who contacted whom to agree a meet? Why the bloody hell is she there, with him?

My mind is in overdrive. So many questions and no answers. How the hell do I get the answers I need? I can't rightly go and speak to Steve, as a man. And I can't approach Aisha, if she's even still alive. I'm not going to rock up to Aisha's hospital bed or doorstep, wherever the hell she is, just in case she's dead and Pete is now inhabiting her body. No chance. But I need answers somehow.

Perhaps Steve tried to contact me after I went around to his house, declaring my love to him, begging him to believe my ludicrous body-swap story. Instead of him contacting me, unknowingly he contacted Aisha, thinking it was me. Aisha will know the truth. She will know that I was still seeing Steve, even though I'd told Tom that the affair was over. If Aisha knows, did she tell Tom? I can't bear this, not knowing the full story, being so out of control. I can't remember the last time I actually had control of my life. Or of anyone else's.

I think back to when my counsellor asked me, 'What do you think would happen if you didn't have control of a situation?'

And I replied, 'I always have control. I *have* to have control otherwise things will go wrong, and I will only have myself to blame.'

Am I to blame for everything that's gone wrong in my life since losing control? No, I'm not. It's a warped, sick twist of fate that's brought me to where I am now. If only I knew back then, how out of control my life would become.

There's only one way I'll find out the answers I need. I will *have* to go and visit Steve, looking how I do now. I have no option. I have no idea how I will get the answers from him, how I'll convince him I'm Zoe. I mean, look at me! It was one thing rocking up at his door looking like Aisha, saying I was really Zoe. But it's another thing turning up at his house and telling Steve that this big ugly bloke standing in front of him is actually the woman he fell in love with. I mean how ridiculous does that sound?

However, one thing's for sure, if I have to go and see the love of my life looking as grotesque as I currently do, I cannot go and see him stinking to high Heaven. I need a shower. I need to clean my act up and there's only one way I can do that. I have to go to Pete's house.

*

The satnav built into the dashboard sends me right outside his house. Well, I assume it's his, if I memorised his address correctly. Although, judging by the state of it, I really hope I've got it wrong. It's a two-up two-down end of terrace house. Its grey walls are only that colour due to the years-worth of grime that's evidently been building up on the brickwork. The front concrete weed-riddled drive is occupied by a ghastly caravan that's rusting away and leaning on its flat tyre. A patch of grass is overgrown and full of stingers and dandelion roots. Three pairs of different sized Wellington boots stand on the doorstep, abandoned in disarray.

Great. Fucking great. Home sweet, freaking, home. Although, it doesn't surprise me in the slightest. I wouldn't have expected anything more than the eyesore that stands in front of me. I start to doubt the possibility of hot water, maybe not even any electric awaits me inside.

I leave the car parked on the road and walk up the driveway sideways, mindful not to brush past the filthy caravan. Well, this is it. This is the moment I have *not* been waiting for. I inhale sharply and with a trembling hand, I turn the key in the lock. The door is already unlocked. Shit, that means that someone's home. His wife maybe or his kid? Realistically probably both. Shit, shit, shit. My heart is in my throat, throbbing away. My knees are trembling. What am I going to find on the other side of this door? This is my abuser's house, his family, his life. I don't belong here, but I have no choice. OK, let's do this, rip it off like a plaster. I open the door.

The hallway walls have torn shards of eighties wallpaper hanging down like sad, dismal bunting. The staircase ahead of me is wooden but not polished. Oh no. Instead, it's got splodges of white paint trailing up each step. The dirty green carpet underneath me is balding, its edges frayed along the skirting. Even if I do have a shower, I won't feel clean for long after.

There's a smell of wet dog, mixed with stale fags. I start to itch all over. Desperately, I scratch my face and try to stop thinking of all the potential fleas that could be jumping on me. This is a pit. A dump. Whatever you want to call it, it's hell. I can't possibly be made to stay here, I can't. But, I have nowhere else to go. I'd like to say it beats sleeping on the streets, although I'm not too sure.

My tummy rumbles. I glance at the mobile phone I put in my pocket and see the time is almost two o'clock. No wonder my belly is rumbling. I bet this is the longest that this body has ever gone without eating something. But, looking again at the state of the house, I swallow the hunger pains. I'm not eating here. No way.

I hear a rustling coming from the room ahead of me. Then the sound of a plate and cutlery clattering followed by gushing water. The door to the room, the kitchen I assume, opens and the blonde woman from the photo stands, staring at me uneasily. She's tiny. Can't be more than five-foot tall and there's nothing to her. I know I was skinny, but I was muscular. She needs to put weight on! Her hair is greasy and scraped back into an untidy bun. She's wearing no make-up and dressed in a holey shirt that's buttoned to her neck and leggings. A far cry from the pretty-ish woman I saw in the picture.

'Oh …' she says timidly. Her voice is quiet and coy. 'Hello.'

Hello? Her husband has been out all night, she hasn't got a clue where he's been and he wanders in stinking of shit, yet all she can say is, 'hello'? What can I even say in response other than … hello?

'Um … hello?' I say back.

From behind her, a little face appears. He's got a mop of ash blonde hair. He hugs his mum's leg, buries his head into her thigh and shields himself behind her.

'Uh … Finley's missed you,' she says nervously, her head bowed and her tiny hand gripping the door frame. 'Um … where have you been? Are you OK … what have you done to your arm?'

Shit. What do I say to that? I can't exactly tell her the truth. I mean what can I say? Sophie, I've been in an accident, switched bodies, ended up in this fat rapist's body, roamed the streets all night and now I'm stood talking to his wife. No, I certainly can't say that.

'Um … out and about. Had a bit of an accident,' I say.

The nerves I felt upon entering the house start to fade. If anyone appears anxious it's Sophie. And as for little Finley, he looks like he's quaking in his tiny boots. Where's daddy's welcome home hug? If he's missed his dad so much, why isn't he running to him for some love and attention? This doesn't feel right at all. If I were to say, 'boo!' I swear they would both jump out of their skins and fall in a heap of tears. I'm not exactly comfortable in this situation but it seems, ironically, that I'm the one who's most cool, calm and collected.

I need to put them out of their misery and make like a tree. Let them regain their nerves, calm the fuck down.

'I'm going to take a shower … sorry … I smell like shit … I mean, sorry I don't smell good,' I say, suddenly conscious of swearing in front of the little boy. I turn on my heels and start walking up the stairs.

Not that I have a clue exactly where I'm going, but most bathrooms are upstairs right? Wrong. Upstairs are two bedrooms. One with Finley's name on the door and the other with a double bed in. Great. Looks like I'm on the sofa then, no spare bedroom for me.

Opening the door to the main bedroom, the same wet dog smell lingers. It's vile and *everywhere.* Where is it coming from? Please say they don't have a dog, I hate dogs. And cats. In fact, most domestic animals. Ironic seeing as I'm vegetarian. I just don't get why you'd have animals living in your house, getting their fur everywhere, bringing fleas in with them and stinking out the place. What's the point?

The room is surprisingly big, stretching the length of the house. Not that you can really tell the true size of it, considering the floor is completely littered with clothes. Piles and piles of dirty clothes, possibly once clean but left there to rot. There's a massive built-in wardrobe along the one wall, why not use that? Reaching across a massive heap, I slide open the wardrobe door to look for 'clean' clothes. Oh, that's why. It's bursting at the hinges. Male and female garments but no order what-so-ever. My idea of a living hell. There's no organisation, no structure. They're all just thrown in there without a care in the world.

There's a stack of towels on the top shelf, I grab one and tentatively give it a sniff. It doesn't smell as bad as I feared. After some digging, I find some jeans, boxers and a jumper. A shiver runs down my spine as I think of who would have worn these before. But there's nothing I can do about it; I can't stay in these pungent rags.

I run back downstairs with the clothes and towel tucked under my sling. Where is the bathroom? The front room is the lounge, the room ahead is the kitchen I assume. That's where they were standing, and I heard the sound of plates from behind the closed door. I barge through the door, unintentionally. I don't know my own strength as Pete. Behind the kitchen worktop, Sophie crouches, quivering with Finley hugged tight to her legs. She seems utterly terrified. What does she think I'm going to do to her? What has Pete done to her in the past more to the point?

'Sorry … I didn't mean to startle you,' I say. Her eyes widening, confusion spreading across her brow. 'It's OK, I'm not going to hurt you. Just going for my shower.'

There's a door leading off the kitchen, oh please be the bathroom, otherwise I'm going to look completely insane walking into a kitchen saying I'm going for a shower. I open it, yes, it's the bathroom. Well, if you want to call it that. It's more of a cupboard with a toilet, sink and shower in. Filth and limescale coats the plastic shower door. And the toilet … Oh my God, it is despicable. There is no excuse for these poor hygiene standards. Have they never heard of bleach before?

After making a crow's nest out of toilet paper on the toilet seat, just so I can have a wee, I sit down. Realisation dawns on me that in order to pee sitting down, as a man, I need to physically push *it* into the toilet bowl to avoid pissing all over the floor. No way I'm touching it. I scoop the paper into the toilet and flush. As gross and shameful as it is, I'll pee in the shower. That's certainly no worse than pissing myself last night. When I need a poo, then I'll have to face reality. But not before then. I'll get away without touching it for as long as I possibly can.

I get in the shower, awkwardly and without looking down. I'm still not ready to view the body I'm being forced to occupy. There's not enough room to swing a cat but I clean myself as well as I possibly can.

Clean-ish and dressed, I wander back into the kitchen. They've moved now, maybe into the lounge. I am ravenous. I don't want to eat here, amongst this filth, but my body is insisting. What do they have to eat? I dread to think. Opening the cupboards, I find tins of beans, alphabetti-spaghetti, ravioli and tuna. There's open cereal boxes, pasta and rice. The fridge is full of beer and cheese. And the freezer is stuffed full of pizzas, ready meals and processed crap. Where are all the veggies? Where is the goodness? My heart sinks and my tummy groans. I have to eat something, anything. I've not eaten for at least a day. Reluctantly, I put a cheese and tomato pizza in the oven and sit and wait for it to cook the minimum amount for it to be in any way edible. The oven is filthy too, it almost makes me change my mind, but I just tell myself the germs will be killed by the heat.

Eventually, the pizza is ready to eat. I scoff it. It tastes remarkably good. The stodge and the dripping tomatoey cheese is so tasty. Perhaps it's because I'm so ridiculously hungry that I'll eat and enjoy anything. Or perhaps my tastebuds have changed too. After all, they are Pete's.

As I take my last bite, there's a knock on the kitchen door. What do I do? She's knocking to get into her own kitchen. That's so freaking weird.

'Um … come in?' I try. I mean, what else do you say when someone knocks on a door?

In she walks, without Finley. As quiet as a mouse, she says, 'Just came to get some water. I'll wash these up too for you.'

She reaches over me to clear my dirty plate away, her hand quivering as she picks it up. I swear she's going to drop it, so I reach over to steady the plate in order to avoid it dropping to the floor. I needn't have bothered. As I reached out to help, she flinched and jerked, causing the plate to clatter to the tiles below, smashing in two.

What the hell did Pete do to this poor woman?

'It's OK,' I say, crouching down next to her as she picks up the broken fragments of crockery. I gently place my hand on her arm, causing her to flinch once more. I pull away and start picking up the pieces one-handed. 'I'm not going to hurt you. Let me help.'

She glances up at me through her long, black eyelashes, still clearly terrified. Her eyes are dark and the bags under them are accentuated by the light shining in through the kitchen window. She looks knackered and older than her years, a deep sadness embedded within. Such a waste of beauty and such a waste of a gentle character. I can tell she's kind and tender. Pete would have taken advantage of her good nature and abused it. That's for certain.

'It's OK,' she says meekly, continuing to pick the fragments of the broken plate up from the floor. 'It's my mess, I'll clean it.'

'Joint effort then. Just be careful, I don't want you cutting yourself,' I say, smiling at her. I want to put her at ease. I don't want her to be scared of me.

Picking up the last piece, I say, 'There. All done. No harm done.'

She stands, confusion mixing with the deep-rooted sadness spread across her face. She waits, as if waiting for me to tell her what to do. She just stands there, staring at me, awaiting orders. Did Pete have *this* much control over her? I feel that if I were to tell her to start cleaning, she'd grab a cloth and start wiping. If I were to tell her to do anything, she'd crack on and do it for fear of the alternative. Whatever that alternative was. Did Pete hit her? Did he verbally abuse her? Or … worse?

'Sit down,' I tell her, tenderly. I need to be mindful of how my gruff voice can sound. I don't want to intimidate her. 'Please.'

She does as she's told. But horrifically, she starts slowly unbuttoning her shirt, her fingers shaking with every fastening.

24

'Woah! No, no. Stop please,' I say putting my hand in the air to signal to her to stop. This isn't what I expected. Is this how Pete would have punished her? Would he have expected her to apologise for breaking a plate, by giving herself to him? She's done nothing wrong. These things happen. For crying out loud, their three-year-old son is in the other room! 'Like I said, no harm done. Please, button yourself up, that's not what I want.'

Her neatly trimmed eyebrows furrow as she rapidly buttons back up. I can see she feels self-conscious and utterly baffled. She offered herself on a platter to me, but I rejected her. Of course, I bloody did. No woman should feel that she needs to service a man just to avoid a more brutal punishment. I get the strong feeling that this isn't something she's used to. She clearly doesn't know how to react. She just sits there, in what I can only describe as shock.

I decide not to draw any more attention to what just happened and take a seat next to her at the table. I'm thoroughly embarrassed and she's … what exactly is she feeling? She deserves a whole lot better than this miserable life that she's being forced to live. I want to tell her that her bully of a husband is dead, that she doesn't need to live in fear anymore and that she's free. I want to tell her to run, live her life and take her boy with her. But I can't. I don't know for sure that Pete *is* dead. Only when I know for sure, can I tell her everything will be OK and truly mean it. I must find out if Pete is still alive or not, not just for me anymore but also for her and that little, innocent boy.

'Have we got any money in the house?' I ask her. Her eyebrows rise in surprise at my question.

'Um … yes,' she says in her soft, mousy tone.

'Could you get it for me please?' I say. I know she will do as I ask. I have total control over her, not that I want it. For once in my life, I do not want control. I don't want this poor woman to feel like I control her. But right now, I need her to do as she's asked. 'I can't remember where I kept it.'

She scuttles off and returns shortly after with a black shoebox. She places it on the table in front of me.

‘Thank you,’ I say. She stands hovering above me. ‘Please, go and check on Finley if you like.’

I feel as though I need to give her permission to do everything. She can’t make decisions for herself. This is control gone mad. Her presence is making me feel ridiculously uncomfortable. She nods and exits the kitchen.

Lifting the lid of the shoe box slowly, I catch a glimpse of money. Lots of money. I whip the lid off. What the hell? Counting them, there are seven bundles of fifty-pound notes. Seven grand! Stashed away but for what reason? No-one nowadays keeps money like this stashed in their house, unless they’re old, right? There are also some other items tucked in between the bundles. I pull out a flashy watch, a sovereign ring and a thick gold-chained necklace. Did Pete think he was some kind of gangster or something? Did he use this money and wear this jewellery to lure women into his bed? No chance. No woman in her right mind would sleep with Pete, but perhaps if he was flashing the cash, they’d stupidly think he was rich and try and see what they could get from him. Not knowing that he had a much darker side and other, more sinister intentions. I take out one bundle and shut the lid. I get the feeling it’s dirty money but it’s money all the same. And Pete owes me.

Hearing the TV playing cartoons on the other side of the lounge door, I knock out of respect before barging in. Sophie knocked to come into the kitchen when she didn't need to, so I want to show her the same consideration. Plus, I don't want her to jump out of her skin again and take her protective stance with Finley once more.

'Hi,' I say, again mindful of my tone. 'Here, I want you to have this. Go, take Finley away for a couple of days. Take him to the sales, buy him something nice or go to Longleat to see some animals or something. Have a get-away and refresh. On me, yeah?'

I hand her five hundred in cash, keeping five for myself. She cautiously takes it. Reading her face, subconsciously she's asking me what the catch is.

'There's no catch,' I say. 'It's just about time you enjoyed yourselves, I think. Have a bit of time away from … this house.'

She nods, appreciation mixed with bewilderment in her eyes. She looks down at Finley and says, 'Fancy a little trip away with me yeah?'

She looks back up towards me and says, 'Are you sure? … Thank you.'

I can tell she's still not convinced that there's no catch. Pete would never have done something as generous as this. Never in a million years. I wonder if she knows what Pete does to other women and I wonder if she knew he was stalking me. I doubt it, he wouldn't have wanted her to know. But even if she did find out, she'd never have said anything. Pete would have been able to get away with murder and not worry about her ever standing up to him or leaving him. She would have been far too frightened, for her safety and for Finley's.

I tell her to go pack and leave as soon as she can, I say that there's no time like the present. I'm kind about it as I don't want her to feel as though I'm kicking her out of her own home. The truth is, I kind of am. I can't be tiptoeing around her, living in this awkwardness. Not while I have other things on my mind. I need to gather myself for my visit to Steve. That's my priority, not her right now. I need to get to the bottom of what Steve and Aisha talked about; I need answers.

*

The last time I saw Steve I told him he'd never see me again. Yet, here I am, looking like a man standing outside his house. I guess I was right, he *will* never see me again, not in Aisha's body and certainly not in my dead, decaying one. I haven't had time to think about my approach properly. It's been so rushed. I have no idea what I'm going to say to him, but I need to find out what was said between the two of them. I can't believe she met up with Steve and kept it all to herself.

I'm going to have to tell Steve what happened, that I switched bodies with a man. He'll never know who the man was and what he did to me by the canal side that day. However, the only way he'll tell me what was said between him and Aisha is if he miraculously believes me. I convinced him well when I saw him last, so well that he rejected me because he didn't fancy me anymore. Hopefully, I will convince him again.

However, he cannot tell Aisha and Tom that I'm still alive. I can't ever let Tom find out that I switched bodies with Pete. I never want Pete's name to be brought up in conversation, ever. I don't want any little revelations cropping up in conversation because I never want to be in the situation where I have to say what he did to me. And importantly, I don't ever want them to question who the twins' father is. No, what happened to me needs to remain secret, so I need to convince Steve to stay shtum.

Steve answers after I rap the familiar five-knock-beat on the front door. My mobile phone is clasped in my hand. He cocks his head to one side, wrinkles his lips and frowns.

'Can I help you?' he asks, quite rudely, I think. I guess it's not every day you answer the door to someone who looks like a big thug.

'I'm sorry to disturb you,' I say. 'And this will sound crazy but please hear me out.'

I turn the phone on and show Steve the photo of him talking with Aisha, outside his house. The one that was taken after we'd switched bodies. The one that got my blood boiling. 'See this picture of Zoe …?'

He edges closer to the phone, brows still furrowing and says, 'Sorry … who exactly are you? Where did you get that picture from?'

'Never mind that, for now. It's not important,' I say. 'What is important is that we both know that's *not* Zoe … it's a woman called Aisha.'

Steve's eyes shoot up to meet mine, he looks unsettled and on edge. He takes a small intake of breath and opens his jaw slightly as if he's about to say something, but words fail him. Slowly he peers down at the picture again that's held in front of him.

I need to prevent Steve from slamming the door in my face. He needs to hear me out right now. I think of the only person I can possibly pretend to be. Fingers crossed Steve's never met him before.

'I'm sorry, you don't know me … I'm … Luke. Aisha's husband.' I say, trying to fill the awkward silence but inadvertently making it even more uncomfortable.

His eyebrows twitch and realisation flickers in Steve's eyes. This revelation has obviously made him nervous. 'Luke? Yeah … um … I've heard about you. What exactly do you want?'

'Well … it's a crazy story, but Aisha died … and somehow swapped bodies with a woman call Zoe … but … you know all this already,' I say. 'What I want to know though, is what are you doing in this photo, talking to *my* wife?'

Steve looks very shifty, shuffling his feet as he stands. 'Well … um ... look … what exactly is it you want from me? I wasn't *seeing* Aisha if that's what you're concerned about. Once I knew she wasn't *my* Zoe anymore I wasn't interested. Not in that way. I mean … I haven't been seeing Zoe either for months … um … not like that …'

He's obviously panicking about saying something he shouldn't regarding our continued affair and he's starting to get tongue tied. As far as he's concerned, he thinks I'm Luke and doesn't know exactly what I know.

He continues jabbering on, 'Um … what I mean is, Zoe's dead. Well … I mean, her body's dead and I'm not interested in your wife's body mate, so I won't be seeing her again … oh … shit sorry, I didn't mean … Your wife's spirit must have died, inside Zoe's body? This is so bloody confusing … I'm … um … I'm so sorry about your loss, Luke. I heard the twins survived which is good news but … I guess, that's probably not good news for you. I … I don't know what to say … I'm just babbling now … I'm sorry.'

It's now clear that Steve believes the body swap. I thought I convinced him last time we met, now it's confirmed. He knows that Aisha was in my body. But he also knows my body died in the accident. He thinks Aisha's soul died though, maybe it did. Hang on … he knows about the twins? He knew Aisha was carrying my babies, potentially *our* babies and yet he seems so cool about it. Does he not wonder if they could be his or not? I need to come clean now, tell him who I really am, I need answers.

'Look … I've not been entirely honest,' I say sheepishly. 'I'm … not Luke … hear me out! I'm … shit … I'm Zoe … I'm *your* Zoe … Stephanie.'

His face darkens, I'm not sure how he's going to take this revelation, if he'll even believe me. But I have to try.

'Please, hear me out,' I continue. 'I know it sounds crazy because I'm a freaking man! I get it. But I *am* Zoe. You believed me when I told you a few months ago what happened during the car accident, I know you did. Well, it happened again, only I didn't manage to get back to my body. I switched to this God-awful one. I said last time we spoke that you'd never see me again … well … *surprise*?'

I take a breath and wait for the door to be slammed in my face. Instead, surprisingly Steve just shakes his head, resignation swept across his brow.

He says, 'Do you know what, it wouldn't surprise me in the slightest if you *had* actually swapped. None of this makes sense … this whole situation is just …'

'Crazy?' I interrupt. 'Ridiculous? Horrendous? All of the above … But it's true, Steve.'

'I know … I believe you,' Steve says. 'But I'm at the point now where I'm losing the will with this whole situation. I don't need this drama in my life. I'm over it all. I just want to get on with my life and forget I ever met Zoe Young, ever met *you*!'

He goes to close the door, I stop him, wedging my foot in the doorway. I'm a hell of a lot stronger nowadays so I am not letting him slam this door in my face. Not without getting the answers I came here for.

'I know you met up with Aisha. Just before Christmas ages after we last spoke,' I say. 'Why? What did she want? What did you tell her? Does Tom know about us, about how we kept seeing each other?'

'What the fuck are you on about?' he shouts at me, still pushing the door against my foot. 'Why do you even care? He'd never take you back now you're a man anyways! So, who cares if he knows or not! They've moved on, so if you *are* Zoe, I suggest you do the same.'

'Please, Steve,' I beg. 'It's important. Why did you meet up with her?'

'You never told me,' he says, hatred filling his eyes. 'You never said anything about being pregnant and that I could be the dad. How dare you not tell me!'

He'd have seen Aisha pregnant, in my body. He's put two and two together and thinks he's the dad. Does Aisha now think that he's the father too? Has she told Tom that she thinks Steve could be the dad? Oh my God. This can't be happening.

'You're not the father!' I say. Even though I don't know this for definite, I need him to believe it's Tom's. I don't want there to be any doubt in anyone's minds about the true paternity of the children. No-one can ever know that there's another potential father.

'I know I'm not!' he shouts. '*That's* why I met up with Aisha. She wanted a DNA test because she suspected you'd still been cheating on Tom. She said Tom was getting one too. They just wanted to know once and for all who the father was. Well, mine came back negative so I can finally move on with my life! I can finally forget all about you and the drama that comes with you.'

Steve's not the father? Tom's got tested too! Oh my God, this can't be happening. What did Tom's test reveal? Is Pete the father? Shit … am I the mother *and* father of my own children? My foot that I was using as a door wedge slips and the weight of Steve pushing on the door heightens. I can't let him slam the door in my face, not yet so I push back.

'Wait,' I beg. 'Just one more thing. You can't tell anyone I was here … what happened to me, that I'm now … a man. Please.'

There's no response.

'Please Steve. If you *ever* truly loved me, don't ever tell anyone what's happened to me. Let them think I'm dead. Please!'

I hear Steve scoff on the other side of the door before it is finally slammed in my face.

Part 4

25

Walking up the grim driveway, I kick the caravan. It bloody hurts but I kick it again, and again. I slam my hand on the aluminium cladding, bury my head in my sling and fight back the tears. I draw in a huge gulp of breath, swallow and tell myself to ‘man up’. Oh, the irony.

I try to think back to the last time Tom saw me in Aisha’s body. He was fuming but not because he’d found out he wasn’t the father, but because of what I had done to the nursery and how horrible I was acting towards them both. He can’t possibly have found out the twins aren’t his. He’d have said. He’d have thrown in some insult during his rage. When you’re angry, you don’t hesitate to say what’s on your mind and you have no composure. Surely, he’d have called me out and shouted at me for cheating on him and making him think the children were his. This leaves two options. Either Tom is indeed the father, which would be the best possible outcome, or he had not yet taken the test when I saw him last. If he hadn't taken the test then, he could still take it now or perhaps he has taken it since. And then what?

I'm not going to find out the answers. Not now. Yet I can't stop thinking about it. Steve isn't the father. Therefore, it's now fifty-fifty between Tom and Pete. The odds are looking much worse for the twins being born of a sick, evil man. The man whose body I'm now haunted by.

With one last slam of my hand into the metal side of the caravan, I pull myself together, inhale sharply through my nose and tilt my chin up. I am strong. I *am* strong. I get this feeling that someone's watching me. I look over my left shoulder at the house opposite. A man, possibly in his late sixties stands by his car, staring at me.

Great, I have a nosey neighbour. Who knows how long he's been watching? Probably saw everything. Saw me kicking the shit out of this caravan, unleashing all my anguish into the lump of metal junk.

'Get a good look, did you?' I shout across the road, rage bubbling in my chest, what little control I have left vanishing.

'Some free entertainment? Piss off and mind your own sodding business!'

His eyebrows shoot up, I see him sneer and roll his eyes. He probably doesn't expect anything less from his neighbour. Without thinking, I raise the index finger of my free hand to my forehead, close my eyes, soak up the anxiety of not being in control and throw this tension to the air in front of me. I see his shoulders tense; a look of shock unfolds across his face. He raises his hands in front of him, defensively, takes a step back and gets into his car and drives off.

Hah! He thought I was threatening him. I actually wasn't this time, but I don't care what he thinks. He can think I was threatening him, it makes no difference to me. Serves him right for sticking his nose into my business.

I head on inside this hovel of a house, that will never, ever be home.

The house is as it was when I left, a filthy mess. There's no sign of Sophie or Finley so they've done as I said, taken the money and fled. For a bit anyways. I'm certain they'll be back once the money runs dry. Five-hundred quid won't get them much, but it will give them maybe three days away from me.

My eyes are heavy. I'm shattered. I've not slept properly for God knows how long. Yet, I can't bring myself to sleep in a grubby bed and I do not have the energy to find clean bedclothes (if there are such things in this house) and make up the bed.

Upstairs I find a throw in the wardrobe after navigating myself around the piles of clothes strewn across the bedroom floor. It's right on the top shelf which I can quite easily reach now that I am at least four inches taller. I grab it, give it a sniff and it's not too repellent. It'll do.

The sofa in the lounge is covered in crap. Books, clothes, opened mail that's been discarded and toys. I scoop as much as I can into the one arm and toss it all onto the floor and repeat.

Stretching out half of the throw over the sofa, covering as much of the grimy cushions as possible, I lie on top and pull the other half over me. Curling up on my side, I scoop the throw under my sling, close my eyes and before I know it, I'm fast asleep.

*

Ding dong … ding dong … bang, bang ... bang! What the …? I peel back my eye lids, reach for Pete's mobile that I put on the side of the sofa last night and with eyes half open I peer at the time. It's three-seventeen in the morning. Who the hell is knocking on the door at this time in the morning?

The door bangs again. As I walk towards the front door, I hear a woman's voice shouting, clearly drunk as a skunk.

'Pete?' she shouts. 'Pete … I knows-ya in 'ere …'

She bangs again and continues her drunken howl. 'Peterrr Wriiight. Open-dis door … righ' now!'

I hear her mutter in a lower tone, 'Tha' bloody boy of mine … bets-ya he's sleepin'. Always bloody sleepin'.'

She shouts, rings the doorbell, and bangs once again. 'Waddaya doin' in 'ere? Open-up … it's ya-mam!'

Pete's mum. At three in the morning. Is she having a laugh? What the hell am I supposed to do now? I don't want to open the door; I can't deal with this. Yet she's going to wake the whole street if I leave her outside, wailing away.

'Go away! You're going to wake the whole neighbourhood!' I shout back.

There's silence, for all of eight seconds.

'Pete …' she slurs a bit quieter this time. 'Will-ya just let ya ol' mam in please? Is cold-out 'ere … pleeeese?'

If I let her in, what do I do then? I don't want to meet Pete's mother, blotto or otherwise. I didn't want to meet any of Pete's family. But then, I didn't want *any* of this. I think back to my own mother and when she turned to drink after my father died. She was vile when she was drunk. She wasn't exactly pleasant when she was sober, but she was certainly worse when she'd had a few too many. God knows what this woman will be like if I let her in. Who knows what kind of verbal abuse she might hurl towards her son?

Yet I can't leave her out there in the freezing cold, vulnerable, can I? Maybe the old Zoe would have. Perhaps I'm turning soft and will live to regret it. But I now know what it's like to roam the streets at night, alone and frightened. No-one deserves that. Reluctantly, I turn the key in the lock.

She falls through the door into a drunken heap on the floor and bursts into hysterics. 'Oops-a-daisy … hah, hah …I knews-ya wouldn't leave ya poor mam out-in the cold. There's-a good boy … Nows-then … gives-us a hand up.'

I hold my hand out to her. She grips it and sways as she stands and smiles a toothless grin at me, eyes red and watery. She must be in her fifties but looks more like seventy. Her grey hair is pulled back in a greasy bun, with dishevelled strands dangling in her eyes. Her cheeks are sunken, and her skin is red and blotchy.

As she sways in the hallway, she knocks a small telephone table so that it rocks unsteadily making a creaking sound. Her reactions are too slow to catch the landline phone before it clambers to the ground and a loud beep sounds from its port.

'Oh … shhh … shhh,' she giggles to herself with a finger pressed to her lips. She attempts to whisper, although unsuccessfully, 'Where's the boy? Gots-ta be quiet … shhh … don't wants to be wakin' him up nows do we?'

'He's not here,' I say.

'Oh … that's gooood. Doesn't wanna be seeing his gran likes this. Now … lets me haves a proper looks-at-ya.'

She places a hand on each of my cheeks, the smell of stale fags wafting from her nicotine-stained fingers. 'There-he is … my beauuuutiful son.'

She plants a sloppy, whiskey infused kiss on my cheek. As she pulls away, she must have clocked my repulsion because without a moment's hesitation, her whole demeanour changes.

'Ah … no, no, no, no … noooo,' she says, her wrinkled face creases heavily into a frown. She starts shaking her head and raises her finger, waving it in my face. There it is. The drunken change. That moment when someone pissed as a fart shifts their mood in an instance. 'I knows whats-ya thinkin' boy. Don'ts-ya be lookin' at me like that. Looking down-ya nose at me. Hyyyypocrite you are. Yes, I've had a few … probabbbly a fews too many. But you say nothin' boy. You can't talk, with ya lager guzzlin'.'

She staggers past me, down the hallway towards the lounge, swaying into the walls as she goes. She's off her head.

Her arms are thrashing in the air as she hobbles with her back to me, slurring, 'Waste of fuckin' space you-are boy … always-has been … always-wills be. Never has time for his mam … never.'

She turns into the lounge and collapses, face first, onto the sofa. Onto *my* make-shift bed. And within seconds, she starts snoring.

I just stand for a while, staring at her in utter disbelief and resentment. One minute, I was fast asleep, enjoying a deep rest. The next, I was woken up to this skank banging on the door. Then I stupidly let her in for her to spit and slobber all over me and hurl abuse at me in her drunken stupor. Now, she's conked out on the sofa, preventing me from having my first chance at a decent night's sleep.

Reluctantly, I grab the mobile and head upstairs. I strip the bed of the crusty, humming sheets and curl up into a ball. I place the phone on the bedside table. Shivering, I try to forget about the woman downstairs and try not to think about who has slept in this bed before. I try not to imagine being bitten to death by bed bugs in my sleep and I try so hard not to think about Tom getting a DNA test. However, my attempts at turning off my mind are futile. That woman downstairs is just another reason why I do not want to be living this life.

After a lot of tossing and turning, huffing and puffing, my mind eventually allows me to gradually nod off once again.

*

Something jolts me awake. I'm not sure what. It might have been a door banging or a loud crash, I don't know. What I do know is that I'm most certainly awake now. I reach for the mobile that I left on the bedside table last night and see that the time is now twenty-past-ten in the morning. I can't say I had a good night's sleep. I was cold, restless and fidgety, but I slept. Thank God I finally slept.

My mouth tastes rotten. I haven't cleaned my teeth for days now. There's no way I'm putting Pete's toothbrush in my mouth. No chance. I'll have to go shopping today and buy one, along with some decent food to last me. I'm still in the same clothes from last night too so all in all, I feel disgusting. I need another shower. Although, that can wait. Something happened last night.

My mind is foggy. How did I end up on the bed last night and not the sofa? I remember clearing the sofa and falling asleep. Then … oh … the early morning antics are hazy although slowly but surely the events start to untangle and grow clearer in my mind. Being woken up by a drunk woman, claiming she was Pete's mother. The sloppy, toxic kiss on my cheek. The slurred abuse spouting from her lips. Her passing out on the sofa downstairs. Me having to sleep in the bed.

Oh, good God, she's downstairs!

How do I approach this? I can't just stay upstairs all day and hope she leaves, can I? No, I can't. I need to go downstairs and face whatever she throws at me. Oh, why the hell did I have to let her into the house? I'm so stupid. What's happened to me? There was a time I'd have just let her rot outside, but not anymore, no. I had to go and be the Samaritan and let the pissed fart into the house.

Creeping down the stairs, I reach the lounge door. I don't want to draw attention to myself. I'm hoping she's still fast asleep so that I can escape and leave her to it. That way, by the time she comes around, hopefully I'll be busy shopping and she'll have left by the time I get back. I peep around the lounge door.

She's not there. There's an empty whiskey bottle discarded on the floor that wasn't there when I left her last night, an ashtray on the coffee table with four stubbed butts in and three empty bags of cheesy puffs crumpled in a heap on the sofa. Next to the empty crisp packets is Pete's wallet. Its contents raided. She's left the credit cards (what little use they have without a known pin number) but the five-hundred pounds I kept for myself from Pete's hidden stash she's pinched for herself.

She's nowhere to be seen. The noise that woke me up this morning must have been her slamming the front door behind her. Well good riddance. I won't be letting her in again. No wonder Pete was a vile species of a human being if *that* was what brought him into the world.

Looking around me, I take in the appalling living conditions Pete and his family have been living in. I can't stand it here. I despise this house. I detest this body. And I hate this life. What is Aisha up to right now? She won't be going through the hell I'm suffering, that's for certain.

Do I really have to play the hand I've been dealt? Do I really have to make do with what I've been given? No, I don't have to. The world wouldn't miss me if I weren't here. I should have died in that car accident. That old crone should never have resuscitated Pete and caused me to switch into his vile body. But the fact of the matter is that it's happened. I either try and learn to accept the horrendous situation I've now found myself in, or I do something about it.

26

The last two days I've spent cleaning. Solidly and with minimal breaks. It's hard work scrubbing, hoovering and mopping one-handed when I'm so out of shape and with lungs knackered by cigarette tar.

This house is still far from my usual standards. Just staring at the peeling wallpaper is enough to make me despair. At least it's clean now and germ free though which is progress. I was able to sleep slightly more comfortably in the main bed last night, knowing that the sheets were cleaned to my standard and the mattress had been hoovered and flipped.

However, I still struggled to fall asleep, knowing who had slept in this bed before me. My mind had been racing on overtime, wondering if he had brought any women back to this bed, if he'd forced himself on anyone, maybe even his own wife, under these bed sheets before. Even though the linen was freshly washed, and the bed vacuumed, it didn't erase the history or the tale-telling stains I'd uncovered on the aged mattress.

This morning I finished my manic housework with window washing. A job I hate at the best of times, let alone when the windows were caked in years' worth of grime. The house stinks of bleach and my hands are red raw from my frantic scrubbing. Now I'm exhausted. And downhearted. I thought cleaning would help. A clean house equals a clean mind or so I thought. I was wrong. The house is bleached so it's a less disgusting place to live, but it's no easier to live here. Knowing who lived here before but not knowing the appalling secrets these four walls could tell if they spoke is hard to say the least. Would I want to know the secrets though? Probably not. But I can only imagine what may have happened before under this roof and constantly imagining truly horrific things is no way to live.

Sitting down on the sofa in the deathly silence, I rest my aching back and feet, and twiddle between my fingers the half full cigarette packet I found on the kitchen table, that had been lost amongst the mail and clutter.

I haven't thrown it away but I'm not entirely sure why. I've never smoked in my life, it's a filthy habit and highly unhealthy.

Whenever I see someone choking down a fag, I turn my nose up at them. If I have to walk past someone in the street blowing out the ghastly plume of stench, I cough repulsively and obviously to try to prove a point. Normally my cough is followed shortly by a waving arm in front of my face flapping to disperse the pungent smoke and a very loud tut in the smoker's direction. I'm one of *those* people.

Yet, this packet is crying out to me, longing me to spark up one of the sticks hidden within. I'm not sure if this is because my body is craving the nicotine it's been missing the last few days or if it's my brain telling me I need that fix. Who knows? All I know is that for the first time in my life, I want to take a drag and experience the relief and satisfaction smokers seem to get from the little white and orange tobacco filled tube.

Fuck it. This body is wrecked anyway. I may as well try it. What have I got to lose? Nothing, that's what. Nothing at all. Not even my dignity.

I take one out of the cardboard packet and flip it so that it nestles, surprisingly comfortably, between my index and middle finger. I threw away the three lighters I'd found whilst I was cleaning. That was before I found this packet of cigarettes and before they started calling to me. So, I turn on the gas hob in the kitchen, not an easy task with only one fully functioning hand and hold the cigarette in the naked flame. Once aglow, I dash out of the back door onto the wonky patio slabs preventing the smoke from lingering inside the scrubbed house for too long.

Holding the cigarette up to my mouth, I clench my lips around the filter and inhale. I feel the smoke travel down to my lungs and surprisingly I don't cough and splutter like I thought I would. Instead, the sensation is shockingly pleasant. I slowly exhale a cloud of blueish smoke out into the crisp air. I take another drag and breathe out. Then another. For someone who's never smoked before in their life, I'm amazed at how natural it feels. This body I'm now in thoroughly embraces it and thanks me for finally lighting one up.

What has become of me? Will it be drugs next? Or beer? I mean, Pete loved smoking and drinking. Perhaps I would like to drink as much as I seem to enjoy this cigarette. With every inhalation and exhalation, I feel the nicotine hitting the spot each and every time. My head is feeling lighter and lighter with every drag, as if it's just going to float away in a minute, away from the shoulders beneath it. All too quickly the glowing end reaches the butt, so I discard it on the stone slabs below and stamp on it, twisting my foot from side to side.

Back inside the house, I can smell the stale fag smell on me. It's repulsive. Why the hell did I just do that? Whatever possessed me to smoke a whole cigarette? Yet the worst part of all is that I enjoyed it. Not the smell or even the taste but the sensation and the release of tension I felt with every exhalation. My counsellor shouldn't have recommended that I use my index finger to absorb the tension I feel of not being in control and release it into the atmosphere. She should have advised me to just take up smoking.

Opening the fridge, I pull a can of lager from one of many six packs and crack it open with a pleasing hissing sound. Without any caution or concern, I take a swig. The bubbles rest on my tongue, titillating my taste buds, before I swallow. Sure enough, it's cold and refreshing with a very satisfying kick. I take another gulp, and another. Before I know it, I've necked the lot. I tip the can up to my mouth, tilt my head back and wait for the very last drop to drip onto my tongue.

That one can just wasn't enough. I grab a second one from the fridge and an ashtray from the draining board, light another cigarette on the hob and slump on the sofa. Who gives a shit about the smell of smoke in the house? Not me anymore. I open the fresh can and between drags of smoke, I swig.

*

After many cans (I've lost track of how many I've drunk) my mind begins to work on overdrive. I think back over the last year and how shit everything is now. It really is shit. Everything is shit. This house is shit. This whole God damn world is shit. I'm shit! … And … I'm drunk.

Hah … I'm actually pissed! I don't think I've ever been this bladdered before, but do you know what? I don't care. If it's good enough for my mothers (both of them, the pissheads), then it's good enough for me.

I've got nothing, absolutely nothing. Well, that's not strictly true, I have beer and fags. Well, five fags left. Sod it, I'll get some more in the morning. But other than that, what have I got? Sweet FA is what!

I've never been one to wallow. Yet here I am, wallowing and drowning my sorrows in beer. I am officially a wallower. I am a hippo. A very drunk hippo. A wallowing, drunken hippopotamus, and the only companion I have is mud. Mud that is in fact beer. Beer! Who would have thought it was so remarkable? I take a swig. Yep, remarkable. Such an amazing invention. Made from hops. Hops! Now there's a bloody stupid name if ever I did hear one. Why hops? Maybe because once they're fermented and then drunk, hops make people go hopping mad! Let's take another swig. Yep, still remarkable.

I raise my almost empty can in front of me. Cheers to an amazingly shit life Zoe! What a class-act you've become. Abso-flaming-marvellous you are! Look at you, you should be ashamed of yourself. What a state. A repulsive, drunk.

I gulp down the remainder of the beer and head off in search of more.

Swaying across the lounge, into the kitchen and over to the fridge, I open the heavy metal door. I blink a few times to try to focus and count eight remaining cans (I think). Sod it, I'll get some more in the morning. I scoop them under my arm, grab a massive bag of calorific tortilla crisps (I mean what the hell, may as well), some peanuts and some chocolate. I dump my supplies on the lounge coffee table, stumble back into the kitchen to spark up another cigarette and then slump back down onto the sofa once again.

*

It's only five o'clock in the afternoon and I'm lying on the sofa now. My stomach is swirling and churning, the beer sits heavily in my belly. I've only got half a can left and one cigarette remaining. Sod it, I'll get some more in the morning. But I want more now. And maybe some chips … with a battered cod. That'll soak up some of the alcohol. Cod? Why the hell do I want cod when I haven't eaten meat or fish for years? Ah, who cares. I haven't drunk beer or smoked cigarettes before either, I may as well try something else different too. The local shop is only a ten-minute walk away and right next door is a chippy.

I need more money though. That alcoholic excuse of a mother stole five-hundred quid from me. I raid the shoe box that I hid under the bed and take out another hundred. That'll be enough to get some more booze, fags, chips and I'll still have a nice sum left. I'm not going to keep so much on me anymore. I need this money and I need it to last me. But one blowout is allowed. Why the hell not? I've earnt my right to a fatty meal, drink and smokes, right?

*

People are so judgmental. I'm back home now but while I was waiting in the chip shop queue, the amount of tuts, scowls and scared looks thrown in my direction was preposterous. Just because I look intimidating, it doesn't mean I'm horrible. Pete was, but I'm not. I'm *not*.

I'm starting to sober up now after my early evening walk and I reluctantly munch a few chips. The taste of the fried potato strips is unsurprisingly pleasant. I'm no longer shocked by my new tastebuds, not after devouring thirteen cans of lager and smoking fifteen cigarettes.

The smell of the battered fish is making me want to heave though. What the hell possessed me to buy fish? Of all things. I pick up the newspaper-wrapped cod and as I go to throw it in the bin, the printed words 'Zoe Young' catch my attention.

Scrambling to unwrap the cod as quickly as I can one-handed, I'm finally able to toss the fish into the bin. I straighten out the crumpled newspaper and hold it closer to my eyes. Trying to focus, my eyes still blurry from the booze, I slowly take in the words. It's a funeral announcement. My body is going to be cremated next week.

My funeral. My body has already started decaying. The realisation sinks in with a lump in my stomach. Even though I've known it, I've refused to allow myself to think about it or accept the facts. My body will soon be nothing but ashes. I will never, ever be able to get my life back.

I am utterly disgusted with myself. My head is pounding now. Oh, why have I done this to myself? I feel so ill. I look at the packet of twenty cigarettes I'd just bought and retch. Is this really what my life is going to consist of? Am I just expected to live out the rest of my days downing booze and looking and acting like a complete yob, whilst my ashes reside in an urn, gathering dust on a mantlepiece somewhere?

I hate who I've become. People are right to judge me. I look like a thug, a waster and that's exactly what Pete was. He lived up to his stereotype, validating people's assumptions of him. I hate him. I absolutely, whole-heartedly *hate* him. Which means, I hate *me.* I can't go on like this. I can't continue to live inside the body of the man who raped me. I've no-one to talk to about this, no-one to turn to. No-one would understand me and what I've been through, they wouldn't believe it. And even if they did believe me, they'd probably reject me anyway, thinking I deserved everything that was thrown at me. Just like Steve did.

Even though it doesn't help, and I know it's useless, I start sobbing. Uncontrollably. I've tried to sort out my life and make things right, but everything just keeps getting worse. How much worse could it possibly get? I've tried to suck it up, but I can't. The truth is, I have no energy left to keep fighting. I'm tired of fighting, tired of trying to be strong. And for what benefit? What is the point of my existence? If I didn't wake up tomorrow, no one would miss me, no one would grieve for me. I don't want to wake up tomorrow morning and have to battle through another day. I don't think I ever want to wake up again.

Without giving it much thought, I head into the kitchen, grab a knife from the block and carry on through to the bathroom. I shut the door behind me and sit on the edge of the bath, tear the sling away from my arm and grip the knife. My left wrist shakes in front of its blade.

27

People have mixed opinions about suicide. Some people say it's a selfish act, the coward's way out. Other people suggest it's an act of someone not thinking straight, a last resort. I think it's dependent on circumstance but one thing's for sure, no one should ever believe that killing themselves is the only option.

My mother killed herself. It wasn't intended but her death was her fault, and I never understood why she risked everything for a drink. She drank herself into such a state after my father died. If she hadn't been such a drunk and stupidly gotten into a car intoxicated, she'd never have driven her car into that streetlamp. She didn't plan her own death, map out the gory details. But she was so miserable and had given up on life that she selfishly put other road users at risk before killing herself. Well, that's what I always thought.

I used to think that people that took their own life were weak. They should battle through, I'd say, not take the coward's way out. Those that would jump in front of trains or walk out into a busy motorway I'd call selfish for putting other people's lives at risk. Even those that chose pills as their ticket out of this world, a pipe connected from their car exhaust to their lungs or decided a belt strapped around their necks would be the best way out, I would call attention seekers.

How wrong was I? Sometimes people just feel they have no choice. It is not a decision to take lightly and not something that someone decides to do on a whim.

My wrist is clenched over the handle of the kitchen knife, my eyes are blurred with tears and the blade is trembling across my vein. After everything I've been through, all the hurt, fear and disgust at what my life has become and yet I cannot make the cut. I do not have the courage to end things. I don't have the strength to take the plunge into darkness. If I kill myself, who's to say I won't wake up in someone else's body once again and this whole nightmare continues once more? This isn't my ticket out of this world. I'm trapped here for eternity, or so it feels.

Yet I won't know for definite until I try. Perhaps because there's intention behind it, I won't switch bodies again with someone else. Perhaps it only happens when it's an accident and not planned. Who knows? All I know is that I can't go on like this, with no one to turn to, no one to help me.

The bathroom door opens.

I didn't even hear them come home. I stare up at her stood in the doorway, her eyes wide open staring first at my tear-stained face and then glancing down at the blade pressed against my wrist.

She gasps at the sight of the knife clenched in my fist.

'Finley stay in your bedroom!' she calls out through the bathroom door. 'Do not move until I get there!'

She takes one last terrified look at me, holding a weapon in my hand, and turns on her heels. I hear her pounding up the stairs as if hers and Finley's lives depended on it, leaving a trail of fear in her wake.

Shit! I drop the knife. It clatters on the tiled bathroom floor. She doesn't realise that the knife was intended for me. She doesn't know the turmoil I'm going through. She thinks the knife is intended for her. Perhaps she thinks I've been waiting for her to return, waiting for my prey, waiting to kill her or Finley, or both.

'No … no, no!' I call after her. 'It's not what you think … I'd never … I wouldn't … I couldn't!'

With trembling knees, I rise from the side of the bath, grab the sling from the floor and follow her. As I get to the staircase, before I can climb to the second step she appears at the top of the stairs, bag in one hand, Finley behind her, looking petrified. She looks behind her and back at me, trying to plot their escape from me. I show her my empty palms so that she knows I no longer have the knife in my grasp.

'I'm not going to hurt you Sophie,' I say as calmly as I possibly can whilst fiddling with the sling, popping my arm back within its comfort. 'Or Finley. Please, you have to believe me. Don't be scared. Please!'

She bends down to Finley and whispers to him, 'Go back to your room love. Everything will be OK. Mummy loves you.'

She turns back towards me; her cheeks are flushed red with terror and her arms are folded in front of her chest in an attempt to offer her a little protection. From me. I hate that I scare her this much. It makes me sick to think about what Pete must have done to this poor woman.

'Honestly,' I say. 'I promise I won't hurt you. It's not what you think. I was …'

How to find the words? I was doing what exactly? Trying to take my own life, attempting to escape the torture of living each day inside this vile human's body, summoning up the strength to end things but failing epically?

'I hate myself,' I say half a whisper, lowering my head to the ground, avoiding eye contact with her. I don't want her to feel threatened or scared by me anymore. 'I hate who I am and what I may or may not have done to you. I just wanted to … end things.'

I raise my head back up and look at her, meaningfully. 'You deserve better than me. I'm sorry.'

Her whole body softens and kindness shines in her eyes. Her timid voice says softly, 'You're … sorry?'

I bet she'd never heard these words come from Pete's lips before. 'Yes I am. I am *so* sorry. For everything.'

My instinct is to turn away, head bowed and walk into the lounge. I sit on the sofa, bury my head in my arms and let out a long sigh. I was so close to ending things, so close to taking my own life. Yet I couldn't do it. Something prevented me, stopped me. Was it because I was weak? Because I was scared? Or was it something else, something more powerful telling me not to do it?

Thank God I didn't. Sophie would have walked in to find me, slumped on the floor in a pool of blood. Or poor Finley could have seen his dad, dead on the bathroom floor. They'd have been left with those scars for the rest of their days and who knows what damage it would have done to them.

I feel the sofa sink next to me and feel her warmth brush the side of my thigh. I raise my head from its burrow and look at the woman sat next to me. Now this, right here, is a prime example of a strong woman. A year ago, I would have looked at someone like Sophie and thought she was weak. Weak for staying with a bully and weak for putting her son at risk. Now, I see her as a strong woman for putting up with years of abuse yet still finding it in her heart to show kindness towards the man that did, God knows what, to her on a daily basis.

'You don't deserve this,' I say to her. 'You don't deserve what Pete … I mean, what *I* did to you. I wasn't going to hurt either of you. Honest … I was … I was trying to hurt myself.'

Her eyes shine and glisten with tears. I continue and begin to sob. I imagine Sophie would have never seen Pete shed a tear before. 'I'm not the same person. I can't explain but the night I dislocated my shoulder, something happened. I'm not who I was … I'm not the arsehole you knew and was frightened by. To see the fear in your eyes and witness your trembling every time I'm near you … It's just too much. When I look in the mirror, all I see is ...'

She places her still-trembling hand on my knee, she can tell I'm struggling, and says, 'It's OK …'

'It's not OK though, none of this is OK!' I say through my blubbering. I can't tell her the real reason why I wanted to end things, why I didn't want to wake up again in the morning. But I can try and explain a little. 'I wanted to take my own life because you and Finley would be much happier without me. I'm a horrible person and I can't go on living in this body knowing who I am and what I've done in the past. But I couldn't do it! I was too weak. I'm a coward.'

'You're not *weak*,' Sophie says quietly but with stern articulation. 'It takes strength to stop. You were strong enough to prevent yourself from hurting yourself. You'll find strength to carry on and face life, face what you've …'

'What I've done?' I say. She can't say the words. She's still on edge for fear of me lashing out and I can't blame her. 'How do I face what I've done? How do I *carry on* knowing what I've done, how I've hurt people?'

'With help,' she says. 'You need help.'

I know I need help! But no one can help me, no-one knows what I've been through, no one could possibly understand. I'm the only person who's gone through something like this, the only person who wakes up every day living hell on earth, the only person who can ever know and understand what it's like to switch bodies.

But I'm not the only one, am I? There *is* someone who knows what it's like. There *is* someone who might be able to understand what has happened to me and why I'm going through such turmoil. There *is* someone who might be able to help me. I just need to seek her forgiveness first, if she's still alive.

'You're right,' I say. 'I do need help, and there's someone who might be able to do just that. Sophie?'

'Yes?' she says, her eyes expressing concern and dread. She starts to stutter. 'I can try … I mean … I have a duty to you. I'm your wife … I can *try* to help you.'

Oh God, no I don't mean Sophie. She can't help me; she needs to be free from Pete and all the hurt that he has caused her over the years. I need to help her, set her free.

'No, you've done enough,' I say softly and kindly, placing a hand gently on her knee in return, trying not to startle her with the physical contact. 'I mean … You're free. If you want to be. Take the money from the shoebox, leave me enough to get by for a few weeks but you take the rest. Take Finley somewhere safe, away from me. Start a new life Sophie. I won't stand in your way.'

She blinks back the tears, a look of confusion and shock appearing across her face. 'Um … really? I … um … don't know what to say.'

'There's nothing to say,' I reassure her. 'There's no catch or anything. I mean it. You deserve more and you can't stay trapped in this marriage forever. You're young Sophie, you can go on to live a life without me holding you back. And as for Finley … he'll be much better off without me as a father and role model.'

Somehow or another, Sophie summons the strength to hug me. This woman, who must have been through utter misery living with Pete, still shows warmth and compassion towards the man who must have made her life a living hell.

'Thank you,' she says almost as a whisper. 'What about you?'

'I'll be OK,' I lie. I'm not OK but her words resonated with me when she said that I was strong to stop myself from cutting my wrist and that I should find the strength to carry on. She was right, I have to remain strong.

'Please, promise me one thing. Seek help,' she says. 'All I've ever wanted is the man back who I fell in love with years ago. See if you can find him. If you can, perhaps I'll still be around.'

I nod and smile at this immensely strong woman. Even after everything, she's willing to forgive. I wish I could be as strong and merciful as this woman sat beside me.

*

It's a crisp, frosty morning and the sun is shining casting orange rays across the white crematorium building.

Dressed in black, my intension was to summon the strength to join my funeral party and be part of my own cremation. Sitting in the car, I can't bring myself to witness my funeral. I mean who can say they've been to their own cremation unless they were ghosts, if you believe in that kind of thing? And even if spirits could go and watch as the curtains pulled across their coffin, would they want to?

A hearse inches along the main driveway, right up to the front doors of the crematorium. The hearse is followed by a few cars, driving in tandem who all park up a few spaces away from me. I'm close enough to see the hearse, but far enough away to avoid drawing attention.

Emerging from the hearse, is Tom. I can't quite see his face clearly from this distance, but his shoulders are slumped and I'm certain there's grief there. Grief for whom though? For his wife whose body he is sending off or for the soul of the woman he truly loved? After Tom, appears Mel dressed from head to toe in black and a veil swept across her face, hiding her emotions from me.

From the car I hear the sound of multiple footsteps, crunching over gravel. Looking through the passenger window, I see *her.* Aisha's stone-faced and followed closely by her parents. The twins are nowhere to be seen. But then it's not long since they were born, and they were premature so I'm guessing they're still in hospital at the moment. The two mites couldn't even go to their own mother's funeral.

Dave and Carol are chatting between themselves about the weather being beautiful, that it'll be a lovely send off and that they hope a few people will turn up to pay their respects. They do not sound like they're grieving the loss of their daughter. As they walk past in front of my windscreen, I can see as clear as day that there are no tears. There's no grief. They have not lost their daughter and they know it. This can only mean one thing.

Aisha switched back to her original body. She's still alive which means she *can* help me. I don't know just yet how she can help but she will understand what I've been through better than anyone. I never thought I'd be seeking support from the woman that took everything from me. But I have no other option. She is the only person I can turn to.

Not only does this mean that Aisha is alive, but it also means Pete is dead. Gone, forever. I beat back the tears of relief, take a breath, and start up the engine. I don't need to watch anymore; I have the answers I need for now. What I need to concentrate on for the next few weeks or months, however long it takes, is how I will pursue forgiveness and seek help from the one woman who hates me the most.

28

Sophie is still packing by the time I return home. But then again, I did tell her that I'll most likely be a couple of hours, so she'd be able to pack in peace. I was only forty-five minutes in total. Watching her pack her belongings, I feel a pang of guilt. Even though I am giving her the option of leaving and escaping her life with Pete, I am technically 'kicking' her out of her own home. My initial thought was to set her free. Now, I'm wondering if that was selfish of me.

She jumps as I enter the bedroom, eyes wide in my direction. I forgot to knock.

'Oh, sorry,' I say. 'I should have knocked, made you aware that I was back home. I didn't need to be out as long as I thought so, I'm back but I'll head downstairs in a moment, leave you in peace. Just one quick question, did you take the money, yeah?'

She nods whilst folding one of Finley's jumpers. 'Yes … um … thank you.'

'Do you know what?' I say, still standing in the doorway, afraid that if I take a step closer, I'll abuse her personal boundaries. I need her to trust that I will not hurt her. 'You and Finley should stay here. This is your home. I'll move out. Set up a little pad somewhere to clear my head a bit.'

'But … um …' Her head lowers, her slender fingers start to quiver as she now folds some small trousers. I can tell she's feeling uncomfortable, more so than normal. Perhaps she thinks I'm trying to trap her, keep her here so that I can still find her and do God knows what to her.

'I promise I will leave you alone here, I won't come back unless you reach out to me,' I say. 'I hope one day you will learn to trust me. But I understand if that will never be possible.'

She nods and pauses with the packing. 'I must be honest; I would like to stay here. But where would *you* go?'

'Don't worry about me! I'll find somewhere. This is your home so you should stay. I'm the one who should leave, set up somewhere else.'

'Thank you,' she says again. Although, she really doesn't need to keep thanking me, she owes me absolutely nothing. She should be kicking me out, hurling abuse at me, whatever. Not showing gratitude for me allowing her to keep the roof over her head.

She reaches into the front pocket of the carry-all bag that she's been busy filling with clothes and takes out the bundles of money. She starts separating them and holds out five wads of notes. 'I can get help to support Finley. If you're happy, I'll keep a grand as that will tide me over until I get a job. It's not right for me to take more than that. It's your money. You're … um … going to need it if you're leaving.'

This woman astounds me. After everything Pete must have done to her to make her so scared and nervy, she still showed such kindness and compassion to me earlier and now she's showing care and generosity. There's no point in arguing with her and telling her to keep the money because I know she'll insist I take it. That's the kind of person she is. And in all honesty, if I'm going to move out, I need a bit of cash to prevent me from ending up on the streets of Taunton again.

'Thank you,' I smile at her. 'I'll head off then. Let you be. Um … all the best Sophie.'

I don't particularly want to say goodbye to Finley. I'm not exactly the most maternal person on the planet. But I never had love growing up and feel that Finley deserves a decent farewell from his father. He probably knows his dad to be a scary man. But I think it best that Finley sees a loving side to his father. A memory for him to hold on to whilst his dad's away. I'm by no means doing this for Pete, he deserves nothing from me alive or dead. But this boy does deserve a goodbye. I want Finley to think his dad loves him and isn't just upping and leaving him for no reason. The poor mite doesn't know his dad is dead and I don't want him to think his father has abandoned him.

'Where's Finley?' I ask Sophie. 'Could I say goodbye to him please?'

She's cautious, understandably. 'Um … he's in his bedroom, playing, I think. But … um …'

'It's OK,' I say. 'I just want to say a proper goodbye. I won't be seeing him for a while and I want him to have at least one decent memory of me, possibly the only one. I can't imagine he has fond memories of his dad, so I want him to know that I'm not all bad and that he is loved.'

'Um …' she hesitates, still cautious. I can tell she's uncertain. So, I try to reassure her by telling her that she can come with me, be there to make sure I'm true to my word.

'OK …' she says and follows me to Finley's bedroom.

'Finley,' I say softly through the bedroom door. He's busy playing with a truck, racing it along a wooden track but I get his attention. He looks up at me. 'Can I come in please Finley?'

He nods slowly so I enter and take a seat on his bed. The small wooden frame creaks beneath my weight.

'I'm going to be going away for a bit Finley,' I start by saying. 'I'm not sure how long I'll be away but I need you to do me a favour yeah?'

He stares at me, waiting for my next words.

'Look after your mum for me,' I say. 'You'll be the man of the house now. I need you to be a big boy.'

He nods and blinks slowly, his face deadpan. I want him to think his dad loved him, I want him to grow up thinking he was loved. He's an innocent boy at the end of the day. 'You know your dad loves you, don't you?'

'Yeah,' Finley says timidly.

I smile as kind a smile as I possibly can. And Finley launches himself at me, wrapping his arms around me, giving me the biggest hug. This takes me by surprise. All I can do is slowly wrap my arms around him in return, feeling his fragile body within my arms. It feels shockingly comforting.

He finally releases me from his embrace and as he pulls away, my natural response is to plant a kiss on the top of his head. I have no idea where this thought came from, but it just felt right.

I look over to Sophie and see her shoulders relax and the corners of her mouth curl ever so slightly. I smile back at her tenderly. 'Thank you.'

She nods. 'OK … take care Pete. Stay safe.'

'You too,' I say, smiling at her.

I grab a few clothes, some other belongings and leave the house I knew I'd never call home.

*

'You've got the shared use of the kitchen, lounge and bathroom. Four other tenants. This would be your room,' the landlord says unlocking and opening the door to the box room at the front of the property. 'You've got your own personal wash basin, wardrobe, bed and set of drawers. The rent's eighty pounds per week, bills included. I expect payment on time and without delay otherwise you'll be turfed out, no second chances. In return, anything you need fixing, text me and I'll be here as soon as I can. What do you say?'

What an arrogant twat. And rude! But it's cheap rent and considering some of the places I've found myself sleeping lately, this is like a palace. It's clean but cramped. It's warm but certainly not cosy. At the end of the day, it's shelter and somewhere I can call mine.

'I'll take it,' I say.

'I'll need two references,' he says. 'One from an employer and one personal reference. That way I know you'll be able to pay on time.'

I have no way of getting references, I have no job for starters and know no-one that could give me a personal reference. Perhaps money talks.

'How about three months up front? Cash.' I say, that'll shut him up. Hopefully. 'I'm between jobs at the moment, but I will be working within three months, I can assure you of that.'

He pauses, mutters to himself, raises his head to the ceiling as if deep in thought for a few seconds and then says, 'Deal. But I expect to receive confirmation that you've got a job within two months. I'll need to see a payslip or something and a standing order set up. If not, you're out on your ear.'

'Not a problem,' I say. 'It's a deal.'

We fill in the relevant documentation, I hand over the cash and he gives me the keys. I have my own pad, my own space to start to try and build some sort of a life. These are small steps in, what I assume is, the right direction. But I still need help. I can't do any of this alone. I need Aisha to believe me, to support me through all of this. She's the only one who can.

*

The last several weeks have been spent following her. Pete kept a log of all my movements and recently I feel like I'm doing exactly the same thing to Aisha as Pete did to me. I'm stalking her. But for totally different reasons. Instead of rushing in, like

I did with Steve, I feel I need to suss her out first, get to know her routine a bit before just turning up at her door, begging for her help. I need to be sensible about this because I can't afford for her to slam the door in my face. Not when she's the only person in the world who could possibly relate to what I'm going through, on some level.

The first week or so, I didn't see the twins. However, over the last two weeks, they've made an appearance. They're out of hospital now, so they're OK. Bizarrely, I'm not sure how I feel about that. I spent the best part of this year resenting the two babies. Resenting what they meant, what they represented and the potential they had for revealing my web of deceit. I wanted them dead. But now, there's a part of me that's pleased they survived. I can't explain it but the hug Finley gave me plays on my mind. After everything I've been through, I can understand that they are innocent, just like Finley, and not to blame for any of this shit.

Every time I've seen Aisha with the kids, she seems to be in blissful motherhood, fully embracing raising my children. I've never been close enough to see the children's faces so I have no idea who they may resemble. One thing's for sure, they're not Steve's, which leaves two potential fathers.

I've watched her shopping in town, pushing the two kids in their massive double-buggy, negotiating crowds, feeding them and soothing them when they cry. Not once does she ever seem stressed or tired. She met up with Mel, *my* sister, for a coffee in the town centre, they hugged and kissed each other's cheek. Mel cooed over the twins and they chatted and laughed like best friends over coffee and cake.

She's been to church with them. I didn't go in. But I waited for the service to finish and watched her smiling, saying her goodbyes to other members of the congregation and accepting their praise for raising a dead woman's children.

There's a youth club called *Young Stars* and I've seen her take the babies in there. I've never heard of this place but considering it has my surname over the door, I'm assuming it's something she set up when she was posing as me.

Today is the first time I've seen Tom present as part of the family bubble. It's a sunny, cool, February day and they've gone to Vivary Park for a walk, the children fast asleep in the twin buggy.

It's strange to be back in this park. The last time I was here, I'd literally just switched into this body. I was so lost, with nowhere to go and nowhere to sleep. I had no one to turn to. I'm still so lost, but it makes me realise that I've already come a way since then. I hit rock bottom when I thought the only answer was to be at the mercy of a kitchen knife. But I picked myself up a bit, dusted myself down and now I'm ready to be proactive. I'm ready to seek help.

They're holding hands as they walk around the stony paths, chatting away to each other as if they haven't got a care in the world. Tom releases his hand from Aisha's grip and moves his arm around her waist, pulling her close to him as they walk, and she puts her hand back onto the pram and rests her head on his shoulder. He plants a soft kiss on the top of her head.

They look totally and utterly in love. Completely consumed by each other's presence, as if there were no-one else in the world. It's clear that Tom is happy raising the children as his own. Perhaps he did take the DNA test and found out that he *is* the father. If that's the case then, on that dreadful day, Pete must have fired blanks and didn't impregnate me with his evil sperm. A happy, freaking ending for everyone. Apart from me.

A heavy feeling of jealously rises from my stomach to my throat and catches my breath. I take a seat on the closest bench to steady my legs and watch from a distance. They are so happy, so content, so blissfully unaware of anyone else's suffering. Blissfully unaware of *my* suffering.

The feelings I used to have come bubbling back to the surface again. I try to swallow them down. They are so happy together. Tom looks much happier with her than he ever did with me. She makes him complete. And this tears at my heart. How different things could have been, if only I had been different.

No-one seems to be grieving for me. Not Tom, not Mel and most certainly not *her*. It's as if they're all relieved that I'm dead. Are they all happy that I'm dead and out of their lives? Are they pleased that I'm no longer around to pose a threat to their unbearably radiant love?

I've been following her over the last several weeks to try and figure out how to ask for her help. But I realise now that that would be futile. She may be the only one who understands to a degree what I'm going through, but I can't ask her for help. They've all moved on with their lives and are so content. If I turned up now and rocked the boat, what good would that do anyone? No. I was right all along. I'm on my own and no-one should help me. The only person who should help me *is* me.

There's that part of me that thinks, if I reach out to her for help now, I'll lose any ounce of dignity or self-respect I have left and worst of all, I'll lose any remaining control. I'll let them carry on with their perfect lives and their idyllic family.

I have to try and find a way to move on. I'm not going to hit rock bottom again. I have to find my inner strength once more. I'll live a 'normal' life while I figure out what the hell I'm going to do. I've been through enough shit over the years, I'm not going to rely on her to help me. I don't need to, not yet. It's time to make a change. It's time to suck it up and sort my freaking life out.

29

It's been four months since I last saw Aisha, Tom and the twins. It's not been an easy road, but I've managed to secure a job and provided my landlord with proof of employment. Three months ago, I started working as a cleaner. It's not the most glamorous of jobs but it pays for the roof over my head. Without knowing Pete's qualifications, not that I expect he had any, it proved hard to evidence my worth on a CV.

All I've ever really been known for or been good at was music and fitness. In this body, my hands are too fat and stubby to reach the piano keys anymore and as for my singing voice, well it's non-existent and forming any career to do with fitness would be just laughable.

So, I swallowed my pride and got a job as a cleaner. I needed to pay the bills somehow and it was the only job going at the time. I clean office blocks and banks four evenings a week and have a regular job at a school for three hours an afternoon. Not only does it bring in an income, but it keeps me busy so there's less time for me to think and dwell on stuff. Surprisingly, I've actually found it enjoyable and rewarding.

I've got a new bank account set up too, by using Pete's ID. When the bank clerk took the driving licence from me, they read out the details. Pete has the very same date of birth as both me and Aisha. The same day, month *and* year. I mean, what are the chances? I'm surprised I never noticed when looking at his details in the gym. It can't possibly be a coincidence, can it?

Unsurprisingly, he had a non-existent credit history, so I had to get a very basic account with no overdraft facility, but it does the job. At least I can be paid directly into an account for me to pay my rent by standing order and withdraw cash whenever I need. It's very hard keeping to a strict budget though. As someone who has never had to worry about money, it's a massive learning curve making sure I spend less than I have coming in each month. No margin for luxuries and barely enough for necessities.

The job as a cleaner is very solitary. I've never been a social butterfly, but the feeling of loneliness has only been highlighted more since scrubbing toilet bowls for ungrateful business owners.

I got chatting to Jason a couple of weeks ago. Jason rents the room next to mine in the shared house. The conversation all started when we were both complaining about the cleanliness of the kitchen and how it seemed that we were the only ones who actually bothered to keep it tidy. Jason told me how he'd battled with drugs in the past, ended up on the streets and how, finally, he managed to get clean, get a job and end up here, in this house. He was on the streets for over a decade. How the hell he survived out there for that long is beyond me. One upsetting night sleeping in the park, being kicked out by the police and winding up in the church was enough to haunt me for a lifetime. Fair play to him.

There was a time when I'd have looked at someone like Jason and thought, 'it's your own fault for getting into drugs in the first place'. However, my whole opinion has changed over the last number of months. People sometimes get thrown a bad hand, hit the crossroads in life and sometimes, quite easily, they take a wrong turn. If you want to call it a wrong turn. Perhaps it would be fairer to call it a 'more difficult' turn. Before they know it, they spiral down this dark and windy road and sometimes, to try to forget the awful hand they were dealt, they end up hitting the bottle, popping some pills, snorting the white stuff or worse, injecting themselves. Every admiration for this man picking himself up after hitting rock bottom and trying to make something of his life. I never, ever thought I would see a man like Jason as an inspiration.

Jason does still like a drink. I mean, why not? He's given up the hard stuff, but a few drinks here and there is nothing in comparison. He invited me to join him at a local pub the other night after I finished cleaning the bank, so I did. We had a few pints together, he introduced me to a few of the locals and we played some pool and darts. I was surprisingly good at both pub games, winning a few rounds too. It was comforting to feel 'normal'. Not *my* normal of course, I didn't feel like the old me. But I felt like I was doing 'normal' things that a man my age would do. And I enjoyed it.

It's nearing four-thirty on Monday afternoon and I'm tying up my third bin liner of rubbish collected from the school canteen. All the teachers have left for the day now and most of the school kids have gone home to their parents. However, as I carry the bin bags out to the wheelie bin cage located in a courtyard around the back of the kitchens, I hear a commotion coming from the bike sheds. The bike sheds are just around the corner from where I am stood. I'm out of sight but I can hear boys shouting. It sounds like a fight. I chuck the bags into the industrial bin and stand by the corner of the grey building, back to the wall and listen.

'What a loser!' I hear one lad shout. 'Kick him in the balls … yeah, let him have it!'

There are scuffling sounds of feet scraping against the tarmac. Soft thumps pounding into flesh. There's laughter mixed with pained yelps.

'You recording this?' I hear a familiar voice shout. 'Look at him rolling around on the floor, crying! Oi … fatso, get up and fight like a man!'

I hear further laughter and can only imagine a poor boy being beaten up, trying to get back on his feet only to be pounded to the floor once more. The feelings of being bullied as a child come flooding back and guilt slaps me in the face.

When Steve started backing me against the bullies in school, the bullying stopped. It wasn't gradual, it literally stopped overnight. They realised that they couldn't pick on me anymore. I had someone who would stick up for me and someone who would put up a fight if he needed to. At the time, this was relief for me. I was no longer the bullied kid and it was the turning point for me to toughen up and start wearing the hard-faced mask I was known for hiding behind as an adult.

However, bullies don't stop. They may have stopped picking on me, but they moved on to their new target. Carly Reed. I haven't thought of Carly for years, probably because I wanted to forget about her. But perhaps I should have thought about her more, perhaps I owed her. Greedy Reedy they called her, and she wasn't even fat. I mean, she was a bit chubby I guess but she didn't deserve what they did to her.

Everyone knew about her suffering. But no-one did anything. No-one reported the bullies to the school because everyone was too scared to stand up to them. Even Steve turned a blind eye once they started bulling Carly. He'd say to me, 'better they bully her than you.'

I didn't report them to the school either. I should have. If I had, perhaps Carly wouldn't have done what she did. Instead, I was grateful. I was relieved that it was no longer me being tormented by these pricks. I was glad that someone else was now the bullies' focus. I was to blame.

There's a part of me that always thought the school must have known about the bullying. It was so public. The bullies were brazen enough to taunt her in front of all the other kids just to feed their own egos. Yet nothing was ever mentioned by the teachers and no action was ever taken by the headteacher. They were either completely ignorant to the torment and abuse that Carly suffered or they all turned a blind eye. Either way, they were also to blame.

Three months after I left school, I read in the papers that Carly had taken her own life. She was only thirteen.

If only I had spoken up back then, told the teachers, done the right thing instead of watching it happen and feeling comforted that it was no longer me being bullied. Even back then, I felt guilty. But I pushed it to the back of my mind, telling myself that it wasn't my fault. It was the bullies' fault that she killed herself. But I know now that it was as much my fault as it was theirs.

Standing here now, listening to these teenage thugs laying into an innocent kid makes my blood boil. I have to do something, anything. No-one should suffer this abuse. Not me, not Carly and not this kid.

Without thinking, I pump up my chest, clench my fists, trying to look as threatening as I can, and stride towards the bike sheds.

'What the hell's going on here?' I holler out to the group of teenage brutes still a distance away. I see a group of them huddled around a boy lying on the tarmac, curled on his side and hands wrapped around his head.

'Move your arses unless you want to be arrested?' I shout. 'The police have been called!'

Obviously, they haven't. I've not made the call, but I lie in order for them to panic and leave. The last thing I want is to be their next target. However, if they continue beating this poor lad, I worry they'll do more damage than even they intend to do.

They all turn around to look at me, startled at my bravery, I think. As I grow closer, I start to see their faces more clearly. And then realisation hits me. It's *them*. What was his name? Boss. That's it, that's what they called him. And sure enough, the same stocky kid called Moose angles his phone towards me, recording me once again.

My heart starts to pound, and I can feel my spine start to tremble. Don't lose it Zoe. Keep cool, they won't do anything to me, not if they know the police are on their way. Surely?

'Go on, piss off!' I shout at them. Then, miraculously, I hear sirens in the distance. What are the chances that sirens would sound at the exact time I really needed them to? What a fantastic coincidence, I'll use this to my advantage. 'That's them boys, hear the sirens … they're coming for you!'

'Fuck it,' I hear Boss exclaim. He turns to the other boys and shouts, 'leg it!'

They all turn and sprint off, out of the school gates and out of sight. None of them recognised me. At least I don't think they did. Perhaps they didn't have enough time to register who I was. To be fair, I was still a good number of metres away when the sirens sounded so they possibly didn't get a good look. And it has to be said, I look a little less like a tramp nowadays so probably look a lot different from how I did when they ganged up on me in Taunton centre that ghastly morning.

I run up to the boy, who's now scrambling from the ground to his feet. His school bag and contents are strewn on the ground around him.

'You're alright, they've gone,' I say, picking up the books that had fallen from his bag during the tussle. I clock his name written on the front of one of his exercise books. Daniel Hardy. He grabs his bag and I hand him the books.

'Here you go … Daniel is it?' I ask. He turns to me and takes the books from my grasp. This is the first time I get to see his face.

Oh … my … God. It's the short, overweight one. The one they called Lardy. I think of the name, Daniel Hardy. Hardy that rhymes with Lardy. He wasn't part of the gang back then; he was *trying* to become part of the gang. He was trying to impress them. Was that why he spat in my face? Is it the case of, 'can't beat them join them'?

His bruised eyes widen, and his bleeding lip quivers. The blood from his nose dribbles down his chin. I can tell that he recognises me as well as I recognise him. He opens his mouth to speak but just a few garbled noises come from his parted lips.

'You!' I exclaim. I thought that if I ever saw the little runt that spat on me when I was most vulnerable again, I would have revenge, give him a piece of my mind. However, after seeing his so-called mates kick the shit out of him, I now know why he spat at me and joined in with the other teenage brutes. It doesn't make it OK, but I understand why.

'I …' he tries to speak, his cut lip still trembling. He wipes some bloodied snot away from his nose.

He stuffs his books in his bag and slings it over his shoulder, turns and hurriedly limps away, occasionally turning back round to check I'm not chasing him.

30

Bullying is unacceptable. Full stop. No child should ever be at the receiving end of another child's fist or malicious tongue. Not I, not Carly and not even the kid who spat in my face when I desperately needed help. This changes my perspective on things. Daniel Hardy was joining in with Boss and his gang for one reason only, to try and save his own skin. I get it. But there's better ways of dealing with this situation, surely? Daniel can't keep putting up with this abuse. If he does, he might end up in prison, become a bully himself or worse, wind up like Carly, taking his own life. Something has to be done about this. Is this my problem? The old me would have said 'no'. However, this has become *my* problem as I cannot turn a blind eye again and deal with the guilt of two bullied kids ending up six-feet-under due to my negligence and selfishness.

It's been a couple of days since I saw Daniel being beaten up by Boss, Moose and the rest of the gang. This evening, I've only got an hour left of my shift, the time is nearing five-thirty in the afternoon. Thankfully, I can just go straight home once I've finished. For the first time this week I don't have to go straight to the bank after finishing at the school.

My shoulder is aching today. Even though it's fully healed, I still get twinges every once in a while, especially after long hoovering sessions. I balance the vacuum hose against the hallway wall and take an opportunity to stretch my arm up above my head. I clench every muscle in my back, shoulder, and upper arm, down to my elbow. I slowly circle my arm and feel the muscles in my back and shoulder tighten and release. It's a very satisfying feeling, releasing all this built-up tension.

As I'm enjoying my final stretch, the door to the English classroom opens and I see Mr. Nolan pop his head around the door. My arm drops to my side and I try to quickly grab the vacuum hose and nozzle I'd carefully balanced against the wall. I don't want him to think I was slacking on the job; all it takes is one complaint from a teacher and I can wave goodbye to my job. However, as I reach out, my fat hand knocks the hose from its precarious perch sending the nozzle clattering to the floor. What a klutz I am.

Whilst I'm embarrassingly grappling at the vacuum cleaner, trying to regain composure, Mr. Nolan says, 'Sorry to interrupt you … um … Peter is it?'

I nod from my squatted position, he continues. 'Could you do me a small favour please? Just listen out for the kids in detention whilst I pop to the little boy's room a minute. They're busy with their homework at the moment, so should be fine for you to carry on out here. But just make sure none of them make a run for it whilst I'm gone, yes?'

Yeah, because *that's* in my job description! Whatever. I can't exactly say no, so I'll clean the windowsills whilst I'm waiting for Mr. Nolan to return, that way I can keep a proper ear out. I'm not going to sit with them though, I need to be out of here by six-thirty at the latest, so I'll clean as I'm listening. I'm not paid overtime. Therefore, I'm not prepared to be made to work on later with no extra pay, especially if it's not my fault.

'OK,' I say. 'But I'm not babysitting them. I'll make sure there's no escapees but that's it. I'll be cleaning at the same time, no time spare to down tools.'

He raises an eyebrow. 'Enough time to down tools to stretch though?'

I raise my eyebrows back at him. Cheeky bastard. I'm not one of his school kids, he has no right to talk to me like that. However, I bite my tongue, knowing this job is too important to risk losing by getting into a petty feud with a condescending teacher.

'Right boys,' he shouts back into the English classroom. 'Got somewhere I need to be for two minutes. Actually … make that five minutes. I'll be back. Don't do anything stupid, else you'll be on detention for the rest of the week.'

Seeing as it's Wednesday, that doesn't seem like much of a punishment or deterrent I think to myself. But hey ho! What do I know? Mr. Nolan nods, mouths 'thanks' and hurriedly scampers down the corridor.

Urgh, I hate teachers. Egotistical pricks. At least all those I've ever had the misfortune to meet have been. I'm sure there are some decent teachers out there, but I've never met them.

Chitter chatter starts building within the classroom and before long, the boys are laughing, shouting and being typical brats. They obviously don't know I've been asked to keep an ear out.

‘Oi Moose, come here,’ I hear the familiar voice of Boss hollering across the room. ‘In fact, all of you, get here now. Got something I wanna tell you before he gets back.’

There’s scuffling, giggling and scraping of chairs. I down my window-cleaning cloth and put an ear to the door. My curiosity is piqued.

With a lowered voice, Boss continues now that the boys are in closer proximity to him. ‘I got a plan … it’s Parents Evening on Friday, so we’ll all be here until at least six-thirty. Lardy will be here too.’

Boss pauses, building suspense and I can hear the other boys snickering in anticipation of what he’s plotting. Boss resumes. ‘I’m gonna get Lardy to …’

He starts laughing a wicked, twisted laugh whilst forcing out the remainder of his sentence. ‘I’m gonna make him burn down the school!’

The other kids erupt in laughter.

‘No way!’ One kid shouts, I think it’s Moose.

‘Fuckin’-a!’ Another one declares. ‘What time and where Boss?’

Still snickering, Boss says, 'Six o'clock. In chemistry lab one. Be there or be square. I'll make sure Lardy's there, you can leave that with me.'

What the …? Shit, this is *not* good. Not good at all. The phrase 'curiosity killed the cat' springs to mind. I should have kept my big nose out of it. Instead, I'm now responsible for the safety of everyone; kids, teachers and parents. I need to stop this. I need to stop Boss. He will never torment another kid in this school once I've finished with him.

*

It's nearly six o'clock on Friday and I'm hiding in chemistry lab two. It's next door to lab one and I'm waiting for them to arrive. Waiting for the events of the night to unfold. I'd contemplated telling the Headmaster about what I heard. But I changed my mind. There was too much doubt in my mind about how seriously he would take it. I couldn't run the risk of there not being enough evidence or the bastards not getting a decent enough punishment. I also didn't want Daniel to be punished for something he was made to do either, that wouldn't be fair. So, I'm going to take matters into my own hands. No-one will be hurt if I have anything to do with it.

Sure enough, at two-minutes-past-six, I hear snickering and excited whispers approaching lab one. I can also hear Daniel sniffling and whimpering. It sounds as though he's being dragged by a couple of the boys towards the room. I imagine his arms to be grabbed and pulled by a boy either side of him and Boss behind, pushing him along, his feet struggling to keep up.

'Get in 'ere,' I hear Boss growl at Daniel. I picture the boys pulling and pushing him into the lab. There's a bit of a commotion as they all bundle into the room, making a racket as they pull out tall wooden stools from underneath their worktop.

I'm struggling to hear now. The door to the lab is still open I believe as I haven't heard it clunk shut. However, they are too far away to hear clearly. So, as silently as my big bulk of a body can be, I tiptoe out into the corridor so that I can hear a little more clearly although I can only catch certain sentences.

'… You're gonna burn it down Lardy,' I hear Boss tell him. He's already started giving him instructions. 'Else, we'll kill you.'

'… Wait for us to leave,' Boss continues, the gutless shit. He's getting this poor kid to do this for him.

'… Lighter fluid … turn the gas on … 'ere's the lighter.'

Oh my God, it's worse than I thought, he's going to *blow* the school up and possibly himself with it. I fight against the urge I have to burst into the lab and put a stop to this sadistic scheme with my fists. I need to bide my time and stick with the plan I have in my head.

'We're off …' I hear the boys shuffling towards the door, so I dart back into lab two. 'Don't let us down Lardy, else we'll come for you.'

I hear the squeaking sound of the boys' feet quickly thudding on the polished floor as they run down the corridor. I poke my head round and see them sniggering as they run away.

Right, time to try to diffuse this situation. I scurry into lab one to see Daniel with tears streaming down his face, the lighter quivering in his hand. The smell of gas starts to permeate the air. I lunge at the gas valve, which a Bunsen burner would normally be attached to, and switch it off. In doing so, Daniel jumps out of his skin at the sight of me, any remaining colour from his face quickly draining away.

'They're making me …' he cries through sobs. 'They're gonna kill me if I don't …'

'I know, I know Daniel. I heard them, don't worry. I'm here for you. But … you might kill yourself if you do!' His face looks shocked as I say this, I don't think in his panic, this thought has even crossed his mind. 'You don't have to do this.'

'Yes, I do!' He wails. 'You have no idea. They *will* kill me!'

'I do have an idea,' I say. 'I was bullied at school too. But I survived, you will too. This is not the way. Let me help you.'

'You can't help me!' He sobs. 'No-one can help me. No-one can stop me. I'm burning this school down and there's nothing you can do!'

He reaches over me to turn the gas back on. However, a loud male voice booms through the doorway, stopping him before he manages to turn the valve.

'Daniel Hardy!' The Headmaster shouts in his direction. 'Stop this nonsense immediately.'

Behind him, I can hear giggling and then Boss's face appears from behind the Headmaster's back. This was Boss's plan all along. He played a dangerous game, thinking Daniel wouldn't go through with it straight away, giving him enough time to dob Daniel in with the Headmaster, framing him for attempted arson. This could have not only put Daniel's life at risk but also himself and the Headmaster, not forgetting me. The stupid, immature idiot.

'Come with me to my office now, you stupid boy,' the Headmaster shouts. 'Your parents will be informed and then we will decide what to do with you.'

'But they made …' Daniel starts but knows any plea of innocence will be ignored so he stops mid-sentence. He glances at me desperately.

I mouth at Daniel without anyone else seeing, 'You'll be OK, trust me. I've sorted it.'

With that, the Headmaster marches him to his office. Boss follows smugly grinning to himself.

31

It's been a week since the incident in the chemistry lab and I've not seen or heard a peep from Boss or Daniel. I'm just hoping my plan worked and Boss got his comeuppance. The last I'd heard was the Headmaster telling me that he would handle the matter from here and that was shortly after Daniel left his office.

Being so out of control over the last number of months has made me realise that I'm not always going to be in control of *everything* and sometimes you just have to try to make the best out of a very shitty situation. I've always been the person to take things into my own hands, sort it out and make it right. I mean, if a job needs doing well, best to do it myself. Or so I thought. However, after everything I've been through during the last year, I'm starting to come around to the idea that I don't need to have explicit control over everything. I *can* hand control over to other people and sometimes this is necessary to achieve the right outcome.

Whilst plugging in the school vacuum cleaner in the main school corridor I hear a boy whisper, ‘psst’. I turn around to see Daniel.

‘What did you do?’ he asks me. ‘I mean … I think it was you … whatever you did, thank you.’

‘Why, what’s happened?’ I ask him, hoping the Headmaster did what he promised when I decided to hand him the reigns.

‘He expelled him,’ Daniel says, a hint of a confused smile sweeping across his face. My heart bounces. The Head did do as he promised. ‘How d’you do it?’

I smile back at him. ‘I overheard Boss and the rest talking about getting you to start a fire on Wednesday last week. The silly boys even revealed when and where they would meet with you. Well … I got there first and planted my phone in the chemistry lab. Recorded the whole thing.’

Daniel’s mouth widens as he tries to comprehend what I’ve said and his smile fades. ‘But why didn’t you just try to stop them in the first place? I was so scared, and I almost did it.’

'But you didn't. I knew you wouldn't do it because you're a good kid really,' I say. 'But if I tried to stop them beforehand, they would have still given you the lighter. Who knows when though? He'd have chosen a different time and day and I would have had no way of helping you then. I'm sorry you had to go through that, but I had to prove that they were being so mean to you, framing you for something you didn't want to do. The Head would only do something about it if he had proof. Well, I got him the proof.'

I can see Daniel pondering over this. I can understand his confusion. Believe me, I contemplated beating the shit out of the wankers and making them stop by threatening them. The old me would have had no issues doing this. But that wouldn't have been the right thing to do. The right thing to do was to take evidence to the Head for him to take the most appropriate action. And thankfully he did.

'He's gone now Daniel,' I say, wanting to convince him that his whole, horrid ordeal was now officially over. 'The other kids won't bother you now, not without their ringleader.'

He nods ever so slowly. His mouth turns up slightly at the corners. 'You think?'

'I know,' I reassure him. 'They're weak without Boss telling them what to do. The Head will have close eyes on them from now on too. You are the one in control now. You are the strong one from now on.'

His eyes start to well with tears of relief. 'Thank you,' he whispers. 'And … I'm sorry I spat on you.'

I smile at him. I know he's sorry. He isn't a bad kid; he's suffering just like Carly did. Just like *I* did. 'OK Daniel. Just promise me one thing. Make sure no other kid gets bullied in this school. Don't turn a blind eye. If you see or hear anything, tell your Headmaster straight away, OK? You can speak to him in confidence you know.'

'I promise,' he says. 'I never want anyone else to be as sad or as scared as I was. I'll do you proud.'

'Make *yourself* proud,' I say. 'That's the only thing that truly matters.'

With that, he heads home for the day. A new skip in his step as he walks through the main school doors.

Thinking back to the second car accident with Aisha, the moment I switched into Pete's body, I look at how far I've come as a person, what I've been through, what massive obstacles I've overcome and the daily battles I'm gradually defeating. It's still not an easy ride and I still refuse to look at myself in the mirror, but I'm really trying to keep busy and move on. Every step I take, I feel stronger. I think for the first time in my life, I feel genuine self-pride. I'm not proud of my figure, my wealth or even my relationships anymore. I think that was more arrogance and vanity. Instead, I feel proud of *me* and my accomplishments and the hurdles I've surmounted this year.

*

After my shift, Jason suggests the pub. It's Friday night, I have no work tomorrow so what the hell. I've got a bit of surplus cash which I've managed to save, a bit of a blowout won't do any harm. The early June weather's starting to warm up so a beer garden would be lovely now that the days are longer. I suggest to Jason that we go into the town centre, rather than to our local so that we can make the most of the warm British weather whilst it lasts. He's hesitant as he's not got much money to throw away at the moment. What little money I have, I'm willing to share with Jason and offer to buy him a couple of drinks. He's been more than a house mate to me since moving in, he's become a true friend, my only friend.

Standing at the bar, I've finally weaved through the crowds of drinkers and my arm's now perched on the bar, bank note in hand, and I'm waiting to buy our second round of drinks. It's a young, male bar tender serving, and I can't help but notice that I seem to have been waiting a hell of a lot longer than some of the young, pretty women waiting at the bar. I'm sure this is just a coincidence, but there's a part of me that thinks if I still looked like *me,* not Aisha or Pete, I might have been served long ago. I lean over the bar and stretch my twenty-pound-note out in front of me and wait to see if the woman next to me still gets served before me. I'm going to test my theory. Sure enough, with her ample cleavage resting tidily on the oak bar, the male waiter can't resist asking her for her order before mine.

It's on the tip of my tongue to hurl some abuse at the barman, but I fight the urge. I've learnt that as a big, grotesque hulk of a man, any lip from me will only result in me being escorted out of the bar by security. Surprisingly though, the busty woman waves her arm towards me and says, 'he's first'.

Fair play love. That's pretty impressive as I've seen five other women being served before me and not one of them had the same common courtesy.

'Thank you,' I smile at her.

I take the drinks from the bartender and as I turn around, there's a woman stood right behind me chatting away to her boyfriend – I presume. One of my full pints collides with her shoulder causing half of the lager to tip all down her arm. She gasps.

'Oh shit,' I say. Without even thinking, my natural response is to be annoyed rather than apologetic. I mean, I've been waiting so long to be served and now I'm half a pint down because some idiotic woman doesn't understand personal space etiquette. 'Shittin' hell, I didn't know you were right behind me, I've spent ages waiting for these drinks.'

She's wiping the liquid off her arm with her hand, trying to brush away as much of it as she can but I can see she's clearly soaked.

'For fuck's sake, look where you're going …' she says angrily still trying aimlessly to wipe away the spillage. Then she raises her head to probably hurl some abuse in my direction but as our eyes meet, she catches her breath undoubtedly recognising me, recognising Pete. She looks genuinely scared.

'Sorry,' I say, even though I know it's not strictly my fault. She shouldn't have been stood so closely to me. But I can tell she's intimidated by my presence, so I don't want to escalate the situation any further, not that my apology sounds entirely sincere.

Then her boyfriend pipes up. 'What the fuck you done mate? You gonna apologise properly yeah?'

'Leave it Josh,' she whimpers. 'Can we just leave please?'

With jaw clenched, his nostrils flared and the corners of his mouth facing downwards, her fella threatens me. 'You escaped this time mate. Next time you might not be so lucky.'

'Josh, come on,' the girl tugs at his sleeve desperately wanting to escape the same breathing space as me. 'Please, just leave it. I need to leave. You coming?'

Reluctantly, the boyfriend agrees, they turn around and get swallowed by the crowd. What the hell was all that about? She knew who I was, and she was scared. Did Pete do something to her? I bat away the vile feeling in the pit of my stomach and try to excuse it away. She probably just thought I looked intimidating or perhaps she thought I was someone else. I can't afford to think of the other, more probable option.

Returning to Jason sitting patiently outside, he says, 'Took your time mate!'

I tell him the whole debacle, sip on what's left of my pint and request that he get the next round in using my money if needs must. There is no way I'm queuing again for a drink. We chat away about this and that, but I can't stop thinking about how that girl reacted when she saw my face.

A few pints down and I can feel my head start to fuzz and my stomach start to bloat. It's nearing closing time so Jason and I down the rest of our drinks and start to make our way from the beer garden back home. The shared house is only a fifteen-minute walk so it saves on a taxi fare.

There's a cut-through shopping arcade from the High Street through to a carpark which we take as a short cut home. The arcade is narrow and not well lit. It's the height of activity during the day. But by night, it's eerily quiet and menacing.

I can hear raised voices towards the end of the walkway. It sounds like a struggle. A male voice and then a female voice. Then a female shouting. Then sobbing. Then shouting again.

'No …' I hear her shout. 'Please, stop!'

Both Jason and I look at each other for a split second and then I hoof it down to the opposite end of the arcade, the sound of Jason's footsteps closely following mine. In a shop doorway, a man is straddling a woman lying beneath him on the cold, concrete floor. I grab the back of the man's shirt, clenching the fabric in my fist and heave him back on to his feet, away from her. Jason lands a punch on the man's face and he thuds to the ground. The man struggles back to his feet, spits blood onto the flagstones of the arcade and then scarpers as quickly as his feet can carry him.

Jason reaches his hand out to the woman. 'He's gone. Thank God we turned up when we did,' he says kindly. 'Are you alright?'

Gently, Jason clasps her trembling hand and helps her to her feet. The moonlight shines and I catch a glimpse of her face over Jason's shoulder. She's only in her early twenties I'd say, tear-stained make-up is smeared over her cheeks. If she weren't so heavily made up, I'd imagine she'd be pretty.

'Yes … I think so. Thanks to you two,' she says to Jason as she wipes away the tears rolling down her cheeks.

She looks over Jason's shoulder towards me but instead of looking relieved, a fresh, new look of terror encompasses her face.

'No!' she cries staring eyes wide in my direction. 'Not you! Get away from me.'

She turns her head back to Jason and shouts, 'Let me go!'

Jason quickly releases her hand that had still been firmly in his grasp and says, 'Of course. Sorry … you misunderstand … we're not the enemy.'

'He is!' she yells pointing at me and then she frantically totters away in her ridiculously high heels.

That vile feeling in my stomach avalanches, I think I'm going to be sick. I can't vomit in front of Jason. I have to hold it in. If I throw up, it'll make me look guilty. Jason has been a good friend to me, I have to deny any involvement with that woman. What the actual fuck? I wasn't the only girl Pete abused. I know this for definite now. That's two women in an evening who recognised me and not for good reasons. How many more are there?

My God. Was I the first woman out of many that Pete molested? If I'd have spoken up at the time, got him locked up, would these girls have been safe? Would their suffering have been avoided? If I hadn't had been so self-obsessed back then and worried about looking weak or having my secret affair revealed, perhaps these girls wouldn't have fallen prey to Pete's perversion. If I had reported him at the time, Pete wouldn't have stalked me, he wouldn't have been at the crash site and I may have found my way back to my own form rather than his despicable body. Perhaps I would have died and not swapped back to my own body, but that would still have been better than me living this hell every day. Things could have been so very, very different.

Then the even more sickening realisation hits me, full pelt in the chest. What if one of these girls *does* finally do the right thing and report Pete to the authorities. It won't be him on trial, it'll be me. I might even go to prison and we all know what happens to rapists behind bars. I've been roaming around, looking like Pete for almost six months now. Anyone could have seen me, reported me.

To think I was starting to feel proud of myself, thinking I could face this alone, that I didn't need help. I don't know what to do anymore, I don't have any answers for this. I need to speak to someone, and not just anyone. I need to speak to the one person who would believe me and possibly show me the forgiveness and compassion I'm not sure I deserve. It'll destroy her and Tom's little love bubble, but I have no other choice. I was worried before about losing any ounce of dignity I had left by reaching out to her for help. Well, having a strong inkling about what Pete did to the two women tonight has destroyed any remaining dignity. There's nothing else for it. I need to speak to Aisha.

32

Waiting for the eighteenth of July has been agony. But I know this is the best way of getting her attention, letting her know that I'm still around, that I didn't die like everyone thinks I did. I'd contemplated knocking on their door, but standing on a doorstep, trying to convince someone that I am who I say I am has backfired on me before. I'd thought about rocking up to their kids' club, what was it called? *Young Stars*, that was it. But I would have looked far too weird standing there without a child in tow.

Without being able to access my Facebook account due to my password being changed by Aisha, I wasn't sure how much information I would see on their walls when I decided to Facebook-stalk the pair of them. However, there was a public post posted by Aisha which Tom was tagged in saying that they were planning on getting the children Christened in July. I knew that would be my best option. They didn't state a time for the Christening on their Facebook post, but a date and location were good enough. I'd make sure I was there early enough and just wait. Wait for them to arrive and wait for my best opportunity.

Sitting in Pete's car far enough away from the church yard not to draw attention to myself but close enough to see the gate, I wait for the guests to arrive. It's ten-past-eight in the morning. I have no idea what time people will start to turn up. Christenings are normally nine or ten o'clock I believe. But who knows really? It could be the afternoon for all I know, but I will wait for as long as it takes.

The clock on my dashboard is slowly changing, minute by minute. Finally, after forty-five minutes, a familiar car pulls up outside the church gate. Thank God for that, I was starting to doubt I'd got the right church. If the Christening is due to start at nine o'clock, they're cutting it fine. So are all the guests. Perhaps the start time is nine-thirty or ten o'clock even.

Tom is the first to exit the car, opens the boot and battles with the massive dual buggy. Once assembled, he opens the passenger door and takes a crying little bundle of white lace out of their car seat and gently puts her in the buggy. He walks around and opens the other passenger door to release an equally grumpy baby from the comfort of her car seat and puts her next to her sister. All the while, Aisha stays sitting in the front, no help offered, she just lets Tom do everything.

Then she exits, mobile in hand. I hear her start to speak, so I wind down my window enabling me to hear her a little more clearly. Although it's still a bit of a strain to hear the words. 'Sorry Tom, that was Auntie Rose needing directions. Thanks for sorting the girls.'

She plants a kiss on Tom's lips, 'We made it.'

'We certainly did,' he replies. 'Today is the day!'

They start their walk up the church path. Now is my chance, before anyone else gets here. I clutch at the door handle just as another car pulls up. Bugger. Now is *not* the time. It's Dave and Carol. They're closely followed by Mel, linked arms with a man I've not met. She looks radiantly happy, not grieving for the sister she lost as far as I can tell. More guests arrive and finally, there's quiet.

I never had a plan. Not really. I mean, how exactly do I tell Aisha and Tom what's happened? I just knew I had to be here as this was my best chance at seeing them, telling them what had happened. I used to have a plan for everything. I *had* to be in control, I had to know exactly what I was doing and when. But circumstances have drastically changed. No planning can help me here, I have to just find a way, some way or another.

I'm not sure what possesses me, but before I know it, I'm out of my car and walking through the graveyard. In the distance I can hear an organ playing *Toccata and Fugue in D minor* by Bach, an obvious choice but nice all the same. The grass is adorned with a blanket of daisies, it really is beautiful. Flowers are not something I would ordinarily notice, but the beauty gives me a sense of calm. I have nothing to lose, I am strong, I can do this. I'll go in and sit in the congregation and watch from a distance, wait for my chance.

As I reach the porch of the old stone building, the music stops and the hinges of the big oak door clatter as it closes.

'Thank you all for gathering here today,' I hear a muffled female voice say through the solid wood. No doubt the vicar. 'Today we welcome the families of Eva and Livia who will be Christened today …'

Eva and Livia. They wouldn't have been my choice of names. But then again, I'd never given baby names much thought, never needed to. There's a sudden ache in my gut, an odd feeling, almost of loss. I never wanted the children, after all I was going to get rid of them. For good reason at the time. But I can't shake the feeling that it should be me in there. If things had been different.

Regret is a feeling I'm not accustomed to. But that is definitely what I am feeling right now. If only I hadn't been so self-obsessed, a cheating wife and a money-hungry snob. I've realised that I have been so judgemental of others, yet the one person I should have judged was myself. Perhaps I would have done things differently then and maybe karma wouldn't have needed to be such a bitch to me. Have I learnt my lesson? Yes, I believe I have.

My eyes are welling as I think about what could have been and what is instead. There is a strong likelihood that these twins who are loved by so many are the offspring of an evil man. Yet they are innocent and deserve this love. I see that now. They didn't ask to be conceived in such a horrific way. They shouldn't be hated by me or by anyone else. They are worthy of loving parents and I am happy for them. I just wish I thought of this before. Perhaps, I could have found it in my heart to love them too.

The more I think things over in my head, the more I want to speak to Aisha. I want to apologise for everything. I want her to know that I'm so very sorry and desperately need her to listen to me. The secrets I've been holding on to for too long need to be revealed and to the one person who will whole-heartedly believe me. I just hope that she forgives me.

Well, I can't rightly stay here until the service is over. From what the Vicar was saying, there's going to be coffee and biscuits after too so that's going to be at least an hour from now. There's a small table to my left and on it is a white, ornate box made of cardboard, with the word 'CARDS' written decoratively on the front. Now, *that's* an idea. Perhaps I can leave a card for them, write in there what's happened to me, let her read it at leisure and wait for her to hopefully contact me. It's always better in writing isn't it? That way she can re-read it and fully absorb my story. If I'm quick, I can make it to the shop down the road and back and write my note before the service ends.

I move as quickly as this body allows, pelt it down the pathway and back to the car. I'm huffing and puffing by the time I strap into the seat. I'm still not used to being so unfit. I start the engine and drive to the shop which is ten minutes down the road. Looking at the dashboard clock, the time's already five-to-ten. Twenty-five minutes since the service began. I really do need to haul ass.

I park haphazardly at an angle beside the pavement. No time to straighten up. I dash into the shop and ask the shop assistant where the cards are. She shrugs and continues bleeping her machine against the baked beans. Nice one. Thanks a freaking bunch love. Whatever happened to customer service?

There's a poxy little stand with about fifteen cards to choose from. I speedily scan the choice. Several birthday cards, a few with 'Congratulations' written on them, a couple of wedding cards, one 'With Sympathy' and a 'Thinking of You' card. Shit. Nothing for a Christening. I hover over the 'Congratulations' one but hesitate. That would come across as sarcastic surely. Congratulations on the Christening, oh and by the way, I'm back from the dead! No, that wouldn't work. Well, the only other option is the 'Thinking of You' card, because technically I *am* thinking of her. I've thought of nothing else for the last few weeks. I take the card to the counter and pay.

Bugger, I have no pen and I doubt there's one in the car after I deep cleaned it. So, I ask the woman behind the counter where the stationery is after she's just taken my contactless payment. She points to a corner of the shop behind me, so I quickly go and grab a pen and return, only to find an old lady being served. Oh, come on! I know I shouldn't pass judgement. I need to try and turn over a new leaf but seriously? When I'm in a rush and don't want to miss the one chance to have my voice heard by the one person who can help, an old woman is dawdling with her purse. I stand behind her, tapping my foot and I'm conscious I'm sighing. Loudly.

Finally, the old lady finishes.

'Sorry, my love,' she says to me as she turns around. I recognise her now. Her grey hair, her glasses perched on the end of her nose. 'Am I holding you up? Somewhere you got to be?

'You!' I gasp. What the fuck is she doing here? Every time I'm on the cusp of doing something important like trying to find my way back to my body as an example, she's there, messing things up, meddling where it isn't necessary. She's the one who brought me back. She's the one who resuscitated Pete. She's the one who ruined my life.

The things I could say to her. But I can't, not here. Not in public. I don't have time for this. She's held me up enough, I swear it's intentional.

'I don't know what your game is,' I say to her, quietly enough that the shop assistant can't hear. 'But you're not going to mess things up again for me. I won't let you.'

'Pardon love?' The old crone is deaf as well as crazy. 'You'll have to speak up.'

I cast her a glare, snarl and say to myself, under my breath, 'leave it.'

I throw a pound at the shop assistant and rush towards the exit, push the old woman to one side as she's still stood there, trying to stop me from leaving. The shop assistant shouts after me, 'I need to scan it!'

'Go and get another one to scan!' I shout back at her through the doorway and dash back to the car.

No time to think about what happened. No time to wonder why the old witch was there. No time to do an awful lot. The dashboard now tells me it's twenty-past ten. The only parking space available outside the church is the one I left empty, so I dump the car in the space and leg it up the pathway, card and pen in hand.

I can hear chatting from inside the church. The service has now ended. Coffee is being drank. People will be leaving soon to enjoy the sun. No time. No time to think about what to write. What do I write? How do I tell her it's me and what's happened to me when time is against me? I need to tell her I'm alive. I need to let her know it's me. I scrawl two words in the card, seal it shut and dump it on top of the card box. No time to write anything on the envelope, no time to write anything much. She'll know it's me when she reads it, she'll know what I mean. Then I'll wait and watch. I'll wait. However long it takes.

*

The guests start leaving one by one, chatting and bustling back to their cars, their voices full of excitement and good cheer. They're off to a celebratory party I hear someone say. I feel like a spy or secret agent hiding behind a tree amongst the gravestones, watching and waiting. Patiently.

The numbers of guests leaving the church starts to dwindle and finally I hear the scrape of the buggy leaving the church.

This is it. Has she noticed the card yet? Has she read it? Does she know?

I move my head from around the tree and sneak a peek. But it's Tom and Tom alone pushing the twins. No sign of Aisha yet. Unless she's already left, and I missed her? Shit, I hope that's not the case otherwise all of this would have been for nothing. Tom's trying to push the buggy one-handed whilst his other hand attempts to shield his eyes from the blazing sun. He looks blinded by it. The sun beats down into the porch, illuminating it, giving me a good view. I know that if the sun is in his eyes, I'm harder to see. I can see in, but no-one can see out easily. This gives me the upper hand. He heads off down the path with a bounce in his stride. He's so happy. I don't think I ever made him that happy.

A few minutes after, I catch a glimpse of Aisha carrying bags and toys into the porch. She stops where the card box is. *This* is it. This is the moment she sees the card. She picks it up, stares at it for a bit and moves it towards the letterbox at the top of the box. No! Read it now, please! Don't put it in there, open it!

As if she read my mind, she puts the bags and toys down and opens the envelope. She opens the card and now she's reading my message. What is going through her mind? I can't begin to imagine. I wish I'd had more time to write more. Maybe she won't understand my message. Perhaps she'll discard it thinking it was left there as a mistake. No, she has to twig. Come on, don't let me down Aisha! I move out from behind the tree and as I do so, I cast a shadow on the ground in front of me.

She's seen the shadow; she turns her head. She can't see me clearly, so she raises her hand to shield her eyes from the sun's glare. She won't recognise me looking how I look now. How do I make her know it's me?

Then I realise, there's one distinctive move I've made a number of times in her presence. The move my counsellor taught me. The one that is supposed to help me release my tension and pass it into the atmosphere when I feel I'm losing control. The one I've used to pass control over to other people. What better way to tell her I'm back? I slowly raise my hand and place my index finger on the middle of my forehead. I can tell that I have her attention now. It's working. I move it firmly and meaningfully in her direction. She knows it's me now. I'm going to sort it out and make everything right, all she has to do is let me.

Epilogue

Zoe

She stands, staring at me. For what feels like forever. Her hand is still shielding her eyes, she's frozen to the spot. I contemplate moving towards her, but my legs refuse to budge. This is such a big moment, a pivotal one. I mustn't do anything to jeopardise this. I've got her attention; I need to maintain it without scaring her off. I have to be patient.

There is silence apart from birds chirping in the trees above and the distant sound of a plane that roars across the sky. This affirms to me that the world is still turning, and time has not stood still. Although it feels that way. Everyone has now left and we're alone, standing metres away from each other yet entirely connected.

Eventually she places one foot in front of the other slowly, painfully slowly. Is she going to make a run for it? Then what do I do? She's out of the porchway now, still staring in my direction. I can tell she's trying to figure out who I am, the cogs turning inside her brain. She stops walking and breaks the eye contact. She looks towards the graveyard gateway, planning her escape no doubt.

A twig crunches underneath my foot causing her to swing her gaze back towards me. I can see she's frightened now; her eyes are glazed and wide. A shadow falls across her face allowing her to see me a little more clearly. I raise my hands to shoulder height, palms facing outwards in a gesture of peace. I need her to realise that I mean no harm.

'Hello Aisha,' I say, hoping she can hear me from where she stands. Without startling her and still with hands raised, I gingerly step a little closer. She takes a step back. We're still far apart but I'm close enough for her to see me in all my hideous glory and for me to hear the next words that come out of her mouth.

'Who … um … who are you?' she asks warily with an air of hostility.

'I think you know who I am,' I say. 'It's been a while Aisha.'

'But … you *can't* be.' She looks shaken, yet she stands strong. She's not the weak woman I once thought she was. 'You … um … well you're …'

'A man,' I interrupt her. 'Yes, I am. But I *am* Zoe, Aisha. I am, and you have to believe me.'

'But it's impossible …'

'I know it's impossible, don't you think I know that?' I realise how this comes across. I hold back my impatience and bite my tongue. I know how intimidating I come across to people, especially now when I look like I do. I don't want to scare her off. 'Yes, it is impossible, but you and me switching was impossible but *that* happened. Sorry … I didn't mean to come across sarcastic or … um … intimidating … or anything.'

I step a little closer again. She allows me, her feet glued to the stone pathway beneath her. I tentatively edge closer again. She moves one foot back, again, in a defensive stance, so I stop.

'What do you want?' She's stopped stuttering and her confidence is growing. She sounds more pissed off than frightened now. 'I mean, it's been over six months … You died ... or so I thought. But now you turn up here … as a man …

that's if it *is* you. Have you come to finish off the job? I mean … you tried to kill us …'

'No … no I didn't. Yes, I wanted to switch back and at the time I was so angry, so self-obsessed, so determined to get my life back, I would have done anything. But when I turned up at your house that day, Pete … um … this man,' I gesture at my body. 'Well … he was *not* a good man and he was in the back seat of your car. I was trying to save you both.'

She scoffs. She stands tall but I can see the fear in her eyes. 'Save us? You honestly expect me to believe that? You wanted me dead, you said so yourself.'

I can't argue with that. 'I did want you dead, but I also wanted to die. Only for a moment so that we could be resuscitated again and switch back. But when I knew *he* was in your car I couldn't let him get to you. He was a bad man … a very bad man and I switched … oh God … if you only knew.'

I feel my voice break slightly. If only she knew the truth. What happened to me and why Pete was such a vile person. But she doesn't know, not yet and she shows no compassion towards me. I mean, why would she? She shakes her head, her lips scrunch and her nostrils flare. She loathes me. I can't blame her, I loathe myself.

She turns and starts striding down the path muttering, 'I can't deal with this. Today was supposed to be a *nice* day.'

'No, wait! Please!' I shout after her. I can't let her go, she's the only one who will believe me, the only one I can reveal my story to. I have to seek her forgiveness. 'I'm sorry!'

She stops. She turns slowly. 'You're … sorry?'

'Aisha. I am truly sorry … for everything. Please … shit …' She has to realise how hard it is for me to say this. 'I need your help.'

*

Aisha

The last six months had not been easy for me. The letters I sent to everyone was just the start of me proving to those I loved who I really was. They eventually accepted me and loved me. But the nightmares got worse.

I had people around me to support me through the dark times, the traumatic flashbacks, and the incessant worry that bad things would happen once again. People told me to stop worrying, that everything would be OK now. Now that *she* was gone. My counsellor advised me that the past was history, the future a mystery, and the present was a gift which was why it was called the present. This resonated with me and I worked so hard to rebuild my confidence, trying to curb the anxious thoughts and focus on the present.

Well, now the past has most certainly come back to haunt me, smacking me full pelt in the face and destroying my present. The future once again looks terrifying.

Meet in a public place I told myself. Make sure people are around. Get a coffee so that my hands have something to focus on. And most importantly, don't show any signs of weakness.

Now that I'm here, in the park, waiting, I start to have second thoughts. Do I really want to hear what Zoe has to say? Do I want to step back into the past? No, I don't. But I don't have much of a choice. She … do I refer to her as a 'she' or a 'he'? I know *her* as Zoe so I will refer to her as a female ... She has given me no choice.

She said she needs me and that she's sorry. Over six months have passed, and she's waited until now to approach me. Surely if she meant me harm, she would have hunted me down way before now. Even though I'm reluctant to meet with her, I can't bat away the niggling feeling that she would have been through a lot and that she must need someone to turn to. Of course, I don't want that someone to be me. But I am the only other person that can relate to what she's going through, on some level.

It's been two days since the Christening. I needed the time to decide if I was going to meet with her or not. She asked to talk on Sunday afternoon, but I said Tuesday. I had to go to the Christening party and plaster a fake smile on my face which was hard to do to say the least. However, the main reason why I said Tuesday was to give me time to think about everything. That way I could duck out of it if I needed to.

Tom knew something was up even though I tried to hide it. He noticed my obsessive counting had worsened again and my cleaning had become irrational once more. He tried to talk to me about it, but I pushed him away. I shouldn't have but how could I tell him what happened? I don't really have any answers myself yet, certainly not enough to explain to him. I have to hear her out, not just for me but for Tom too.

Sitting on a park bench, coffee in hand, I hear an unfamiliar deep voice say, 'Hi Aisha'.

There she is. A massive, balding man with a stubbly chin. A far cry from the beautiful blonde she and I once were.

'You happy for me to sit?' she asks me. I nod and allow her to sit beside me. My grasp on my takeaway coffee tightens. Here goes. I wait for her to speak first.

'Thank you for meeting me,' she says. 'I wasn't sure if you'd show, but I'm pleased you did.'

Her whole demeanour is different. She sits hunched, arms folded, chin close to her chest. Every now and then she raises her head to glance around the park nervously, as if she's not sure who may be watching her. She's lost all confidence; I can see that undoubtedly. I know what it's like to lack confidence and she's obviously had the wind well and truly taken out of her sails.

'An old woman once said to me, look out for side roads, you don't want to let them pass you by,' she says. 'Well, I've been down some roads, I tell you. But I've come to a dead-end

Aisha. I don't know where to go or where to turn anymore. I'm lost.'

An old woman? Side roads? The same old woman who I kept bumping into, giving me strange advice? No, it can't be, can it? When I first met her on the bus, just after bumping into Luke and Zoe at the supermarket, I thought she was kind if not a little weird. But her words stuck with me. Then, a few months ago, she turned up at Church. She sat next to me and the twins and after the service she told me that 'he needed me' and that 'our paths would cross again so I needed to be ready'. At the time I thought she was a batty old lady but maybe she knew more than I once thought.

'An old woman?' I ask. 'In her seventies, grey hair, glasses perched on the end of her nose, spouts weird stuff about everyone being on journeys through life and that she gets weird feelings about people?'

Zoe raises her head and looks directly at me for the first time.

'Fuck me … you've met her too?' She says, a mixture of hurt, fear and disbelief showing in her wide-open, bloodshot eyes.

'Yes … who the hell is she?' I ask. I can't believe Zoe's met her too.

'She's the one who did this to me,' Zoe says, signalling to her body.

What is she saying? How could an old lady be responsible for what happened to her? This is insane. There are so many questions bubbling away in my mind.

'Right then, time to start talking,' I say. I need to find out what's going on. I don't trust Zoe in the slightest and have no idea what her intensions are. But I need to know what's been going on. I have to find out what's happened. This is the present and I can't afford to worry about the past or the future anymore. I need to know what I'm dealing with and I need to know everything.

'I don't know where to begin,' she says with a big sigh.

'Start from the beginning,' I say.

To Be Continued …

Acknowledgements

Firstly, and most importantly, I would like to thank all my wonderful readers who took the time to read, enjoy and crucially review *Time's Ticking*. Without your support throughout this whole process, I wouldn't have had the confidence to continue on the *Junction Trilogy* journey and *Still Ticking* would just be a mind map of plot themes and ideas, rather than the novel it deserved to be. I cannot express my gratitude enough for all the wonderful feedback received from *Time's Ticking* (the first book in *The Junction Trilogy*) and I know in my heart that you will continue to support *Still Ticking* by reading and reviewing it. The third book in the trilogy, *Time's Up,* will be released in December 2021. This last novel will tie up all the loose ends for each of the integral characters, further twists and turns will be revealed and mysteries solved.

My social media followers and supporters. Thank you for your shares, likes and comments of appreciation. All of which have raised exposure and increased my confidence as a writer.

This book is dedicated to Bethan and John. My parents. They have consistently been on the end of the phone, offering support and guidance. I am truly blessed to have them in my life. The lockdown of 2020 that continued through into 2021 has meant people have not been able to see, socialise with or hug loved ones for an exceptionally long time. My heart goes out to all those who have not had an easy ride over the last year and who have faced exceedingly difficult situations or experienced heartbreak. Together we can fight the virus and hopefully this trilogy can be a means of escape to those trapped within the confinement of their homes.

Carl. What can I say other than thank you? Two words that will never demonstrate exactly how appreciative I am of your love, your reassurance, and your words of encouragement. Without you, *The Junction Trilogy* would never have been published, let alone finished. You gave me the confidence to get it out there and make it available for the public to read. When I've stumbled, you've picked me up. When I've needed to shut myself off to write, you've understood. And when I've lost momentum and writers block threatens to make an appearance, you've talked it through with me and given me clarity. Thank you from the bottom of my heart.

The Junction Trilogy

L. A. Evans

Junction: Time's Ticking

Junction: Still Ticking

Junction: Time's Up

Junction

Time's Up

L. A. Evans

Due to be released in

December 2021